Entanglement

Alina Leonova

Cover design by Maria Levene
https://www.marialevene.com/

In case of any questions, please contact the author
contact@alinaleonova.net

Table of Contents

CHAPTER 1

Cay had to act quickly, as he only had a couple of hours before Limea's return. He'd made up his mind. Was it a mistake? Probably, but he couldn't pretend anymore. And he surely wouldn't wait for the fixers to come after him.

He packed a couple of charged batteries and a sample of solar fabric, some clothes, snacks and water. He made sure to enable alternative security measures that allowed him to access his encrypted private cloud without an implant. To do that, his fingerprint and a passphrase said in his voice with the right intonation was required. He also had a copy of the most important things, including technical specs and documents related to his invention in a button of his smart jacket.

Cay looked around. Their home, a magical place that kept all troubles away, their common creative space. Even the plants he didn't feel quite comfortable around–all of that was soaked in memories and feelings, a projection of their connection.

He sighed and focused on the task at hand. There came the messy part. Cay injected a painkiller in his arm and took a small household laser already configured for his needs. It was very thin and precise, Cay had always admired its thoughtful design. He waited for the painkiller to kick in and steadied his hand. Took a deep breath. Okay.

He had practiced the exact movement he had to make multiple times with the laser off. The implant was a biotech that integrated with his flesh and was impossible to distinguish without special equipment. To get rid of it, Cay made an incision right at the base of his thumb, slid the laser down, slightly to the right and up again. He cut out a piece of flesh 2 centimeters long, 2 millimeters wide and 5 millimeters deep in a smooth, decisive motion. The laser cauterized the wound, so there was almost no blood, and the painkiller did its job well. Still, he had a strange feeling looking at his mutilated palm.

A citizen without an implant was technically disabled. He couldn't interact with any of the city's software and machinery, which meant he was unable to enter some of the buildings, participate in any transactions, use any means of communication or transportation. Even his home AI wouldn't listen to him. He couldn't use an ordinary passenger drone. But he also turned invisible. No one knew who he was or where he was. He disappeared from all the radars. He didn't exist anymore. He was no one. A blank canvas where anything could be painted. That was the tradeoff he was willing to take.

Of course, living without an implant was impossible in any city, and living outside the city was impossible by default. Cay wasn't stupid enough to try any of that. But there was a way to get a new implant accompanied by a new identity. The problem was, one couldn't come close to the people who did it with an actual implant. It was essential to get rid of it before getting near the facility, otherwise he wouldn't be admitted. Maybe he would even be killed? Cay didn't know for sure. Anyway, this part was done. Now the trick was to actually get there.

He took the last glance at their apartment. Without his implant he was a stranger here. His home assistant didn't even detect his presence, probably considering him some kind of animal.

"Bye, Risa," Cay said anyway, but the AI ignored him.

He took two decisive steps and stopped suddenly at the door, then sat down right there, on the floor with his back to the wall. After leaving the apartment, he would never be able to come back here. He needed one last moment. His mind started racing through the familiar loop of explanations of what might be happening to him, and he gave in to it.

The first one was that he was in a simulation which felt like days on his subjective timescale, while in real time it only took minutes. Simulations that felt longer than a day had been illegal since the infamous series of lethal and insanity cases, but, of course, he might have wanted to try one anyway. Would he be able to find a way if he decided to have a go? Definitely. Would he choose a scenario like the one he was experiencing now? Hardly. But it could be a sim with a hidden or random script.

Normally, a person who wanted to experience something beyond their ordinary life, conquer a fear, work on a trauma or test themselves in a dangerous situation would go to one of the multiple simulation manufacturers. They had all types of plots from the most fantastical to the really mundane ones. They would interview a customer to find out about their expectations and possible problems and then offer over a dozen scenarios.

The customer would study them in detail and make adjustments if necessary. After everything was agreed on, a personalized sim would be prepared, the client would be put into stasis and their recent memories blocked to prevent them from remembering they were in a simulation. It would last up to five minutes in real time and up to one day on a subjective timescale.

Some people preferred not to block their memories, as knowing they were in a simulation allowed them to have superpowers or satisfy the fantasies they wouldn't dare to in real life. But there was a black market of sims offering those searching for adrenaline a wider range of more extreme and dangerous options. He might have decided to try those. He'd done that before. And hell, didn't he and Limea have fun on the outskirts of their consciousness.

Limea occupied an essential chunk of his thoughts and was a part of most of his recent experiences. But could she just be a simulation's construct implanted into his memories for the sake of the plot? It was another illegal feature banned a couple of years ago, as it was responsible for mental disorders, depression and several suicides. After emerging from the experience, people would deny something that felt so real could be just a construct of a sim. They wouldn't agree they could have loved someone who'd never existed in the first place. They'd break up with their partners, abandon their families and friends in search of a person who was to be found nowhere but in the virtual world. They were ready to give up their real lives for a simulation that suddenly made them so happy and complete.

The thought scared Cay, but he had to admit to himself that anything could happen on the sim black market. Deep in his heart he didn't believe it though, as he felt that the simulation wouldn't be able to create their intricate bond. It could make him feel love, but it wouldn't turn him into an antenna tuned to her frequencies. It was more than just chemistry easily recreated by technology. It was quantum entanglement on human level. A beautiful dance of their melanas' internal fire if one

4

believed in melanas in the first place. Cay didn't, but he'd always appreciated the elegant beauty of the idea.

According to the legend, the first image caught by the eyes of a baby in the moment of birth formed a melana, the inner stem of a person that made them who they really were. It was the reason many mothers found beautiful and meaningful spots to give birth before science proved newborns couldn't see well enough to make out the environment. Many mothers would still do it, as science had always been incapable of changing people's beliefs if they were emotionally committed to the idea.

Anyway, what was between him and Limea couldn't be simulated. It was too unique, too deep, it reached the very bottom of his being and further. It glowed in the darkness like a billion dancing galaxies. It was a mystical experience that extended beyond the three known dimensions. It was rooted in his every cell.

On the other hand, Cay had questioned the reality of their relationship many times because it seemed too good to be true. He'd never experienced anything like this before, and he didn't know anyone who had. At times he thought that maybe he'd designed the whole thing for himself, because it was impossible for two people to connect in all those sophisticated ways.

What if it felt so unbelievably good precisely because it was constructed by a simulation? No wonder people lost their minds and didn't want to go back to their partners after that. Normal human relationship seemed a tasteless parody of the real thing. The thought threatened the fragile remains of confidence Cay was still holding on to. It was scary to lose Limea but knowing she had never really existed was terrifying. He inhaled deeply and moved on to the rest of the options he had.

Well, those options weren't optimistic either. If he really was in a simulation, it could have malfunctioned. Such things happened once in a while, especially with illegal ones, mainly because of viruses. It could get really unpleasant. Cay heard about a sim that put its user on an infinite loop, repeating a day of his life in every detail over and over again. The sitter noticed unusual brain activity on the third minute of the simulation and decided to pull the user out, but by then he'd already had ten thousand four hundred twenty-two years five months and seventeen days of repetition in subjective time. The guy was too far gone by the time he got out. They said even the fixers couldn't make him better.

Some people got the scariest scenarios exploiting their inner weaknesses and fears. They often came out broken, mere shadows of who they used to be. Maybe that was happening to him. The good news was that it wasn't real. The bad news was that it could last for years of subjective time before someone noticed, and when they did, it could be too late.

Another option was that he'd lost his mind. It looked plausible, too. Being realistic, Cay's experiences with simulations and neuro-stimulations rather predisposed to it. He'd had his fun, and his brain might have eventually decided to avenge itself. He'd tried all kinds of sims, some of them illegal and not properly tested. Sometimes he forgot who he actually was inside of those sims and had to rediscover himself again after coming back. Together with Limea he took part in a group simulation where a common consciousness was formed by thirteen con-

6

tributors. Those contributors weren't exactly the sanest people. Cay felt like parts of their minds remained somewhere inside his brain.

And with neuro-stimulations different parts of his brain were excited by electrical impulses changing his perception of reality. Sometimes he expanded beyond himself and merged with the Universe. Sometimes he went to another one to communicate with the creatures from out there. Sometimes he became something else, and often inexpressible things happened.

All of those influenced who he was. And even though Cay was mostly pleased with their impact, he also realized they gradually erased an imprint of normality he might have once had. Maybe it wasn't that bad. It hadn't been until this strange time anyway.

Cay shook his head. He'd been through these options before. What he was going through was too weird to be real, but there were no definitive signs that it wasn't. He was in a sort of a limbo where he didn't trust himself, questioned and doubted everything but couldn't do anything because he just wasn't sure about any of it. However, what happened several days before made him finally take the radical steps he was taking.

He and Limea were together in their living room. Cay was looking into her eyes. They were still beautiful, but the emerald fire of nature, the portal to other worlds was replaced by still water of a lake. Cay felt he could reach the bottom of it. Observing her physical beauty that still pleased the eye, he knew that the most alluring and fascinating part of her was gone.

Could she be some kind of an elaborate machine, Cay thought? What would he find inside if he cut her open, he wondered? He glanced at a knife she'd brought from the kitchen to cut fruit.

For a moment, he considered doing it, almost sure he'd see short-circuiting wires instead of blood. His hand even twitched a bit in the direction of the knife. He backed out appalled by the thought. He had to go out of the room to hide his terror and calm his trembling hands. The thought that he could actually hurt the woman he loved was unbearable. Cay couldn't just sit still and wait for the disaster to happen.

Could the woman he loved have been replaced by someone or something that looked exactly like her? He didn't think so. There was no way that he knew of. Yet, this was how it felt.

Whatever it was, he had to do something. If it was a simulation, he either had to find a way to unlock its subsequent levels or just do something to stay sane until he could be pulled out of it. If it wasn't, he had to get away from the people who managed to replace his bonding partner with an intricate and persuasive copy and find out what had happened to her. If he was insane, he had to get away from Limea before he hurt her and end up in the fixers' hands. He'd made a decision. It was wrong for so many reasons. It was right for so many others.

It was time to say goodbye to their home. Cay got up and looked around one last time. So many memories and emotions he had to leave behind. He glanced at the sim-set and recalled something. There was one more thing he had to take with him. He stepped on the treadmill, slipped the glasses on and entered his virtual storage unit. There, on the left, behind the door with all the things that held sentimental value for him was Limea's wedding gift.

8

It was a virtual project she'd made. From a distance, it looked like a painting of his eyes. They were alive, gleaming with emotions, thoughts and questions. There was childish curiosity and bewilderment, courage and strength, intelligence and kindness, understanding and acceptance, care and love, ambition and confidence, knowledge and vulnerability, happiness and uncertainty. There were many desires that drove him, excitement, bursting energy, but also some tranquility and peace in the very corners.

Cay felt that in this painting Limea managed to capture his inner world, the stem that lay beneath all the external layers. He never stopped being amazed at how well she knew him.

As he came closer, more details emerged, and the painting began to move and change. He could see the Universe gleaming behind the eyes. It became more evident with every step he took and began to flow from the eyes and fill the space around him until he was wrapped and lost in it. There were supernova explosions and galaxies whirling around black holes, pulsars shooting their beams across the Universe, gas clouds enshrouding newly born stars and planets orbiting their suns.

He could choose one and take a closer look at it. Some were teeming with life, wild or technologically advanced, others were dead and empty, some destroyed by cosmic bombardments or their past inhabitants. He could also take a step back and see the bigger picture: galaxies binding into groups, clusters, superclusters and finally luminous filaments, the cosmic web of energy and life floating in the void. Expanding into infinity, which had always fascinated and startled him.

This was how Limea saw him. He had to take it with him. This had to stay when he became a new person. He copied it to the memory button of his smart jacket.

Before leaving his life behind, he habitually looked in the mirror. His grey eyes seemed darker than in the artwork he'd just seen. There were dark circles below them, and a couple of lines between his eyebrows. His brown hair was a slight mess as always. It was probably time to get it cut. He forgot to shave, so stubble was growing on his cheeks. His brown smart jacket was old, but it was his favorite one. A yellow T-shirt with an image of an alien asking for water was a reference to a movie he and Limea loved, a gift from her.

As the door closed behind him, Cay didn't look back.

CHAPTER 2

Being alert and vigilant as always, Vietra saw him before he made his first move. The way he walked holding his right arm close to his body under the coat, and his left hand clenched in a nervous fist. The fierce look on his face, the troubled eyes dispersing hatred and pain, the tight pale line of his lips. The rest of the people paid no attention, of course.

She was too far. Even though she started running towards him the very moment she noticed him, she didn't have enough time. Rushing through the unsuspecting crowd she couldn't believe no one had noticed anything yet. Floating in their thoughts, immersed in virtual reality or drawn to each other by conversations, they felt so safe!

The man took the knife from under his coat and sliced right through the soft belly of a plump teenage girl who was interfacing with someone, laughing. He cut deeply and widely, mutilating her intestines, leaving her body wide open for everyone to see the inside of her. Most of the people still haven't noticed and only started turning around when they heard her first scream. At that point the girl was more surprised than terrified, but the pain quickly caught up to her, and the tone of the scream changed into a more agonized one, disturbing more people.

Many stopped, looking around perplexedly, searching for answers in each other's faces. Those who were closer bluntly repeated the screaming, multiplying the girl's agony and making it part of the overall chaos and panic. Some started running away. Meanwhile the man with the knife cut the neck of a by-stander who didn't hear anything, separated from the outside world by music in his earphones. The cut started right under his ear, destroying his carotid artery, leaving him little chance of survival in this mess.

Vietra could see the attacker clearly. His movements looked slow and predictable to her, unfolding into a precise curve of attempted future. But she was already close and broke the trajectory of his next stab with a decisive strike on his throat which made him collapse immediately.

She wanted to kill him. It would be easy with the mixture of skills and anger she was filled with. Just one more strike. One or another. One of a couple dozen.

Imagining it caused a tickling sensation all over her body and made resisting it more difficult. She couldn't let anger take over, that's what the Master had taught her. It was too easy to cross the line under the influence of emotions. Once it was done, there would be no way back, because most people would stand no chance against her. Power always messed one's head.

She wasn't the one to decide who should live and die, especially while being irrational. Her skills were to be used for a certain purpose, the one only the Master knew. Right. And yet... she was so pissed! Pissed at the people feeling so safe they didn't even look around. Because they delegated the responsibility of defending them to someone else. The police. As if they were always around. But the people felt relieved, because none of them liked responsibility. They preferred to pretend against all common sense they were actually safe this way. It meant they could relax and do nothing. They got so used to it that they began feeling powerless. And a vibrant rainforest ecosystem that had been breaking all the obstacles and crushing all dangers standing in the way of its growth suddenly became a soft, harmless mass that had no idea what to do when someone attacked it.

The mass got surprised or upset, the mass tried to get out of danger's way but by no means to protect itself. Just one man with one knife, and so many people around who could have put him down in an instant before he did any damage, the very moment they saw his face. Even without any special skills or strength, just by the number of them, if only they could remember how to be survivors instead of spineless victims. If only they could unite and stand by each other.

Vietra despised the mass. All of it was so annoying that she had to kick the attacker in the balls to prevent herself from killing him. She did a couple of breathing exercises and realized it was time to get out of there as the distant sound of sirens touched her ears. She wanted no part of it.

"You did it again," the Master said as soon as she entered the Nest. Vietra heard disappointment in his voice, so she lowered her head and clenched her hands behind her back, looking at her toes like a little girl reprimanded by her father.

"I'm sorry, Master," Vietra said. "It won't happen again."

"It will, and you know it," the Master's voice became colder. This time he was really displeased, she realized with slight surprise, maybe even angry. "You disobeyed me the third time, and you are lying to me. Such behavior won't be tolerated. You will be punished."

"No!" Vietra uttered more emotionally than it was acceptable, raising her head and looking into the Master's eyes.

They were cold like interstellar void. Everyone turned their heads to her. She blushed. She knew she shouldn't have reacted this way, but the Master got her by surprise. She'd always thought she was his favorite, and he would allow her a little more than the others. She also didn't think what she'd done was such a big deal. It wasn't the kind of disobedience that required punishment. After all, she helped those people. Didn't good intentions count?

Apparently, they didn't. And if she had a chance to avoid or soften the punishment had she accepted is gracefully, after this shameful public outburst it was lost. She lowered her head again to conceal her panic.

"Should I escort you to the room?" the Master asked in a voice that inflicted punishment by itself.

"There is no need," she answered, raising her head and looking him in the eye again. She had no right to be weak now. She couldn't afford to evoke his contempt. That would be the end of everything. She still remembered Mroolic. That poor boy who was too sincere to realize some things couldn't be said and some feelings couldn't be shown. Not to the Master. "I will go."

"How long will I stay there? Tell me it won't be long!" her inner voice screamed. But she knew she couldn't say it aloud. That would be very unwise, another manifestation of her weakness that would toughen her punishment. She had already done enough, and she was angry with herself for that.

Vietra turned around and headed to the sensory deprivation room. She had to pass all the other Nestlings still looking at her with surprised disapproval. She was staring straight ahead as she was walking through the huge, oval room that she knew

14

so well. White bare walls and a high ceiling, no windows, just harsh electric glare coming from strip lights surrounding the room. Nothing in the room, but the large black couch in the middle, where some of the Nestlings were now sitting, and some chairs put in random places. Vietra had always found the lack of aesthetics in the room and the whole building tiring. She wanted more colors, more objects that would make the room cozier, but the only person she dared to talk about it was Mroolic, who was now gone.

Vietra wanted to slow down, but it would be taken as another sign of weakness. Everything inside her was turning upside down, and every step was harder than the previous one. So close to the black door that unhelpfully slid open for her. To the grey, narrow corridor behind it. It took exactly seven steps to reach her destination from there. No slowing down, even though no one was watching anymore.

"Vietra!" a familiar voice called out. "Wait!"

"I can't," she said taking another step. "I have to get my punishment."

"You'll have enough time for that," Tyssdin said blocking her way. "Why did you do it again? You knew how it would end!"

"Are you here to reprove me?" she replied coldly. "I'm pretty sure I've already got it, thanks."

"No," he answered quietly. "I'm here to tell you I think it was the right thing to do. A humane thing. You care. I care too." He looked her in the eye like a puppy expecting approval. Tyss was shorter than her, which made him look up and intensified the effect. It made Vietra feel slightly uncomfortable. Did he really mean it, or was he saying so just to make her believe they had something in common?

"But you know the rules. It's not about being humane. It's about obeying and doing exactly what you are told, no matter what. That's what the Master expects from you. You shouldn't have done it. Not for the third time. He won't forgive you. You don't want to end up like Mroolic, do you?"

"Listen, Tyss, I really appreciate your concern, but it's already done. I can't change the past, as far as I know, and unless you have a revolutionary technology to offer, I'm afraid I have to go."

"Are you in a hurry?" Tyss curved an eyebrow in a sarcastic expression. She had to admit he looked attractive when he did that. It moved something deep inside of her. Something like a long-forgotten memory. Something warm and safe. "Come on, V, I know how scared you are. You don't have to pretend with me. Everyone feels this way. It's not weakness. It's human nature."

"I'm not scared," she said.

"He can't see us now," Tyss said lowering his voice. "He isn't watching. We have two more minutes before he comes to set it up for you. Two minutes is not much, but isn't it better to spend them with a friend?"

"How do you know he isn't watching?" Vietra asked. She knew it was a mistake, but she wanted to trust him. Or maybe to trust anybody at all.

"I..." he hesitated for a moment, probably also weighing how much he could reveal to her. "I just know. It's not the point. You are safe for now. I know how frightening it is."

16

"How would you know? You've never been there!" she tried to keep a note of disdain from her voice, but she didn't succeed because Tyss looked a little hurt.

"I just know," he repeated and suddenly hugged her. It shocked Vietra so much that she didn't move for a couple of seconds. They weren't emotional, weren't supposed to be. They were above it. Emotions made them vulnerable and weak. They were bound by respect as partners, and they were ready to give their lives for each other if only it was necessary for their purpose. As well as leave others to die if that was required. They had to be driven by logic alone. See the clear picture. Not get attached to one another.

This wasn't the right thing to do, especially now, when she'd already brought the Master's disapproval on herself. But there he was, another human being offering her consolation. A warm, heavily built, middle-aged man with brownish skin and dark eyes. A temporary escape from fear. Vietra huddled up to him and felt she wasn't alone anymore. Her terror was now shared between two and, surprisingly, diminished.

"That's it, there's no more time," Tyss whispered. "You have to get in there now. He's coming. Hang on there," he looked her in the eye with a new expression and disappeared in the corridor.

Vietra entered the room, feeling a little dazed. Strange, she thought, but a hug didn't make her weaker, on the contrary, it gave her a little more strength. She felt safe within Tyssdin's arms. Now though, after he was gone, it felt as if she'd been shaken out of a cozy bed into the cold. Probably it was true. All these emotional expressions weakened them after all.

She was in the sensory deprivation room. The absence of sound was that of outer space. Nothing reached one's ears, even the sound of one's own voice. It was also completely dark, so that there was no difference between having one's eyes open or closed. Vietra had been there before, and she knew that after a while she would completely lose sense of time and reality. She'd be totally disoriented, and hallucinations would take over her mind soon. There was no point in fighting them. She always lost this battle. They were too vivid to tell them from reality, even if she knew they were mere constructs of her brain.

Distorted sounds and terrifying creatures would fill the room. They'd surround her and creep around and come closer and try to touch or bite, they'd appear unexpectedly, jump at her out of the darkness, stare in her eyes, examine her. Sometimes she thought she actually came in contact with aliens. Sometimes it felt like forever, and she began to forget who she was or where she actually was. She thought she'd never get out of there. After leaving the room, she found it difficult to focus and perform her normal activities. It took time to tune her body and mind back to normal.

Vietra remembered the first time she got into the room. When the first hallucinations began, she knew those were her mind games, so she enjoyed them. She imagined herself on another planet, studying its bizarre alien life. It was fascinating, but just for a while. The more time passed, the more troubling the images became, and the more anxious she got. She tried to remind herself it wasn't real, but her mind seemed to ignore it. After that, she could never enjoy the hallucinations again. The anticipation of the forthcoming horrors kept her unsettled from the very beginning, and it got worse every time. Nothing frightened her like the sensory deprivation room.

"You disappointed me," the Master's voice suddenly broke the cosmic silence, and Vietra was immensely grateful for that.

"I know, I'm sorry," she tried to say but couldn't produce a sound. It made her desperate. At least she could hear the Master, but who knew, maybe it was a hallucination too?

"You disobeyed me," he continued, "lied to me and expressed improper weakness. All in one day. You see how such behavior is absolutely unacceptable. I'm sure you understand that it calls for a more severe punishment than usually. I'm also sure you know I don't want to do it, but you've left me no choice. You are valuable, Vietra, and I need you to be one hundred percent reliable. I don't want to worry about you when the time comes to fulfill your purpose. I need you to be ready. I'm doing it for you and for all of us. For our future."

Even though the temperature of the room matched the temperature of her body, Vietra felt a wave of heat sweeping through her, followed by a shiver. The Master had never said anything before a punishment. The fact that he felt the need to explain it and the *"more severe than usually"* part terrified her. Something really bad was coming, and she had no means to stop it.

Vietra hated feeling helpless. She suddenly found herself on the edge of crying. She couldn't risk that in case she was being watched, but it had never been so hard to control it. Fervently searching for something to draw some strength from, she found and clung to the memory of a hug Tyss gave her.

The feeling was broken by sudden, severe pain. Vietra saw hundreds of small insects eating their way through her athletic body, that she'd been trying so hard to keep healthy and fit, making tunnels inside of her, coming in and out. She was watching her pale skin turning red and blue and violet with blood and bruises. Each of the tunnels was a separate source of unbearable pain. Vietra didn't know something could be so agonizing. Seeing the insects busily destroying her body made her suffering even worse. She was writhing and shivering and rolling on the floor. She was screaming, but there was no sound. It was playing out in absolute silence. She couldn't see anything but herself and the insects, complete darkness surrounded them, as if nothing else in the world existed. Somewhere on the outskirts of her tormented mind there was the knowledge that it wasn't real, but it failed to alleviate her pain. It was a torture that would probably leave no traces on her body but would definitely maim her mind.

Suddenly she saw her mother. She'd never known her parents, as she was an orphan just like the rest of the Nestlings. The Master was the one who took care of her for her entire life. But Vietra immediately recognized the woman in front of her. She knew it was her mother, she felt it, the tenderness, the warmth, the special bond. They looked alike too: her mother was a bit taller than Vietra, and her greying hair still had playful redness in them. Her body was curvier than Vietra's but looked athletic as well. Her skin was suntanned though, which Vietra could never achieve.

For a moment, her mother's presence gave Vietra hope. She wanted to call out for her, come closer, give her a hug, look into her eyes, find out their color. But she couldn't move, and her mother didn't see her. She was looking around, and Vietra could tell she was scared. There was still blackness all around, as if only her mother was in the spotlight. Then three men emerged from the dark. They were wearing creepy animal masks and clown suits, and they were carrying grotesque weapons, dark blood dribbling from them.

Her mother didn't seem to notice them, but her movements became more nervous. Vietra wanted to warn her, to protect her. She knew she could easily deal with those three, but she couldn't get up. She saw that the insects had eaten her legs completely, so she started crawling towards her mother, but it was too slow. She felt like something heavy and sticky was holding her back. Every move was a struggle.

The men were coming closer. The events were unfolding as if in slow motion. Vietra's concentration had always slowed the world down for her, but this time it had gluey texture of a bad dream. Her own helplessness was unbearable. She didn't want to see what would happen as one of the men reached her mother and started raising his axe over her head, but she couldn't close her eyes or look away.

It was a different kind of pain. She'd been hurt many times in training. It never got easier or less terrifying–in fact, quite the opposite happened. She usually met the pain with the graveness of a weary soldier, head on. But seeing her mother hurt and being unable to do anything about it had a new and alarming quality. A feeling of unfairness pierced Vietra. She was nothing better than a child, deceived and betrayed for the first time in the face of this new anguish. She was overpowered by sorrow and shock; she didn't know how to deal with the emotions mauling her.

Suddenly, there was darkness and silence. The image of her mother fell apart, and Vietra realized with clarity that the woman was a stranger to her. It didn't make her feel better, but the next moment she fell into nothingness, free.

CHAPTER 3

Cay put his earplugs in to protect himself from the noise of passenger and delivery drones buzzing around, went up onto his roof and crossed the bridge to the nearest public drone platform.

The next part of the plan was tricky. It was only possible to get to the place Cay was looking for in a passenger drone, but no drone would accept commands from a person without an implant.

Luckily, there was a way. The drones hadn't always been flying autonomously and activated by implants. Older models had initially been steered manually. They were rebuilt later, when the number of accidents caused by people not trained to use the new kind of transportation urged engineers to come up with a solution. Cay had to find an old model and hack it to allow manual steering.

He looked around. It seemed like it was his lucky day. Among the four drones waiting on the platform, one was clearly what he was looking for. He rushed to it and got inside.

The pain and confusion and all the doubts were still there, but he was now filled with something new, something bigger than all that.

For the first time in his life, he had no idea what to expect of tomorrow or even of the next hour. It gave him a kind of chill, which turned out to be surprisingly refreshing. Like electric charges rushing through his veins, spreading power and alertness through his body. Yes, Cay realized with amusement, it felt strangely good. It moved the troubles that had been worrying him for the last few days into the background, pushing survival to the top of his priorities. Every moment became acute and sharp. It felt like he reached a higher level of consciousness.

Cay wouldn't have known how to hack a drone, it wasn't his area of expertise. He needed help, and he managed to find a shady person online who agreed to assist him for a substantial sum of money. As a result, he received detailed, step-by-step instructions and code. He had no idea whether it actually made sense and had no way of checking, so he was acutely aware that he might have been conned.

Half expecting the police to show up, Cay took the display panel off using a small automatic screwdriver. So far so good. The ECU was right behind it, and Cay connected a cheap terminal he'd just bought to the JTAG port. He made a backup of the ECU software and ran the exploit provided by his mysterious hacker. For a couple of seconds, while lines of code where flickering on the screen, he went completely still. As a simple green line of text confirmed he got root access to the ECU, Cay realized he'd been holding his breath. He exhaled and ran the program that was supposed to overwrite the control module to receive commands from his terminal. He could hear his heart beating.

Cay's gaze was transfixed on the terminal while he was willing the software to do its job faster, so he was startled when he noticed movement on his right from the corner of his eye. Even before he turned his head to see what exactly it was, icy cold spread all over his chest and stomach, and his brain built several possible scenarios: the police were notified by his suspicious activity with the drone, the fixers found out he'd got rid of his implant, Limea was looking for him after not having found him at home.

Instead, the intruder turned out to be a tall, muscular woman with dark skin and unruly hair, thumping angrily on the window shield. Apparently, she'd been trying to get his attention for a while, but Cay couldn't hear her because of the earplugs. He didn't remember having locked the drone and felt grateful he had. The window shields were obscured from the outside, so the woman could only see the outline of his figure, but she couldn't know what exactly he looked like or what he was doing. Cay looked around and saw that the rest of the drones were gone. She needed to get somewhere and wanted to join him in the drone, but Cay couldn't help her with that.

The program finished its work, notifying Cay with a gentle chime that he could now steer the drone manually from his terminal. The hacker, whom Cay was beginning to respect, had provided him with software for that too. He touched the controls on his terminal, starting the propellers and making the drone twitch. The woman jumped, startled. She burst out screaming, shaking her fists at him, but the drone was already rising in the air.

Steering it manually and trying to keep it in a straight line was difficult and required more effort than Cay had expected.

He'd never actually steered a drone: when they first appeared, it was still possible to get around by other means of transport, which he preferred. But as the plague was spreading, steadily making the ground inaccessible, drones became more and more popular.

25

Small and handy, they were designed to take in one or two passengers and transport them to short distances, replacing cars. By the time Cay had to use one, they'd already been made autonomous. They communicated with each other to calculate routes and avoid accidents, so they were perfectly safe. But as the number of drones had grown tenfold in the last half a year and continued increasing incrementally, the software behind the whole system began to lag behind. When a hundred drones met at a certain spot, calculating routes could take minutes, to say nothing about larger amounts. It created air jams with people suspended helplessly in large, immobile swarms, waiting for their drones to decide on the right way to avoid each other.

As Cay was struggling with steering, trying to avoid crashing into other vehicles, he ran into an air jam. He could keep flying, but that would attract attention, so he suspended his drone in the air too. He looked down at the city that had changed so much in the recent years. Light structures built on top of old buildings, creating living space for people who had to escape the lower levels of the city. They used to look futuristic and slightly postapocalyptic to him at first but were now so familiar. Roofs turned into platforms for passenger drones and places for public meetings with cafes, bars, markets, playgrounds, art installations, sports equipment, exhibitions and all sorts of things, with people hanging out and going about their business even now. Bridges connecting buildings, where people could walk and ride their bikes. It was so strange that they were living their regular lives as if nothing had happened, while his life was falling apart. And of course, there was an inaccessible sea of green below, slowly creeping up.

Cay inhaled deeply and exhaled slowly. He could use a break. His consciousness seemed to be drifting away with the air seeping from his lungs. Judging by the amount of people hanging in the air around him, it would take at least 10 minutes for the drones to find their ways. Well, Cay could wait. He noticed some time ago that air jams created a perfect setting for thinking, and his brain took on the task of summing up all his recent troubles.

He noticed something was wrong a week before, on a Tuesday afternoon. He got up to find Limea in the living room, drawing. He came up to her to give her a kiss and tell her about a lucid dream he had after she'd waken him up in the middle of the night. As she raised her eyes and shared a warm smile with him, Cay felt a small electrical charge of warning in his stomach. He didn't understand what it was at first, but it felt strange. The cold of it spread across his body and gave him a little shiver. It felt uncomfortable, as if something was nagging and scratching from the inside, like a cat behind a door.

"Is everything okay?" Cay asked searching for the answer in Limea's eyes.

"Yes, everything's great!" she replied and added with warm concern: "You?"

"I'm not sure. Something feels wrong."

"What is it?"

"I don't understand, it's just a feeling. Some unease. Hard to tell."

"Maybe you've had a bad dream?"

"Maybe," Cay shrugged.

He didn't remember what he was dreaming about before waking up, but it seemed to have been unsettling. Limea was smiling, and he loved her smile. Her thick red curls were gleaming, and her porcelain skin seemed almost transparent where sunlight was touching her cheek. She had probably spent some time outside because there seemed to be more freckles. Her touch soothed Cay's suspense and lulled the subconscious trying to reach his attention. For a moment he felt good again. She was wearing only a thin nightgown, and he could feel her slim body so well through the soft fabric. She smelled like fruit and paint and herself. Her kiss tasted good. The world narrowed to just the two of them, and Cay took Limea into his arms and brought her to their bed.

He didn't quite remember how they got undressed, but the moment he entered her was vivid as always. The sweet merging into one, accompanied by her moan, the perfect synergy of their bodies, her orgasms caressing him, and in the moment when he felt the invincible wave of pleasure washing him away, he looked into her eyes, and that was when he realized. Cold terror impaled him with sudden dreadful clarity, breaking the magic spell of their intimacy.

Cay continued staring into Limea's eyes, completely appalled by what he saw there or rather by what he didn't see. It was gone.

At first, he mistook it for the lack of feeling. Standing alone on top of the mountain, exposed to the harsh wind, naked and bitten by angry snow would feel a little warmer than what he felt when he thought she stopped loving him. But he soon realized it wasn't that. No, no, it was something deeper, something that couldn't be taken from a human, no matter how they felt. It could hide behind masks and strong emotions, could be diffused by weariness, could shadow in the corner of the eye, but it was always there. The inner core, the stem, the melana, the essence of personality, the blaze of self, the light, the character, the inimitable nameless that makes us who we are. Whatever you call it.

Cay knew Limea too well and adored the reflection of her inner world that shone through her eyes, just like she knew and adored his. It was the magic of their connection, deep communication happening through mysterious channels lying beyond human understanding.

"What's wrong?" Limea asked seeing the look on his face.

What should he have said? Cay had no idea. He didn't understand what was going on, so he mumbled something and went to the shower room.

A massive cloud was waiting for him, and he chose a tropical downpour to wash away his bewilderment. Heavy drops broke against his body and went through the filters in the floor into the atmospheric systems that would turn them back into a cloud within 10 minutes. Some of the water would be filtered and transferred into the irrigation system for the plants and crops growing abundantly all over their apartment.

Cay imagined the water working its ways through the pipes, connections and hubs. Being filtered and processed into vapor in the atmospheric system, condensed to create a cloud. Reaching the roots of the plants, ridding them of their thirst. Cay didn't have to look in order to see the whole system at work. He designed it. He made the floors and pipes transparent because he wanted Limea to see it too, and she loved watching the water flow.

Cay never felt quite safe around the plants. He wanted to have at least one room free of any vegetation, where they could hide in case mutation happened. Limea argued that if their plants got infected, no room would be capable of saving them, and even if they were able to get hold of the protective materials that would keep the greenery away, they'd die a slow death anyway, unable to get out of there. It was reasonable, so Cay agreed, but he still thought he'd feel better if they had such a room. It would be some psychological trick that would give him comfort.

Limea, on the other hand, was fascinated by the flora. Even the plague was something she admired, discarding all the damage it had caused. She must have also been drawn to the danger of it, thrilling excitement resonating with the wild in her. It was beaming through the tropical verdancy of her panther eyes.

The drones around started moving, snatching Cay from the depth of his memories. He hardly managed to put his hands back on controls when they got hung up again. He had to wait longer, so he let his thoughts drift again.

It was hard to believe what he'd seen because it made no sense. The tropical rain partially washed away and alleviated his fears. It was absurd, it must have been some kind of mistake or a trick of the mind. But after he'd noticed it, the emptiness was brazenly staring from his love's eyes every time he looked, impossible to ignore.

Every time he turned away, he started thinking it wasn't real and almost reassured himself. Every time he looked back into Limea's eyes, the black hole in his chest devoured a bit more of him... but what was it? It seemed so bizarrely obvious and elusive at the same time. It was right in front of him but faded away as soon as he reached out for it. He felt it with grave certainty, like freezing wind howling through hollow, corroded pipes. At the same time, his mind couldn't grasp it.

Later that evening, he was standing behind Limea's back, looking at her drawing. She always started like this, with paint and a piece of paper. She said she had to feel her work through the smell of paint, to have tactile contact with it when it was born. It gave the painting depth and emotion. When the scene was ready, she would digitize it, uploading it into her virtual cabinet, where she turned it into a detailed holographic scene her observers could walk into and experience.

In her virtual spaces one could visit distant worlds and get acquainted with their technologies, try their entertainment and get lost in the mysterious wild forests, meet unearthly creatures and discover hidden dimensions, break on through to the other side and experience another Universe. This time, she was drawing aliens traveling to explore a newly discovered planet in their outlandish spaceship. It was so like her: the style, the lines, every little detail, the adventurous, surreal mood. The drawing calmed Cay down and lulled his agony.

"Limea," he said, finally ready to tell her about his delusions. She would know what to say, and they would laugh at that together.

Limea looked up at him and shattered his alleviation. There was one thing about her: when she was drawing her alien landscapes, her mind wondered billions of light years away. She wasn't really in the room, it was just her body transmitting distant cosmic signals into images. She was among them. Somewhere there, lost between the strokes of her painting. If she was distracted from drawing, the reflection of the faraway worlds continued gleaming in her eyes for a few seconds before it faded away. It was like waking her up and catching her in transition between dream and reality. Her eyes carried alien experiences. At times, she looked a bit like an alien herself. This time, when she raised her eyes, there was a kind inquiry and love but absolutely no trace of her space trip. And that was when Cay realized with sudden disillusioning clarity it wasn't Limea in front of him.

"It's a beautiful painting," he said.

"Thanks," she smiled and turned back to her work.

Cay turned away to leave but stopped and asked quietly:

"Who are you?"

Limea looked at him in a puzzled manner. She touched her ear as she often did when immersed in her thoughts and colored it green and yellow.

"I'm a mixture of everyone I've ever known and everything I've ever experienced, everything I've learned and thought about, every place I've been to, every idea I've encountered, all art that I've consumed, nature I've been surrounded by, atoms of people and animals long gone, cosmic particles passing through my body, dreams... I guess I'm an empty vessel filled with all of this stuff and shaped by it. I am no one. I am a work in progress," she said after a minute of thinking.

That sounded like her. It seemed to Cay he'd already heard some of those things from her before. He came up and looked closely into her eyes. No. She wasn't there.

"Are you okay?" the stranger who was impersonating his love asked. "You've been weird today. Weirder than usually," she added with a smile.

"I don't know what to say."

"I'm worried about you. Tell me what's going on, Cay. How can I help?"

And the worry was in her eyes. And so was love, and tenderness, and empathy. The questions were perfectly right. But she wasn't there!

"You can tell me where Limea is," Cay said.

"Now you are frightening me. I'm right here. What's wrong, babe? What do you mean?" she got up and put her hands around his neck. She was looking into his eyes, and her gaze was loaded with emotions Limea would probably feel in such circumstances. She was scared, and she was reaching out to him, seeking connection and realizing she was denied it. It looked genuine. But her inner world was still missing. It wasn't her. Just a very good copy.

For a moment, Cay considered confronting her and making her explain what all of that meant. Then he thought it was too hasty. Probably, it wasn't a good idea to reveal what he knew to her. He might have already revealed too much. If someone planted her there instead of the real Limea, there must have been a reason for it. And those behind it must be really powerful

33

to make it happen. He knew no way to create an intelligent copy of a person that would look so genuine.

Listening to his own thoughts, Cay realized how ludicrous they sounded. He needed more time to think it all through. And until then, he shouldn't raise any suspicions.

"I don't know," he said. "I'm sorry. I feel weird today, it's probably because of the sim I had yesterday."

"I didn't know you had a sim," Limea looked surprised.

"I didn't tell you. But I did."

"What was it like?"

"I don't want to talk about it yet. Need some time to process it and get back to normal."

"Of course," she nodded. "But remember I'm here for you."

"I know," he said and hugged her so that she couldn't see the terror in his eyes.

The drones finally figured out a solution, bringing Cay back to the present moment and forcing him to focus on flying. Little by little, he was getting the hang of steering, even beginning to enjoy it.

A roof he was passing over reminded Cay of his own. The association triggered a chain of thoughts and memories.

Normally, energy was collected by communal solar panels, stored in communal batteries and distributed among all apartments in a building. Unfortunately, the technology was obsolete and inefficient. The panels produced way less energy than they could, and the batteries stored only a limited amount of it. In theory, all the needs of the residents were supposed to be covered by the system, while in practice, it was hardly enough to power their home assistants, and blackouts occurred once in a while. As a result, people had to buy energy from corporate solar farms situated all over the world and store it in bulky batteries of low capacity. The batteries could only store about 5 kWh and had to be recharged regularly. What is more, they were loud and broke down easily.

Cay knew for sure that the manufacturers only kept such low standards to have people buy from them regularly and abundantly, introducing occasional minor improvements presented as groundbreaking innovations. Some people might have taken him for a conspiracy theorist, but he'd spent four years of his life working on this problem.

Cay had always been interested in solar power. He'd been studying it for years, monitoring innovation. There were lots of open source projects and new research scattered all over the Internet. There were groups, non-profits and individuals working on improving existing technology and sharing it with underdeveloped regions. The problem was that their scale was too small: it was more difficult to organize extensive action in the post-plague world. And the open source projects that, in theory, allowed anyone to build their own panels and batteries were highly technical, so only a handful of people could actually use them or even knew anything about them. Besides, the materials weren't so easy to obtain.

Studying the work of others online, Cay decided to gather all the relevant information from various sources and see what he could do with it. He meticulously sifted through the data from all over the world, doing his own research and carrying out experiments. He found what worked best and improved some of the innovations, connected others and got rid of unnecessary elements.

As a result, he created powerful solar fabric that could be merged with any material or made into an autonomous solar panel and harvest around a hundredfold more energy through a smaller surface than an average corporate panel, transferring it to compact batteries each of which could accumulate and store up to 50,000 kWh as long as necessary. He put it together in an elegant system that could provide every home with all the energy it needed. The production was easy enough and the cost affordable.

Technically, Cay was working on it with a friend who mostly handled marketing and helped with some minor technical stuff. Broon. He arranged several meetings with the media and got everyone excited about the upcoming product. He also dealt with shipments of manufacturing materials and took care of paperwork. They had a company together.

When everything was almost ready, three people in expensive suits paid them a visit. They were from Sunny–one of the energy corporations that supplied a huge part of the world with solar panels and power. Cay remembered them well. Two tall, elegant women and a fat man, whose eyes emanated slight contempt and slug superiority. Their formal, calibrated smiles rather reinforced that impression. They said they were impressed by the innovation and wanted to buy it. They wanted intellectual property. The money they offered was huge. Broon was excited.

"If we agree, when will you start selling it?" Cay asked.

"When the time is right," one of the women said.

"This year? Next?" he inquired, even though he already knew the answer.

"When the market is ready for it," the man added with a dismissive movement of his fat arm.

"That's not an answer," Cay said ignoring the look on Broon's face that was urging him to shut up.

"It shouldn't bother you. You are getting paid really well for your idea. Isn't that the point?" another woman said, and her smile became vulturous.

"That's only part of it," Cay shrugged. "The other one is to make the world a better place."

"The world is well enough," the man said chuckling. "But your position in it can be much better. You can have anything you want. Your dream life."

"My dream is to do something worthy."

"This is such bullshit, son," the man patted his shoulder with a wet, unpleasant laugh. "You are too young to be good at bargaining. But I tell you what, I'll encourage you with a small concession for trying."

And the man offered them a slightly bigger sum of money. Cay couldn't remember how much it was exactly. What he remembered was his complete certainty that their project was going to be buried. Sunny didn't need it. It would cause a huge loss of sales. People would only have to buy his product once to be supplied with all the power they needed. Sunny wanted to buy it to make sure it would never get out of their tomb of bright ideas. Cay tried to imagine how many they'd already bought. Were there dozens? Hundreds of innovations that could change the world? Collecting dust. Forgotten. Abandoned.

"Let us think about it," he said.

"Don't think too long, the offer might be a little less attractive next time. The longer you'll think, the less money you'll get. The clock is ticking. But I'll give you two days before anything changes. We strongly recommend you get back to us before that. After all, we all know you are going to take the offer. So, do it on the best terms you can get," with these words Sunny representatives left.

"We shouldn't take it," Cay said as soon as the door closed behind them.

"Are you out of your fucking mind?" Broon burst out. "This is our chance to be rich! To be free, just like we wanted! To be independent, to finally stop selling our time for money! Think about it, you can have anything you want, go anywhere you like any moment. You will never have to work again. Only do the things that you like. Create more devices if you want or write a fucking book on success, travel or buy a habitat on the Moon. It's a dream come true! How can you have any doubts?"

All of it sounded appealing. Independence was one of the things Cay craved most in life. He wanted to break free from the system and did his best to achieve this goal. But he knew his creation could change the lives of many people for the better, especially in poor and undeveloped regions. It wasn't all about money for him. Freedom was so tempting though, and it had never been so tangible and close. Broon was probably right. Cay wasn't sure. Later that evening he spoke to Limea about it.

"I don't think you should do it," she said after a pause. "The knowledge that they've buried your project will devastate you. You'll keep returning to the thoughts of what might have happened if you hadn't agreed to their deal. You'll be thinking about the difference you could have made. These thoughts will haunt you. Besides, this isn't just work for you. This project is your child. You've made it to improve people's lives. It has a purpose. It has your heart in it. You want it to live."

"It's true," Cay said. It never stopped astonishing him how Limea seemed to have the ability to read deeply in his thoughts and beyond. Sometimes when he was confused, she seemed to understand him better than he did. "My instincts told me not to. But on the other hand, there is freedom and everything we've dreamed about. Traveling all around the world, living in different countries without being tied to one place, free from jobs or deadlines. Waking up when we want to. Turning our ideas into reality, creating what we are really crazy about. Meeting people, discovering places, having adventures, visiting festivals. Going to space."

"We can achieve it anyway. This is not the price you should pay. You'll be unhappy if you do it. Maybe it'll take more time without Sunny, but it will feel well-deserved. The impact will be your reward. When you will watch the news and see how people have energy where they didn't use to. Can you imagine the feeling?"

"I hope we'll experience it soon," Cay smiled. "Broon and I can sell it on our own like we planned initially. We won't earn that much, and, of course, it will take much longer, but we'll be able to do some good in the meantime."

Limea kissed him on the nose and threw her arms around his neck.

"You inspire me," she said. "I want to be a better person when I look at what you do. I want to be more creative and smarter, and I want to grow like a tree and never stop."

"You have the same effect on me."

"We're a good influence on each other," Limea laughed. "I guess we're really lucky."

"We certainly are."

They looked into each other's eyes savoring the light. Limea kissed him on the neck, behind the ear, on the nose and on the lips. She ran her nails through his hair. The kiss was long, it washed reality away.

When Cay told Broon about his decision on the next day, his friend wasn't enthusiastic.

"Come on," he said. "Of course, we can sell it on our own, but where is the guarantee that it'll work out? Sunny will mess with us anyway. What if they destroy us? You know they can. And all our work will be for nothing. This way we'll make sure we'll get paid well."

"It will be for nothing if we sell it to them," Cay argued. "You know they'll never let it out into the world if they lay their hands on it."

"You are exaggerating. Maybe they'll hold it down for a couple of years to sell their planned products first, but after that they'll release it. Think how great it would be for their reputation! They won't miss this chance."

"They don't care about reputation, at least not when it comes to losing profit. Our invention is a disaster for them, it's the end of their market."

"Then you should understand they won't let us sell it anyway. At least they offer us a decent deal for it. We'd better not stand in their way."

"We'd better try. We'll figure something out. We should act fast, release a prototype, give it out for testing, send it around the world. We can even share the manufacturing details online for everyone to be able to build it if they try to stop us from distributing it legally. Many companies will start making it then. I prefer to earn nothing at all, but to see our product make its way into the world than to get rich for burying it. We can stall for time until we get everything prepared, so that they can't do anything."

"You are fucking crazy," Broon tapped his forehead in disbelief.

"I just don't want to give up easily. And I don't want to play by their rules."

"You'll be left broke. You are naive if you think Sunny will let you pull this out. Be reasonable, man, we are in the real world. We can't compete with such giants. Being broke is probably the best-case scenario. You might end up in prison or even worse. It's within their reach, they can do anything they want. But they are offering us a fair deal. They kindly give us the opportunity to walk away with dignity. Later this chance will be gone, and you'll regret not having made this deal."

"I won't."

"It's not just for you to decide, you know. We've been working on it together, so I have a say too."

"I don't want to sound cocky, but I've made it. You did useful and important things, dealt with a lot I didn't have time for, and I really appreciate it. But I'm the inventor. It's my idea, my design, my calculations, my research, my execution. I think I have the right to decide what to do with if we can't agree."

"What? Are you trying to say you have more rights to it than I do? That my work hasn't been valuable all of a sudden?" Broon crossed his arms and looked fiercely at Cay. He was boiling with righteous indignation.

"It's been very valuable, but now you are trying to destroy it. As for the rights, I wouldn't put it this way, but yes, I believe that as long as I've made it, I can decide what to do with it. I don't want to do it this way, I hope we can reach an agreement. Let's not rush and make this decision under the influence of emotions. We can get back to it tomorrow."

"Tomorrow the two days they've given us will be over," Broon said angrily. "But you've already made the decision, of course, so you don't care. You'll just keep trying to convince me until I give up. I don't have a say in *your* project," the emphasis he put on the word "your" made it clear what Broon thought about Cay's argument.

Seeing how pissed off his friend was puzzled Cay. He thought it was pretty fair, considering the amount and quality of work they'd done. Later he regretted having mentioned it. It was a mistake. He'd hurt Broon's feelings and made him indignant about being treated unfairly. But Cay was emotional too. It was the first argument like that, and he wasn't ready. He decided Broon was just upset, and he'd see reason as soon as he calmed down. He didn't. He closed up and turned passive aggressive, making normal conversation impossible. He got even more bitter after the time Sunny had granted them for thinking

42

was over. He said almost nothing, and when he did, it was a sarcastic comment seeping with poison.

Cay tried to reach him and call for a sincere dialogue where they'd attempt to step into each other's shoes, but Broon wasn't interested. He said Cay didn't want to step into his shoes, his only agenda was to make Broon agree with him. Cay had to admit to himself it was true. He wasn't going to change his mind, but he believed he could convince his friend to do so. A couple of days passed this way, and Cay started getting edgy. He was tired and stressed. Broon didn't pick up, so he decided to have a good rest with Limea, and they went away for a weekend.

When they got back, there was a message from Broon saying he'd sold the project to Sunny, and Cay could get his half of the royalties if he wanted to. He couldn't believe it was true. Broon had access to all the materials of the project in their private cloud so that he could add his occasional contributions. It never crossed Cay's mind his friend would just steal it. No, it must have been a bad joke, a twisted way of teaching him a lesson, anything except for what it seemed. Broon wouldn't betray him this way.

After unsuccessful attempts to contact him, Cay set out to his place. When Broon finally opened the door, he looked as if communication with Cay brought him physical discomfort.

"Are you here for the money?" he said. "You could have just texted, I'd transfer it to you."

"I'm here to ask what the fuck have you done?" it was difficult for Cay to stay calm, but he was trying. He wanted to hear an explanation. He was hoping Broon would say he hadn't actually done it. *Please, Broon, be the person I know!*

"Listen, I don't really have time to talk to you."

"Really? But you had time to sell my project to those fuckers?"

"And here we go again. Your project. *Your* project! It's always all about you! It was our project, and I did what was best for it. You know, talking to you is really depressing. I don't think I ever want to see you again. You've lost my trust and respect. Just send me your account details and I'll transfer the money to you."

"I've lost your trust... and respect?" Cay could hardly pronounce the words. His throat seemed too narrow to let them through. It was true then. Broon actually did it. It was all over his face, lurking from his eyes, weighing on his shoulders. "After you've stolen my project and sold it without my consent? Knowing I was against it? Knowing I wanted it to help people? *I've* lost *your* trust and respect? Not the other way around?"

"Damn, you are a broken record, aren't you? Face the truth, it wasn't yours, you arrogant prick! And don't do anything stupid, the project is legally Sunny's now, it's their intellectual property. As a representative of our company I signed the agreement saying we would never try to release it or anything like it. They'll legally destroy you if you do. This is my last advice to you: let it go. That's it. I never want to see you again. You'll get the money as soon as you send your account details to me. You are lucky you got to work with a decent person like myself, someone else would have kept all the money," and with a smug look on his face Broon shut the door.

"Shove the fucking money up your ass, traitor!" Cay shouted through the door hitting it with his fist.

He actually never requested the money, though he regretted it many times afterwards. Broon appeared in the media announcing the project turned out to be impossible to complete due to some technical obstacles. Probably a part of the agreement he signed.

It was the first serious betrayal in Cay's life. It hurt and burned, it didn't let him sleep at night and sent him heavy dreams when he finally did. He didn't know people could do such things. Not the people he knew, anyway. He couldn't understand how someone he considered his friend and partner could do it and believe it was the right thing. His thoughts were on a loop, revolving around the event over and over again. Limea helped him through that time; it still hurt a lot, but her presence was soothing.

Later he found out Broon got a managing position in Sunny's innovation research department. Probably tracking and buying other ideas that could change the market to bury them.

Cay got over it after a while, and his faith in humanity was restored, though severely corrupted. He still built the tech for himself and hid it in the structure of the roof to never buy anything from Sunny again. Their apartment needed a lot of energy for all the plants, and they got it directly from the sun. They kept about 20 fully powered batteries and managed to occasionally share energy with friends, family and poorer neighbors, hiding the actual source. Cay worked on other things, but thinking about this one always had a sour taste to it. Even now, after all these years, he shuddered at the memory.

Cay took a moment to appreciate how natural steering the drone had become since he could dive in his thoughts like that, keeping only part of his attention on the controls. He should probably be more careful.

He still couldn't believe he had actually removed his implant. He thought it was good that they were now put into palms. It had only been the case for several years, and Cay still remembered brain implants vividly. It seemed that they were there just yesterday.

When the technology was invented, it raised lots of concerns, but it flooded the market with unbelievable pace as people began to see a world of new exciting possibilities it opened. Enhancing memory and senses, accelerating brain work to speed unimaginable before, linking people into networks of shared consciousness, making telepathy a mundane reality, enabling communication without boundaries, reducing the process of learning to downloading the necessary data directly into the brain and much more. It was unbelievable. People felt like gods, it was like they suddenly evolved into a new species, and nothing seemed impossible anymore.

Interstellar travel was within reach and so was immortality, as the implants could detect the slightest signals indicating possible health problems, while scientists were working on nanobots which were to repair any damage, including in the DNA. As soon as the nanobots were ready, they would be stored within every implant, capable of self-replication if needed to make humans forget about diseases once and for all.

The number of scientists increased drastically since it didn't require decades of meticulous studying anymore. They linked up into creative networks, solving one problem after another, and nanobots were a priority for many, so it seemed like they were just a year or so away.

Brain to computer interfaces emerged and evolved, becoming more and more precise and elaborate. Enhanced humans looked down on the "naturals" as a kind of a primitive species. Something like apes for previous generations. So similar, yet so far behind. The gap between the two groups grew every day.

Cay was among the first people to get an implant. He was fascinated by its possibilities. The limits of human brain had always felt too tight for him. He aspired for more. There was too much to know about the world. Getting an implant was like breaking out from a cage. The limits vanished. He had access to endless knowledge, and his brain processed the most complex information within milliseconds.

Making decisions, analyzing, building complex systems in his imagination and transmitting them straight into a computer was easy and accurate as never before. He had a broader perspective of the world, he finally understood complicated theories and ideas, he saw what he had been blind to before.

The Universe suddenly seemed much vaster, but also much closer. Some questions, like those about his own place in the world became irrelevant and died out in the face of more sophisticated ones. Connections became more evident, his thinking became more structured and logical with every thought leading to another one, building a constantly expanding network of facts and ideas. Sometimes it seemed like it could go on forever, and infinity was much scarier than ever before. He had to stop on purpose, learn how to control his thinking before it built constructions so bulky even his enhanced mind failed to comprehend.

The process of creation became astonishingly easy and somewhat devalued. Anyone could do anything now. It was not a matter of skills and perseverance but of mere willingness. Cay knew he could be anyone, and in anticipation of a very long, if not endless, life he was going to try it all. He hoped to see other planets. The fear of death finally let go of him. The existential dread that had sometimes pervaded him before redesigned itself into something new, much vaster and more horrifying. Everything became deeper, more complex, more detailed, more entangled. The entertainments he used to enjoy seemed too primitive. His brain craved for more intricate problems to contemplate. He got bored easily. Not using the full potential of his thinking machine was like flying a spaceship slowly above the streets of his hometown.

He also remembered how the implants first got hacked and how quickly it became common practice. How people began using firewalls and elaborate security systems for their brains, and how all that failed to protect them. Personal data and secrets got stolen, the deepest, most intimate thoughts and desires got exploited, turned into VR and simulation experiences, used for blackmailing.

More dreadful things began to happen when hackers managed to take control over an implant and, with it, all brain activity. People got killed in an instant or painfully and slowly as their implants instructed the brain to make their heart stop or gradually destroy their kidneys. A wave of political assassinations wiped out half of the world government. Whenever anyone died from a disease, it raised suspicions. People became paranoid. Protests bloomed across the world. Religions called implants evil invention. Many people got rid of theirs.

But even that was nothing in comparison to a revolutionary technique invented by a group of criminals that allowed to gain control over people's actions through their implants. It was ironic how the power granted by implants made petty thugs and psychopaths brilliant scientists and engineers. They made people commit all sorts of atrocious crimes, sometimes for profit and sometimes just for the fun of it. People killed, raped, robbed, beat others to death, ate their relatives alive. Sometimes they were completely unaware of what they were doing, and sometimes they were silent observers of their own actions, unable to do anything.

Even more people removed their implants. It was considered too risky now. Cay wasn't one of them. He believed he could protect himself well. Until he found out his friend Martil killed himself.

Martil was a nice and friendly guy. Not too intelligent, he was a person who was always kind to people and helped others without expecting anything back. He just seemed to love everyone and enjoy his life. He didn't need much to be happy. He was a subway operator who worked his hours and liked to go to a bar afterwards, talk to people, discuss some news, gossip a little. It was about simple pleasures for him. He wasn't ambitious, he just wanted to live his life and enjoy it. He was a little sluggish and couldn't defend himself, but there had never been any aggression in him. Even when somebody tried to insult or humiliate him, he answered with a friendly remark and offered the offender a drink. He got beaten for it a couple of times, but he also made a few friends that way. He had lots of friends because it was easy and warm with him, one always felt comfortable and relaxed in his company.

Martil fell in love and got bonded the old-fashioned way. His partner, Campry, wanted more of him. She wanted him to be ambitious and rich and more dominant of others in general. That wasn't who he was, but Campry made the typical mistake so many bonded people make: she thought she could work on him and change him into someone she preferred. She wasn't a very intelligent woman either, but she believed she didn't have to be, as she came from an obscure religious cult with archaic patriarchal views which taught her from the very childhood that she only had to look good, and the rest was men's business. It never occurred to her she could try to achieve her goals herself, she just wasn't raised this way. Cay had always believed she didn't deserve Martil, but his friend was so sincerely in love with her that there was nothing anyone could do about it.

Martil wasn't so easily manipulated though, and he tried to teach Campry to be happy with what they had, to enjoy life as it was. He didn't want to spend most of his time working on complicated problems and come back home exhausted, unable to see, or smell, or hear, or talk. He wanted to spend long afternoons walking with the woman he loved and talking to her, having sex and watching movies, dining out once in a while. He wanted to enjoy the birds' singing and his friends' laughter, the flavor of his favorite food and the touch of cool breeze on his skin on a summer night.

Soon they had a daughter, and Campry began to press harder, as it was time to provide for the glorious and carefree future of their child. The love he felt for his daughter was completely new to Martil, it was so pure and overwhelming he couldn't comprehend it. He wanted her to be happy.

And then automation eliminated his job, as a machine was a much better subway operator than any human. He wasn't prepared for that, even though it had been happening all over the world for a while. He needed money for his daughter and bonding partner who wouldn't think of taking a job even in time of crisis. Martil realized with sudden terror that automation had taken all the simple and pleasant work he could do, that there was no place for him in the world anymore. He had no other choice but to get an implant to be competitive on the new labor market.

Martil was miserable on that day. He didn't want it. But he did it for his family. After that, he wanted to try and become an artist, but Campry explained it wasn't valuable anymore, and he couldn't earn their living doing it, so he became a data analyst. He got drunk with Cay on the day he got the job, and for the first time he didn't smile even once.

He would be unhappy with all the knowledge cramming his brain and shielding the real world from him, but his daughter was his light. Playing with her Martil became his usual self and laughed happily. Little Amy brought the world back to his senses.

Then his implant got hacked. He had a great firewall installed by his company and all sorts of the most modern security systems and protocols. It didn't help. He was hacked by a sick psychopathic shithead who made him torture his three-year-old daughter for hours until she died in his arms. Martil was aware of what he was doing but had no control over it.

He loved his daughter more than anything in the world. He couldn't take it. As soon as he regained control of his body, he started banging his head against the wall until he cracked it. The paramedics said the injuries were severe but not lethal, so they were quite surprised he had died. Cay wasn't. He was sure his friend died of agonizing grief and pain, of being unable to live with what he had done to his daughter, of having betrayed her most precious trust. It was the day he got rid of his implant. Soon brain implants were announced illegal and replaced by palm implants that allowed enhanced communication with machines but left the mind out of it.

CHAPTER 4

Limea had been trying to figure out what had happened to Cay since he disappeared. Thinking he'd just decided to leave without an explanation hurt so much she could barely stand it. They were extremely sincere with each other and shared everything, however painful or ugly. They were best friends. They trusted each other, and she didn't understand why he would do such a thing. What hurt most was not that he had left her–however excruciating, she could accept that–but the fact he hadn't said anything. She was afraid it involved some incurable disease or an unspeakable danger he somehow brought upon himself by confronting a mighty enemy. He might have also just stopped loving her. She sincerely hoped it was the latter.

Limea didn't know what exactly had happened, but she knew when it started: the day she came back from a trip home. She returned in the middle of the night and even though Cay woke up when she slipped into bed, he was actually half between the world of his dreams and reality. He cuddled her, patted her, kissed her and muttered the words of love, then fell asleep again. He must have been working late, because she was the first one to wake up the next day.

She had already had breakfast and begun painting when Cay got up. Meeting him after a break was such a joy, and she could see in his eyes that he felt the same way. They had great sex and then suddenly something broke down. Limea had no idea what might have triggered it, but Cay started acting weird. He grew alienated and didn't let her break through the walls he built around his feelings. He looked into her eyes with an expression she didn't recognize. Distrust, uncertainty and fear were there, mixed with a dozen of other emotions.

She tried to get him to talk to her, but seeing it wasn't working she decided to wait. She thought he'd reveal it to her when he was ready. She did nothing, and now he was gone. Possibly in trouble. Limea blamed herself for not having done more.

She recalled Cay telling her something about having had a sim. Could that be a trigger that finally drew him mad? She knew how much he liked crossing lines and pushing limits, they had that in common. The sim could have ruined him while she was gone. It didn't bring her closer to finding out where he might have gone though. Probably if she could find the sim, it would help her understand what had happened. Unfortunately, none of their friends had spent those days with Cay, but Limea believed she could find the people who did. Someone would know someone who would in turn know someone else. It might not be necessary though. Bialta was calling, and Limea hoped she had good news.

"Hey Lim," she could tell by the sound of her friend's voice that the news wasn't good at all.

"What's happened?"

"We need to talk. In private. Let's meet on the McCintie's roof in half an hour."

Well, that was worse than Limea had expected. Why wouldn't Bialta want to talk over the network? Either it was so bad she had to tell it in person, or it was something she didn't want overheard. Her friend might be a little bit too cautious as was usually the case with tech people, but one thing was certain: there was no reason for Limea to expect anything good.

There was a cold whirlpool in her stomach all the way to their appointment spot. She got there early and had to wait for Bialta for about fifteen minutes, making nervous circles around the roof, passing carefree people who were chilling, having drinks, sunbathing and playing games. It was sunny, and everyone around seemed happy. Limea couldn't stand still. Bialta's face when she finally appeared wasn't reassuring at all.

"Hi."

"Just say it. At once," Limea demanded.

"I couldn't track him. His implant is gone."

"What do you mean?"

"He must have taken it out."

"What?"

It felt like a hammer fell onto Limea's head. The sounds around her got distant and distorted, the background vanished into a blurry haze. There was only her friend delivering punches.

"It's the only option. An implant can be traced even after the host is dead. It's impossible to trace only if it's been taken out. Which is bad news for several reasons. Firstly, you can't go to the police or any private searching services. They all rely on the implants, without them a person doesn't exist. The police are also very suspicious of the people who get rid of their implants, they put them on a list."

"What kind of list?"

"Let's say a very nasty one. If he ever comes back or is found somewhere by accident, he goes straight to fixers, no other options. From what I've heard, they don't only fix him, but also make him undergo a lot of unpleasant procedures to find out what he's done and where he's been while he was off the radar. The technology they use is very raw and often destroys people's minds to the point where they become vegetables. And if he manages to get out in one piece, they'll keep him under surveillance for the rest of his life. So, I wouldn't recommend using their help."

Limea took a moment to process it.

"Is it true that you can't survive without an implant?"

"Normally, you can't. But there are ways to get a new one without going through the fixers' hands first. It's illegal, of course, but there is a mighty criminal group running the business in the city."

"Do you think it's where he's gone?"

"He couldn't have gone anywhere else, if..." Bialta went silent before finishing her sentence.

"If he's still alive you mean?" Limea said bitterly.

"I'm sorry. For all I know, you can't come near them with an implant, you have to take it out long before you get there. But getting anywhere without an implant is extremely difficult and dangerous. None of the ways you can take guarantees you reaching your destination safely."

"How do you know all that?"

"Rumors and the Web," Bialta shrugged.

"I need to know more about the criminal group. I need to get there."

"No way. It's too dangerous."

"I have to find him."

Bialta looked at her intensely, then shook her head.

"What I know isn't enough. I have no idea where to find them."

"But you are good at finding things out. That's all I need from you."

"Do you realize what you are asking of me? Getting you this information might mean getting you killed. And it'll be me who will have to live with that after you are gone and don't care anymore," Bialta said angrily.

"I know," Limea replied softly. "But that's what friends are for, aren't they? I'd do that for you."

"I doubt it," Bialta grunted.

CHAPTER 5

Cay heaved a sigh of relief when he saw the building he'd been searching for and managed to land on its roof. He almost stepped out of the drone and got angry with himself for being so careless. He closed the door, uploaded the backup copy of the original software back to the ECU and put the display panel back where it belonged, silently thanking the hacker who did such a good job. He left the drone behind and came to the edge of the roof, looked around to make sure no one was watching and threw the terminal he'd used down. Leave no traces, the hacker had said, and he or she had earned Cay's trust by now. After a moment of hesitation, he also threw the screwdriver away. Where he was going, he was unlikely to need it.

There was nothing special about the roof where Cay was now standing. It was no different from all the other roofs with drone platforms on them: landing spots marked in blue circles, pathways for people marked in green lines, some drones waiting for commuters, bridges and walkways leading to nearby roofs, Sunny solar panels around the edges. Cay was aware that his destination lay well below the usual levels of human activity, as he had to descend to the twenty-fourth floor. He tried to recall the last time he'd been so close to the ground, but he couldn't. Everything changed since the plague took over.

It began with some random mutations of plants in different parts of the world. Some of them started growing unbelievably fast to the size dozens of times larger than the norm. People thought it was pollution, chemicals, genetic modifications, climate change. It raised some concerns but was mostly amusing. People took photos with the oversized plants, came from the nearest cities to see them, created all sorts of memes and jokes. But the situation was changing so rapidly that it didn't give anyone a chance to really adjust to it.

The mutated plants contaminated the nearest ones, and the epidemic spread all over the globe. They didn't only grow bigger, their look and properties changed, too. Crops suddenly became poisonous. Everyone who ate them died in pain within minutes, and there was nothing anyone could do. Animals started mutating as well, adjusting to the new environment. Most of them turned aggressive and killed people in violent attacks. Many didn't do it for food, they just teared humans apart and left the remains. Slaughterhouses revolted in what seemed to be vengeful mayhem. Caged birds broke free and pecked their owners' eyes out. Some cats and most of the dogs stayed with their owners though, even when their bodies changed, which created many curious and surreal companions strolling along the streets. Many of these animals grew twice their pre-plague size. They acquired huge claws and fangs, extraordinarily strong muscles, reinforced senses, increased speed, some new unexpected colors and body shapes. They protected their humans from their feral congeners. It was inexplicable from the scientific point of view. The animals and plants affected by the plague changed within their lifetime, and every other generation was more bizarre than the previous one. Curiously, the plants were only poisonous for humans, so the herbivores didn't suffer much.

The greenery was growing fast, seizing more and more territory, killing people who didn't manage or refused to leave. It kept evolving, too, perfecting its destructive mechanisms. Soon it developed organs capable of capturing those who were careless enough to come too close, almost like hands, and claws, and pincers, and ropes that would hold the victims tight, while it poisoned and digested them.

Nothing people used to stop the spread of vegetation worked. They tried to burn and freeze it, destroy it with weapons and chemicals–all of it only worked for a short while. Too many times it gave people false hope. The plants began to retreat, withdrawing from the occupied territories only to hit back harder a couple of weeks later. They adapted and became resilient to the means used against them, so nothing would work twice. What is more, they included the new methods into their own arsenal of weapons and turned them against humans. They learned and evolved too quickly for it to be a natural process.

The plants could also thrive in dark places where very little or even no sunlight reached. The scientists speculated that the vast system of roots connected them to those having access to the sun, allowing them to share nutrients. The newly acquired digestive system would come in handy too. The plants seemed to prefer people, but they could kill a careless animal if they had to. Anyway, no one could study them to be sure.

But as horrible as it was, the plague sparked ingenuity and innovation. New methods of construction allowed building light and solid structures on top of the old buildings, allowing people to escape the spreading greenery at least temporarily, leaving it far below. New means of transport and infrastructure, new technologies and gadgets that met constantly arising needs were being created and improved all the time.

Space programs also got a major kick. A huge orbital station capable of holding about a tenth of the remaining human population was being built. People were working on colonizing the solar system planets and moons. The first habitats had already been built, and the first colonists were studying the new environment to make it more suitable for a larger population. They'd got much further within years since the beginning of the plague than during previous decades. Humanity had a chance to escape and survive, leaving their beautiful home behind. It also happened to be their only plan, as they couldn't keep building houses up forever.

A dramatic reduction of pollution and the levels of greenhouse gases in the atmosphere was another positive outcome. Some people believed the gods of Nature got tired of what humans were doing to the planet and took it all in their hands. Old transportation and technology had to be replaced by new, green solutions, the growing amount of plants was clearing the air, water balance was being restored, especially taking into account that humans didn't have access to much of it now and had to build closed systems, reusing the same water over and over again. Climate change that was taking its toll every year, bringing humanity closer to collapse, slowed down.

The food industry underwent a major change too. Only several corporations managed to preserve some cattle unaffected by the plague and establish maximum security farms on top of the buildings. Meat was extremely expensive and scarce now, a luxury delicacy only the richest of the world could afford. A thing of status, something to brag about.

The rest of the people who couldn't give up their eating habits even in that situation had to settle for the rotten meat of dead rats roaming the lower levels of the buildings. The rats mutated too, and it was extremely dangerous to attack them as they immediately gathered into large groups and ate the offender alive. To get a rat one had to descend to perilous parts of the city where nature was in the middle of claiming the world back. Still, as long as there was demand, there was also supply. Getting the supply was some people's only way to survive.

The same happened with fruit and vegetables, of course: only a tiny amount of them was preserved unaffected by the plague, and they had to be kept in sterile environments of secure labs where the contagion couldn't reach them. But cultivating them was a constant risk, as the plague had already managed to find its way into a couple of such facilities, taking the lives of people working there. Thus, fruit and vegetables became even more luxurious and expensive than meat. Some of the richest people started wearing them instead of jewelry.

Most of the people had to settle for artificial food produced by newly established companies, which had all the necessary nutrients but none of the taste and texture of the real food. Eating became much less of a pleasure than it used to be, but the companies kept working on their products, so in the future they would probably be able to create something people might actually enjoy. At least such was everyone's hope.

It was different for Cay and Limea, as she was a botanist who had already grown crops of her own at home before the plague. She continued doing so, disregarding the risk, and even brought more plants from her lab to work on them. She wanted to create strains resilient to harsh environments that could be cultivated on space stations and, eventually, on other planets after humans left their home world.

Limea wouldn't concede to life without greenery around. She had a whole forest at home with soil right on the floor and all sorts of trees, bushes, grasses and flowers. There was also a garden of fruit, vegetables and grains. She could have made a fortune selling those to the rich, but she didn't want that. It wasn't a matter of business for her. It was for Cay and her, for their friends and family, for their guests and neighbors, for the hungry. Limea shared generously, always refusing money but accepting gifts or help when offered. She cooked and invited people to delicious, aromatic, spicy dinners on a small lawn amid the trees that took them to a different world. It was her magic and her power.

The corridor of their apartment had to be turned into a sterilizing room, and all the windows were equipped with filters to keep the plague away, but none of those measures guaranteed safety. Additionally, one had to undress completely in the sterilizing room and leave the clothes there, so they kept lots of funny sterile gowns for their guests at home and often had them dressed as animals or movie characters.

That chapter was closed for Cay, and the thought of having to eat artificial food made him flinch. He reminded himself it wasn't even close to the top of the list of his problems.

He had an old-fashioned analogue map of the building's intricate intersections with passages and turns he had to take marked with a green pen. There were also areas marked in red where the plague had taken over. The closer to the destination, the more red there was, and the more impervious the green way looked. He would prefer to have navigation take him there, but not only didn't it work without an implant, the people running the facility also made sure no electronic devices held trace of their existence. The map didn't exist in the virtual space, and all navigation could tell him was that he shouldn't descend below the forty-third floor. Probably it was best not to, who knew if his map was still accurate. Cay could only hope that the green way was passable. He reminded himself he had no choice at that point. He didn't have an implant, and there was no legal way of getting a new one without being subject to the fixers' mind mincing machine. No, thanks.

He entered the building and took the elevator to the fifty-second floor. It was as far as it went. He looked around. There was a small clinic, a legal sim theater and a café. Lots of people were there, and Cay was sure none of them had any idea of what lay below. He could take the stairs nine more floors down. The lower he got, the less people there were and the shadier they looked.

The forty-third floor was dark and somewhat hazy. Little light got here through grimy windows. There was an unpleasant smell of fried, greasy food. Cay didn't want to think what it was made of, though the odor indicated it could be rotten meat. He cringed and hastened his pace to get to a small store selling electronics around the corner. According to the map it was where he could pass to the lower level, as the stairs were inaccessible at that point. A note on the map said he had to say he was looking for a barnockle, which must have been a pass code because it wasn't a real word.

When Cay entered the store, he didn't see anyone at first.

"Hello?" he said. There was no answer.

"Hello!" he repeated louder.

"What do you want?" an annoyed hoarse voice answered, and a blurry iceberg slowly emerged from behind the counter. Upon closer look it turned out to be an overweight person of an undefined sex in a white, stained T-shirt blending with shorts of the same color and an unbelievably pale skin. Cay had never seen people looking that way. The exotic specimen must have never left this floor, eating what was sold there and staying away from the sun for most of their life.

"Hi," Cay said recovering from shock, "I was wondering if I could get... um... a barnockle here?"

"I see," the iceberg said with a sly grin. "We've got an adept of exquisite pleasures here. Follow me, I might have some barnockles left in the storeroom."

And the iceberg floated through the store, hypnotizing Cay with its whiteness and slow, heavy movements. The back door seemed too small, but the baffling person managed to enter it by slightly turning sideways.

"I'm Sharimma, by the way," the iceberg said resolving the mystery of her sex.

"Brot," Cay said. He didn't want to use his real name.

"It's right here," Sharimma muttered moving some boxes and uncovering a crawlway behind them.

"Thanks," Cay smiled feeling his heartbeat accelerate. He realized he was crossing the border between the civilized society and some dark, unaccounted areas. He got down on his knees, but a hand grasped his T-shirt.

"Not so fast," Sharimma said. "You have to pay first."

Cay had no cash and no access to his e-currency account without an implant. He wouldn't pay with it anyway, of course, he didn't want to be traced to this place. He had something else to offer though. The most stable currency.

"How much?"

"It's thirty birkles usually, but you are so cute I'm willing to make a discount," Sharimma smiled playfully. "It'll be twenty-five for you."

"Do you mind if I pay in energy?"

"Energy?" her eyes acquired a lively sparkle. "You are a real businessman. I'll get the battery."

Cay prepared a transmission cable and hooked it up to one of the batteries he brought from home. He wasn't going to take it out of his backpack, as he didn't want anyone to see the tech and start asking questions. When Sharimma got back with a bulky Sunny battery, he connected it to his cable and transmitted the equivalent of fifty birkles to it. He didn't mind paying more, as he believed it was better to be on good terms with this woman from the border with the underworld. Who knew how the acquaintance could serve him in the future?

"It's a pleasure doing business with you," Sharimma grinned. "Now, you want to get your legs there first and lie on your back. This passage is a slide, so you'll get there real quick," she winked. "Keep your arms close to the body and your legs together, it would be a shame if you damaged this gorgeous body of yours."

"Thanks," Cay was slightly taken aback, as despite being in good relationship with his body, he'd never thought of it in terms like gorgeous. He got into the passage the way Sharimma told him, holding his backpack close to his chest, and glided down. It was quite a steep slide, and it took a couple of unexpected turns. It ended suddenly, throwing Cay out onto a pile of rags. It wasn't the softest landing, in fact, it was rather painful. Cay got up and looked around. The place was a dimly lit den. It was full of old bowed couches where people were lying and sitting in weird positions with their eyes closed. They all had metallic helmets on their heads with wires snaking from them to get lost under the couches. It was obvious these people were having illegal neuro-stimulations.

Unlike sims, where a user got into a partially or completely scripted adventure, stimulations got the brain working in unusual ways, allowing it to create an experience or sensation of its own. It could be hallucinations, uncontrollable laughter, trance, dissolving in time and space or having infinite orgasms. It was illegal for a reason though, as it proved to be addictive and highly hazardous for mental and physical health. Heavy users had seizures, memory loss, depression, all kinds of phobias and manias. The number of neurons in their brain decreased, and some neural pathways got destroyed or damaged, which lead to various disorders involving internal organ dysfunctions, motor function violations and many more problems.

After having a really good time several times, Cay and Limea decided it wasn't worth the risk and focused on sims and meditation. He recalled he'd heard about such places before, casually called stim-gardens. He knew some people spent days and even weeks there. Some of them died during their sessions, which was discovered only after their paid time ended. The smell of the place suggested that such a possibility couldn't be excluded. It was also obvious that not all of the catheters meant to address to their bodily needs worked properly.

Cay checked the map and headed out of the den. He didn't want to stay there any longer, as he began to feel dizzy, and he was relieved when he found himself in a dark corridor. Not for long, as he saw vegetation breaking through the opposite wall. Vines with large leaves and sharp thorns looked frightening, even though there were large violet and pink flowers here and there. Cay felt a chill rush through his body. He hadn't seen the plants so close after the plague outbreak. They must have sensed him, as they started trembling and seemed to begin reaching out for him. Cay looked at the map again. It didn't suggest any greenery infected areas until two more levels down. That meant the map might be out of date, which made his whole journey even more questionable.

Keeping as far as possible from the deadly wall, Cay rushed to the next point marked on the map. He was getting edgy, uncertainty taking over his mind. Suddenly, he bumped into someone. Cay could only see a tip of his nose and a vulture smile getting lost in the thick boscage of his dark beard from under a large hood. The man was dressed in black, barely visible in the darkness.

"Hey there," Cay said, immediately realizing what an inadequate thing to say it was.

There was no answer, only a flash of teeth. The man stood there without movement, and Cay didn't want to go past him, as having someone like that behind his back seemed unreasonable.

"Where you go?" the man finally said in a crooked voice with undefinable accent.

"It's none of your business," Cay answered.

"You no like talk, yes?" the man grinned.

"Not really."

"I want talk. You talk," the smirk vanished giving way to a grimace of fury.

"I don't think so."

Without saying another word, the man jumped at him. Cay managed to notice something flash in the man's hand, probably a knife. He jumped aside finding himself dangerously close to the green wall. The man tried to stab him, but Cay's reactions were quicker as time slowed down a bit, allowing him to see everything clearly. He felt detached, his thoughts were brushed aside by acute concentration. His movements were quick and precise, yet it was only a matter of time before the man would get to him.

At a certain point, when he found himself between the attacker and the safe wall, the man still turning around to face him, Cay pushed him towards the wall taken by flora. He didn't think it over, and it wasn't something he wanted to do, rather a reflex. The next thing he heard was a scream of terror. The plants captured the man, quickly twining around his body, jabbing the thorns into his skin, poisoning and burning him with all the armory of chemicals they'd gathered over the years.

Cay couldn't believe how quick the process was. The man was screaming and writhing in agony, his skin changing color frantically, some of it evaporating or falling off in chunks, his limbs twisting, swelling and falling apart. In about thirty seconds it was over. The man began to dissolve, and if Cay cared to continue looking, all his remnants would completely disappear, processed by the greenery within an hour.

Time unfroze and accelerated. Thoughts rushed back to storm Cay's head. What had just happened? Shock and dread began to fill him. He had just killed a man after nearly getting killed. It all happened within a minute or so. He felt a wave of sickness rising to his throat. He turned away from the horrible scene and started walking away. After a moment, he realized he was going in the wrong direction, so he turned around and had to pass it again. He didn't look, but he didn't have to, as the image was burning vividly on his retina. It was too much. Cay didn't expect to become a murderer when he decided to take that trip.

"It's just a sim, just a sim," he whispered to himself, trying to calm down. He would probably lose control if the corridor he was following didn't become much more dangerous, requiring his full attention and pushing his feelings into the background again. The greenery spread to the floor, so he had to watch his step in order not to touch it. He had to jump over large areas and bend down when it was hanging from the ceiling. Avoiding it became harder with every step forward.

When Cay reached the elevator shaft, he had to use to descend six more floors, he was hoping it would bring him some relieve, but instead it filled him with terror. Exuberant vegetation was covering the entrance all around. There was no way of getting in without touching the plants. Cay peeked inside carefully: there was a ladder on the far side of the shaft, and it seemed to be intact, but the rest of the walls were teeming with green life ready to devour him. Anyway, he couldn't get to the ladder. Cay looked around, then studied the map. It was the only way.

Despair began to settle in. He couldn't go back, as there was nothing for him in the world without his implant. For the first time, it dawned on him how irresponsible and stupid his decision actually was. How little thought he had given to it. Why did he actually do it? Maybe it was a good idea to come back after all. Maybe he could figure something out, say a mad person attacked him in the street and cut out his implant. Or he did it while sleepwalking. No way, no one was going to believe that. He would end up in fixers' hands, that was sure. Or he could die a horrible death here, right now, just like the man he'd killed. Panic was taking over.

"No, no, no," Cay said to himself just to hear his own voice. He closed his eyes and started doing a breathing exercise. Inhale, *one-two-three-four*, hold, *one-two-three-four-five-six-seven*, exhale through the mouth, *one-two-three-four-five-six-seven-eight*. Again. Again. And again. After a couple of minutes of doing that, Cay felt a certain clarity within his head. There was room for logical thought again.

He couldn't go back. In the long run, it wouldn't be any better than dying here. He still had a chance to get to his destination though. All he had to do was pick up some speed and jump through the entrance without touching the plants. Then he had to grip the ladder to prevent his fall into the shaft. It seemed hard to do, but it wasn't impossible. Okay.

Cay took a few steps back and started running towards the shaft before he could get cold feet. He didn't want to give himself a chance to analyze it and change his mind, so he ran, jumped, rammed against the ladder, tried to grip it but slipped down, instinctively grasped again, clang to a rung and found himself hanging. He pressed himself against the cold metal, panting, his heart ramming against his chest. He stayed there for a while without movement, trembling. He managed to calm down as much as it was possible in the circumstances and began his descend. It was easy in the beginning, but the ladder was infected with greenery in some places, so he had to take unnatural positions to avoid it.

Sometimes he could only hold on to it with one hand, sometimes he had to avoid several rungs, and his muscles were getting tense, trembling as much because of the stress as the fatigue. He realized he was only holding on thanks to the helpful hand of adrenaline. He had to get out of the shaft before the effect wore off, and, luckily, he could see the exit. It wasn't a trivial task though. Cay positioned himself slightly above the exit, turned his back to the ladder, squatted holding on to the sides of it, jumped and pulled himself up and out. Luckily, the floor wasn't covered with any plants where he was getting out of the shaft. The effort seemed to have taken the last bits of his strength.

Cay indulged in lying on the floor for a while, restoring his breath and giving his muscles a rest. He hadn't imagined the way was going to be so difficult. He had to admit he could have died too many times already, and he was still far from reaching his journey's destination. It was just floor thirty-two now, and he had to get down to the twenty-fourth. He turned over to lie on his back, stretched his legs and did a breathing exercise again.

Then he took the map out of his pocket with a trembling hand and studied it. He had to keep going. Even though he felt exhausted, Cay rose to his feet and continued his way. The corridor was just like the previous one, there were a lot of plants he had to avoid.

Cay was becoming pretty numb, his movements rather automatic. Stress and physical challenges had drained him, and even though he realized it was safer for him to stay alert, his body refused him this privilege. He entered an abandoned apartment, crawled into the ventilation shaft, got out in another apartment, went down through a hole in the floor with the help of an attached rope, went into the elevator shaft again, traversed a couple more apartments, took the half ruined stairs, went into the garbage chute and another hole in the floor with a rope ladder.

He felt so detached at times that he thought he was dreaming. But a reality check when he pinched his nose and tried to inhale told him it was either real or a simulation. The vegetation was close all the time, and Cay observed with impartial amusement how his body coped with all the jumping, climbing and twisting it had to perform.

After taking the rope ladder, he glanced at the map to see what came next and found out it was the end of his route. Puzzled, he looked up and noticed about ten tall, armed men in black uniforms, who looked like professional soldiers, pointing guns at him. Cay raised his arms. He was so exhausted that he couldn't even think anything more than *"wow"*. The men were silent.

A short, skinny girl appeared from behind their backs. She was also dressed in black, though her clothes looked more informal. She couldn't have been older than sixteen, with her hair cut short and her eyes dark. Her small mouth was pursed, and her childish yet fierce face bore an overall expression of distaste. She raised a gun that looked nothing like the weapons Cay knew and, before he could react, shot him in the palm where his implant used to be. Pain pierced him like a million micro bullets leading to a nuclear explosion of agony, destroying his fatigue and bringing him back into the moment. Cay was afraid to look at his palm, as he was sure it was gone now. He couldn't see anything from behind the white wall of burning pain anyway.

"What the fuck!?" he shouted.

"Don't whine and let's go," the girl said, her soft voice contrasting with her ruthless tone.

Someone grasped his arm and slightly pushed him forward, suggesting the direction of movement. Cay walked, a wall of white slowly dissolving and the pain fading away. In a minute, he felt as if nothing had happened, and his vision was clear again. He dared to look at his hand and was surprised to find out nothing changed since the last time he'd seen it. He felt so relieved that he even found a moment to appreciate the clear air in the corridor. He hadn't been able to breathe so well in the last couple of hours.

The girl opened a door and entered a clean white room that contained nothing but a table and a couple of chairs. All the men stayed outside, the door locked behind them. The girl sat on one of the chairs and offered him to join her with a gesture. Her face was still fierce, and Cay began to wonder whether she was capable of changing this expression at all. He took a sit and glanced into her eyes. They were a dark mystery with a rich depth to them. He was fascinated and a little intimidated by those eyes.

"Why did you do it?" he asked raising his palm.

"You didn't cut the implant out completely," the girl said with a slightly scornful shrug. "Parts of it were still there, and even though they didn't seem to transmit any signals, we don't like taking such risks here. I killed it."

"Don't worry," she added with no trace of sympathy in her voice. "It didn't damage your hand, just the device. Now it's gone completely."

"It hurt, you know."

The girl shrugged again, showing it was none of her concern.

"Safety first," she said indifferently. "Now, let's get down to business, I don't have much time. You haven't come here by mistake, you need a new implant with a new identity, and we can give it to you. We can also irreversibly delete all records of your current personality for an additional fee. No trace left in any systems around the world. Police records included."

"No, thanks, I only need a new personality. I hope I might go back to the old one someday," Cay replied. He was absolutely blown away by what she'd said. If that was true, these people were much more powerful than he had imagined. It didn't sound realistic though, and he suspected it might be just a scam to fleece the naive clients of more money.

"I see. Let's discuss payment. You have to pay in advance. It's not open to negotiation. You have two options: either one of the six blockchain-based cryptocurrencies approved by us or energy. I assume it's cryptocurrency for you."

"Actually, I'd like to pay in energy."

The girl glanced at his backpack dubiously. It could probably accommodate one Sunny battery, but their services cost much more, Cay imagined. And the backpack didn't look full, so she must have thought it contained no batteries at all.

"Trust me, I have enough," Cay added.

"I don't trust strangers," the girl said slightly raising an eyebrow as if his words made her doubt his intellectual abilities. "Show me what you've got there."

"With all due respect, I don't want to show you anything. Get the batteries and I'll transmit as much energy as you require."

"It doesn't work like this. Either you show me what you have in your backpack or we make you do it. I don't see a reason for you to choose the second option, but if you are a masochist, I can call the guys."

Looking into her relentless eyes Cay realized she was being serious. He sighed and took one of the batteries out of his backpack. The girl took it into her hands and thoroughly inspected it.

"What is it?" she asked locking her eyes on him. There was something new in them. Suspicious curiosity.

"A battery."

"I've never seen such."

"I made it."

"You did?" suddenly she looked like a child who got a new fascinating toy. She might be even younger than he'd thought, Cay noted with awe. "How much energy can it store?"

"Up to 50,000 kWh. This one is fully charged."

"It's impossible!" the girl jumped to her feet in excitement. All her ferocity was gone now, magically replaced by childish enthusiasm. "You aren't lying, are you?"

There was so much hope in her voice and her face that it was hard not to smile.

"I'm not."

She smiled back, a bit uncertainly, as if she wasn't sure whether she had a good enough reason to do so.

"Get me S with his equipment," she said to no one in particular, and a minute later a boy of about her age entered the room. He was tall and skinny, his long, curly hair shaved on his temples and collected in a ponytail. His skin was of a delightfully dark tone, almost completely black. His whole left arm was covered with a tattoo of stars and galaxies that looked intriguingly real.

As soon as he appeared in the room, the girl turned serious again. She briefly enunciated the whole idea for him; he listened attentively and nodded in silence. Then he took the battery, examined it and connected it to a tablet he'd brought. When the measurements appeared on the display, his face lost its detached expression. It was a fascinating metamorphosis to observe, as if the boy dropped from the unknown world within his head into the ocean of reality with a loud splash. His face lit up with admiration and wonder. The girl, who was discretely watching him, also brightened, and it seemed to Cay she was relieved to find out she hadn't called the boy for nothing.

"I'm Sern," the boy said offering his hand to Cay. "Sorry, I had to check whether what you said was true, because there are always people who try to scam us. But this is authentic!" he wasn't trying to hide his excitement anymore.

Cay introduced himself, shaking the boy's hand.

"Milsa," the girl introduced herself. Cay couldn't but admire the change that happened in her too. She was just a kid now, boiling with emotions she didn't yet know how to contain, curious, impatient. She even blushed a little, and Cay wasn't sure whether it was because of the excitement or the boy. She was a different person now. He shook her hand and smiled.

"Sorry for your palm," Milsa said, "but I had to do it. Most modern implants are capable of reassembling themselves in time and at least partially restore their functions."

"No problem."

"Tell me about it! Did you really make it? How did you do it?" Sern inquired impatiently.

Cay figured there was no point in concealing anything, so he told about the battery and the solar fabric he'd created, explained the basic principles of their work and answered all their questions. Both kids were savvy, and the conversation turned out to be almost professional. It was a pleasure, as Cay didn't get much chance to have such talks with most of the people he knew.

"Why haven't I heard about this before?" Sern asked. "I mean, I've also seen some of the research you've used in your work, but you've connected so many dots and built something exceptional! Why isn't it on the market?"

Cay sighed and told the kids about Sunny. They got furious.

"That's bullshit!" Milsa outraged. "They are all assholes!"

"We can get access to their files," Sern said, "destroy all their records of your deal and of your prototype. They won't be able to prove it was theirs in any court."

"It's Sunny, they have very good security," Cay pointed out. Both kids sneered.

"Didn't you hear me when I told you we can destroy all records of your personality from everywhere, including the police databases? Don't you think we can get to Sunny?"

"I figured it wasn't true."

"It's true though. There is nothing we don't or can't have access to. Sunny's security is fine, but it's not the best. We can offer you a good deal for your invention and be your first customers. If the others agree, of course, but we'll talk to them," Sern said.

"The world needs that," Milsa added. Cay was a little surprised that they cared, but the indignation was sincere. Well, they were kids after all. He didn't believe whoever ran this place would authorize breaking into Sunny's system just for the sake of the world and justice. However, he was almost sure they'd want his invention for themselves, and being on good terms with these people might have its advantages.

CHAPTER 6

When Vietra emerged from nothingness, she was still in the sensory deprivation room. All the horrors ended, there was darkness and silence again. She didn't know how long she had to wait before hallucinations returned, but she wasn't scared anymore. She was furious. Furious for what the Master had put her through. It was too much, and she suddenly began to understand how twisted it was and had always been. Their relationship with the Master and each other, their training to be prepared to obey unquestioningly and fulfill their purpose without even knowing what it actually was.

She didn't know much about average people's lives, and she somewhat despised them for their weakness, but she also felt they had something she didn't. They were connected to each other by emotional ties that were unknown to her but seemed to have some significance and depth.

Vietra also felt a small void in her chest. Now, as she was looking at it in retrospect, the feeling seemed to have always been there, lurking from the shadows of her subconscious, yet she'd failed to identify or even register it. She realized she felt incomplete, as if a substantial part of her was missing. She suddenly knew with firm conviction she didn't want that life anymore. She didn't want to fulfill her purpose, whatever that was, and she didn't want to have anything to do with the Master.

On the spur of the moment, Vietra understood it was not in her nature to obey anyone, especially someone who was trying so hard to make her do it. It all looked like massive madness, and she couldn't believe it took such a cruel torture for her to see it. However, Vietra was grateful that it had happened.

She didn't know when she was going to be released from the sensory deprivation room, and she was aware that asking for it or demanding it would only prolong her captivity, so she waited impatiently. She wondered what life was like outside of the Master's control. She had enough valuable knowledge to find a job, and she hoped she would be able to establish a connection with other human beings. She even felt excited. When the door opened, light slashed her eyes.

"Have you learned your lesson?" the Master's voice said from behind the burning barrier that momentarily separated her from the world.

"I have," Vietra said quietly and rose to her feet. Her vision was still blurred, but she knew the building well enough to navigate her way.

"Where are you going?"

She didn't find it necessary to respond. She was heading to the door with the intention to never come back. The whole world was waiting outside, and she smiled contentedly, knowing she didn't have to conceal her feelings anymore. She could feel the other Nestlings staring at her.

"Fuck you all," she said for goodbye and walked out the door.

CHAPTER 7

Cay was left in another room to wait for someone of a higher rank to talk about his invention. He looked around, but there was absolutely nothing that could betray any information. The walls were white, there were no windows, and it was impossible to guess where they had come from. There was only a grey rectangular table and three white chairs. The room was faceless, and Cay suspected it was made this way on purpose for outsiders like himself. When he had to cross corridors, they covered his eyes with goggles that let no light through. They moved him around a little before leaving him there, and Cay thought at least part of the way had no other purpose but to confuse him.

"Sorry you had to wait," a middle-aged woman said entering the room.

She looked like a typical mother of three who had just come back home with her groceries, ready to prepare dinner. She was wearing jeans and a plain blue t-short, her blond hair was collected in a neat ponytail, she was wearing light make-up and a moderately friendly smile. She was curvy, but muscles showed on her arms when she moved the chair to sit down. She made an impression of a healthy and fit person who exercised regularly. Her fair skin looked being cared for. The look on her face said she had a thousand things to worry about and was only dealing with him because that was what a polite woman should do.

"It's okay," Cay said. "But I'd prefer to wait in a more entertaining place. There is nothing to rest my eye on in this room."

"Sorry, that's the only kind available for our guests," she said with a patient smile. "I hope you were treated well."

"Yes, thanks," Cay said recalling the shot he got from Milsa.

"I hear you've been fed and treated with a drink."

"That's true."

"Good. I have a couple of questions for you."

"I'm all ears."

"First of all, the way you came in. Where did you get the map?"

"It's kind of a long story."

"I have time," she said with an encouraging smile, though her eyes communicated something more like *"Get on with it, idiot!"*.

Cay thought of the day when he got the map. He remembered it vividly. Limea and he had been having guests for about a week by then. People came and went, and as much as they loved spending time with their friends, they also started growing tired of them after a while. They needed a break with just the two of them sharing the privacy of their home. That day, the last guest was gone, and they enjoyed the solitude having light sims and watching movies. In the evening they decided to go to a party.

There weren't too many parties that suited their specific music taste, besides, they were often too busy or tired to go anywhere. But that one promised to be really good, and they figured they couldn't miss it. They were in a silly mood, so they prepared funny costumes, laughing a lot on the way and making stupid jokes. They got dressed, headed to the party and lost themselves in the music for a couple of hours. It hypnotized them and put them in trance, where they weren't in control of their movements anymore. Connected to other dancers like an ancient tribe, uninhibited, floating above the individual consciousness in a world of intertwined transparent fibers. When they got tired, they went to the chill zone and sank into cozy pillows lying around under the glowing trees from another planet.

"I could help make decorations for such parties," Limes said looking at the trees.

"They'd look great here," Cay agreed.

"I've heard what you said," a middle-aged man with a long silver beard and a ponytail said, turning his head to them from a nest of pillows where he seemed to have been sleeping. "Would you like to make decorations?"

"I could try," Limea said. "I like drawing alien landscapes, and I'm working on a simulation room right now, so it would be interesting."

"I'm Prally," the man said offering them a hand. "I own this club, and we have all sorts of parties here, but these are my favorite. I organize them as often as I can with some friends. There are a couple of teams that usually work on decorations, but I'm always open to fresh ideas. You could join them, or you could gather your own team if you want. But I'd like to see your work first."

"Sure," Limea glowed. "I'll show it to you, and I'd love to join a team."

They exchanged contacts and talked, sharing tea that Prally brought from behind the bar. It had a strange taste and a curious effect on their state of mind. Prally refused to say what it was made of, but revealed it was an ancient recipe and a way people got high before sims and stimulations overtook entertainment. It was his private treasure, supply from before the plague.

Limea and Cay went to dance several times and then went back to their new friend. More people joined them, and they drank more tea. After a while they found themselves on a roof on the outskirts of the city with a bunch of people they had never seen before, looking at stars, dancing and talking about life. It was nice, but their minds were hazy, coming in and out of focus randomly, mostly being out. They couldn't recall large parts of the night later. In the morning they sobered up while walking with a stranger. They tried to recall who he was or what they had been doing before, but they couldn't. Cay felt like he woke up in the middle of a conversation that seemed to be about something illegal.

"Anyway," the man continued, unsuspecting his companion had no idea what he was talking about, "if you ever need a new identity, you go to these guys. They are the only professionals in the business. There are others claiming to do what they do, but they are frauds. This is the real deal," he handed them the map. "It's not easy to get to them, their location is secret. But they give out such maps to people they trust. You'll find a way marked here and some instructions. They are situated on lower levels, of course, so getting to them is dangerous, but if you follow the map, you'll find a safe passage through the parts of the building not taken by the plants."

He went on providing more details about getting there and then left Cay and Limea with the map they thought they were never going to use. At that point, getting such an item didn't surprise them, as even though the details were elusive, there was still something their minds were holding on to. Later they couldn't even remember what the man looked like, and the reason he gave them the map was a total mystery. They put it aside and forgot about it. Cay decided it would be unwise to lie, so he told the woman the truth, sticking to the most crucial parts of the story to keep it short.

"Well, this is strange," she said. "When did you get it?"

"A long time ago."

"Try to be more precise."

"I don't know, something like a year and a half ago, maybe two."

"The map must have been outdated even then," the woman said. "It's an old route, which is long considered impassable. It's unbelievable you've managed to get to us, and I've got to say, you are a lucky man," she eyed him for a moment. "And extremely brave. Or stupid."

"Thanks, that would probably be both," Cay grinned.

"I'm concerned about the man who gave it to you. I'd like to know more about him."

"I'm sorry, but as I've said I wasn't quite sober at the time, and I don't remember most of the night. I certainly don't remember him."

"This map is not the kind of thing you just share with a stranger," she said. "We'll have to look into it, so if you recall anything, I'd like you to let me know."

"Sure."

"Now, tell me why you need a new identity so badly."

"I thought you respected your customers' privacy."

"You are not just a customer, you are a potential partner. We have a strict policy of who we work with, so we need to know everything about you. I suggest you don't lie. If there is something you don't want us to know, just say so and the deal will be off the table."

Cay pondered it for a while. If he told the truth, they'd probably consider him crazy and the deal would be off the table anyway. On the other hand, if what the kids told him was true, they probably already knew everything about him. And he could bet they were wondering why someone like him needed a new implant, as he was definitely not a criminal. So, could he make up a plausible story that wouldn't sound insane? It was risky, he didn't have enough time to make it up and get all the details right. There could be some inconsistency in his story that would make them suspicious. What is more, he had no idea how much exactly they knew, which made it even harder to figure out a good lie.

"I assume you already know everything about me," he said stalling for time.

"I won't lie. We do. We have all of your personal data and your most sensitive information. We have all your passwords and know about all your hidden accounts. We have access to your home assistant, Risa would that be? We know who you are, what you do, who your friends are and what music you like.

"Don't worry, we do a background check for all our clients, as we don't like serving murderers and rapists running from the law. We also don't like being deceived, and some people figured a way to make our batteries believe they transferred the energy when in reality they didn't. We like to have our insurance. We never keep the data after a client is gone though. We've never used it against anyone except real criminals who hurt other people or the planet."

"Okay… so… I must admit, I feel uncomfortable."

"You should. I'd feel the same way if I were you. Your motive is the only thing that remains a mystery to us. We believe it was some personal drama."

Cay felt something unpleasant and cold creep inside. He had never felt so exposed, so naked. Lack of privacy had always been a troubling issue for him, and he tried to stay anonymous in the world of exhibitionists who believed every aspect of their lives had to be exposed and rated. But it was impossible to be out of the grid, even when one wasn't on social media. Cay was almost invisible for the general public but not for the professionals who could hack Sunny or the police.

He looked at the woman who hadn't even told him her name with a new feeling. He was angry. If he was considering telling her the truth before, now he wanted to tell her to go fuck herself. His story was probably the only thing they had no way of getting without his help. He wanted to defy their smug certainty of total control. He needed to resist.

"Fuck you," he said and immediately regretted it. Where would he get a new implant?

"Are you sure you want it to be your answer?" the woman asked revealing no emotions.

"Yes, I'm absolutely sure it's exactly what I want to say, though I understand it's not the best answer considering my position. But I'm pissed off because you know so much about me

88

without my consent. Because you want even more to be able to analyze me completely and give your verdict. And you haven't even told me your name. Don't you see a slight disproportion here?"

"I don't like lying, Cay," the woman said with a smile. "I can't reveal my real name to you because I don't trust you yet. I could tell you a fake one, but I prefer to be honest with you. Yes, we know too much about you and want even more. Believe it or not, I understand how it feels. But if you try to put yourself in my shoes, you'll realize it's a mechanism of survival we've developed based on our experience and self-preservation instinct. You must know we are not the government's favorite figures. We also have enough enemies in the criminal and corporate world. Most of them don't know who we are though, and we have our caution to thank for that."

"You are good at it, you know."

"Good at what?"

"Manipulation. Convincing people. I have to admit, I see your point though. I'm still pissed, but I think I'd do the same if I were you. Allow me not to make this decision under the influence of emotions. Give me some time to calm down and think it over."

"I don't have much time, Cay. But there is a matter I should see to now, so I can give you about an hour. I want you to be ready by then. If you aren't, the deal will be off the table."

"Okay."

The woman left Cay still annoyed. He didn't like having no choice, and he was well aware that the one she gave him was just an illusion. He couldn't just walk away from there without an implant. He needed their support. Besides, they were probably the only ones who could actually help him solve the mystery of what had happened to Limea. His emotions didn't matter. Fuck privacy if the lack of it could give him a chance of finding her. It was most likely a simulation anyway. Maybe that's how he'd get to the next level. Or maybe it was real. Anyhow, they wouldn't help him if they thought he was crazy. Cay knew his story wouldn't sound too plausible. His head hurt because of the contradictory thoughts bouncing against each other.

CHAPTER 8

Thinking about Cay never became less painful. Limea might seem in control for an observer who didn't know her well, but it was only a disguise wrapped around a hurt child who wanted to hide under the blanket and cry.

She could only count on Bialta to find a way into the criminal group creating new identities and hope that Cay had managed to get there, too, and was still alive.

The truth was that Limea had no idea what she was going to do after she'd get there. But she couldn't just sit there and do nothing, as it was steadily driving her off track. Cay was in danger, among criminals, probably navigated by delusions.

She hardly slept at nights, and when she did, it didn't bring her relief. The dreams she had were troubled and ill, except the rare happy moments, when she dreamed about being with Cay as if nothing had ever happened. Waking from them to rediscover the truth was like getting stabbed in the abdomen, but Limea was still awaiting them.

She felt she could break down at any point, but it was too early. She had to stay strong.

Limea turned connections off and instructed Risa not to let anyone except Bialta through or in. She needed a moment of peace. She sat down on lawn in the middle of the living room, among apple and plum trees that were growing from the soil spread right on the floor. She picked up an apple from the ground and inhaled its rich smell. She could make an apple pie later, the one that Cay liked so much. She leaned against one of the trees, enjoying the rough sensation and closed her eyes.

It was always the small things when she thought about Cay. The way he smiled when she walked naked around the house, his laugh when they tickled each other, his face when he was focused on work and the way he looked at her. She also thought about simple pleasures of being with him: lying in bed in the middle of the night caressing each other and talking; sitting on his lap and kissing his face; talking about the Universe and nonsense; making stupid jokes and dancing in the most foolish ways. She thought about sex and being close to him, feeling connected and cozy within his arms. About always wanting to touch him and to share everything with him. About studying each other and learning how to be with each other. About inventing their ways to make living more breathtaking.

The thoughts were swarming around Limea's head, and she couldn't concentrate on one for long enough before another one kicked it out to take its place. It was chaotic. It was often chaotic within her head, and now even more so. But those thoughts were the remedy that kept her going. For several moments she could doze off and forget about the present before it besieged her again. She focused on a memory.

It was a weekend not long before the plague, when they still lived on the ground in contact with the nature, unsuspecting of what was about to come. They were in their early twenties, just in the beginning of their relationship, wild and electric with desire and infatuation, deep connection lying beneath. They decided to make a space cake.

It was winter, and the ground was covered with snow glittering in city lights. They ate the cake, and as it kicked in, they went for a long walk. It was the middle of the night when they realized they missed playing Frisbee which they used to do quite often in summer, so they came back home for it and went to a nearby park. There were some lanterns, and the whiteness of snow helped illuminate the scene a little. They played and laughed, and when they got tired, they noticed there was an icy slope nearby. They used their Frisbee to slide down.

They were giggling, toppling and covered in snow, playing and having fun like kids. Then they went to the riverbank and watched the water flow, watched the lights of the city on the other side and the changing colors of the bridge overhead. They let go of everything, just being happy and in love. Just being.

In her memories, that night was soaked in magic. Would she feel that way if living on the ground was still a natural routine? If Cay was still with her?

Limea exhaled a long breath, allowing herself to loll in the bewitching glow of the memory. All the sims and stimulations that certainly opened new horizons and brought lots of interesting experiences could never compare to the simple power of some plants. Plants that could play with human perception, twist and turn it, open some hidden doors. One more thing that the world lost with the plague, and she missed it.

"Bialta is calling," Risa said.

With an inhalation, Limea let the glow slowly fade away, and reality close its claws around her neck. The world narrowed, the light dimmed.

"Put her through."

"Hi, I've got something for you," Bialta said as her image appeared on the opposite wall. She looked tired with dark shadows under her eyes. She also sounded annoyed. Bialta wasn't the kind of person who concealed or even tried to contain her emotions in any way. She disapproved of Limea's idea. "We have to meet."

"My place?" Limea suggested.

"Mine. No smart clothes or terminals," Bialta responded and switched off.

CHAPTER 9

Vietra didn't remember ever feeling so free. As if a hot day was replaced by a cool night, and she shed her heavy clothes to dance under a starry sky with her feet in the sea. For the first time she was completely alone, an independent individual instead of a part of the machine. If she could ever imagine it would feel so good, she would have left the Nest a long time ago.

There was something about solitude, some intangible beauty happening on subatomic level throughout her entire body. She felt light and electrified. The wind blew right through her instead of around. She didn't have a purpose anymore, which meant she could choose her own path. It could be anything! She could see the world, an idea that seemed to have always been somewhere within her thoughts, mysteriously concealed from her. Vietra suspected there was more she didn't know about herself, but now she would finally be able to discover it all.

"Vietra! Wait!" Tyss called out.

Vietra flinched as his voice reminded her of who she actually was. Could she run from it? It felt good to shed her old personality, but the past was still dragging behind her. She didn't want to be stopped though. If it were anyone else, she'd never even turn around, but she remembered the hug Tyss gave her before the sensory deprivation room. She stopped to face him. He'd been running, but when he reached her, his breath was perfectly even.

"Where are you going?"

"Away."

"You can't go away."

"Watch me."

"You don't understand..."

"I don't want to. I don't care anymore."

"We need you to accomplish our goal."

"Yeah? And what would that be? This mysterious goal of yours?"

"I... don't know, but I know it's essential for us to accomplish it."

"Did the Master tell you this?" Vietra felt slight contempt for him, as he'd always been the most obedient of all. The Master's puppet who never failed to do exactly what he was expected to.

"It's not as simple as that," Tyss sighed and looked at her with reproach.

Probably she wasn't fair to him. Probably she didn't know everything about him.

Vietra suddenly realized with bewilderment that Tyss was the only person she knew who had ever been kind to her. Of course, the Master also showed some support from time to time, but it was only when one behaved as expected and followed the rules. It was a strictly dosed encouragement one got for trying hard to please him, like when a dog got some treat for obedience. Tyss helped her when she did the supposedly wrong thing in spite of everything they were taught. It was, in fact, a bold personal protest. For the first time Vietra looked at him differently and saw something more in him.

"I'm sorry," she said. "You should know that I respect you. Not as a professional, but as a person. And thank you for helping me back then."

She'd never said anything like that to anyone, and it was hard to be so sincere, but it also felt good. Deep inside, she knew it was the right way to communicate. Tyss looked confounded. He even blushed a little.

"Thanks," he said after a pause and looked into her eyes with tension. "I… respect you too. And I'm glad I could help. I wish I could do more. I know how horrible it was."

"You have no idea," Vietra said. "It was much worse than anything I've ever been through. But I'm glad it happened. It helped me see how fucked up the Master and this whole thing actually is. And I'm not going to be a part of it anymore. So, thanks for your concern, but there is nothing you can say that will make me change my mind. Goodbye Tyss and take care."

After a moment of hesitation, she hugged him. Allowing her gratitude to take a physical form felt better this time, when it didn't precede torture and was a voluntary act. Vietra though it was the best way to make Tyss understand that he meant something to her. He didn't expect that. But he hugged her back and held her close for a couple of seconds. Vietra wondered if it wasn't a bit too long, but she wasn't an expert in hugging. Tyss looked absolutely perplexed when she let him go. He looked as if he wanted to say something, but he didn't.

"Bye, Tyss," Vietra repeated, but he kept silent. He stood there and watched her go, even when she turned around and couldn't see him anymore, looking as if he had something heavy on his shoulders.

CHAPTER 10

Bialta's face was tense and grave when she opened the door.

"I still don't know why I'm even talking to you," she said after a short greeting hug. "I'm on the edge of changing my mind right now."

"Please, Bialta, I need it," Limea looked at her, hiding nothing of what she was going through. She knew her friend saw it as her eyes reflected the same feelings.

"Sit down," Bialta said remaining on her feet. "The people you are looking for belong to the criminal organization informally called the Orchids. Apparently, they started their activities before the plague, making small forgeries, but over the years they grew into a large business doing all sorts of crimes, including contract murders and personal data stealing. During the plague most of its bosses died, and a new management emerged. They had lots of disagreements as to the future of their organization, so eventually they split up into independent cells. Some of them have already been busted. You've probably tried illegal sims manufactured by the others. But the Orchids, who are the ones dealing with the implants and new identities, are the hardest to find. According to what I've gathered, the most talented technicians, engineers and developers united to form this cell."

"How do I get to them?"

"You don't. You can't. As far as I know, you can only do it through someone they trust."

"Okay, then I'm going to find someone."

"How?"

"I don't know, I'll look on the Web? I'll figure something out."

"The Web?" Bialta raised an eyebrow and pursed her lips. "The police will come looking for you first."

"Well, I'll ask around."

"You are going to get yourself in trouble! And even if you find them, what you are going to do when you get there? Do you have a plan?" Bialta inquired.

"Yes."

"You are lying! See, that's what I'm talking about! I understand that you feel the need to do something, that you want to help Cay. But this way you'll only cause more problems. What's the point of putting yourself in danger if it's not going to help anyone?"

"I hope it will."

"You hope?" Bialta snorted and smiled bitterly. "It's not what you need if you are going to deal with criminals. Tell me what exactly you are going to do after you get there."

"I.. I'll ask them about Cay. I'll tell them what's happened. Maybe they'll help."

"Are you really so naive? Do you think they'd still be in business if they just gave away information about their clients to anyone who asked?" there was contempt and desperation mixed in equal proportions in Bialta's voice. "And do you really think they'll care for your problems? You don't know anything about the world!"

"I don't know what to do, okay? But criminals or not, they are people, and they might relate to my story. I'm well aware that they also might not, but they are my only link to Cay, so I'm going to try anyway!" Limea was losing her temper. The pressure was too much, and now her friend was criticizing her. She understood that it was well grounded criticism, but it didn't help her stay calm.

"Are you also aware that they might as well kill you if they suspect you are a police agent who got into their super secret facility?"

Limea wanted to respond, but she couldn't. Tears started rolling down her cheeks, and she dropped onto the couch, hiding her face in her hands. She broke down.

After a moment, Bialta sat near and hugged her. She just waited for Limea to stop crying without saying a word. Somehow, her friend's hug made Limea want to weep even more, but in a couple of minutes she calmed down.

Bialta went to the kitchen and brought two mugs of tea. She was a fan of tea and herbs who collected various flavors no one else knew about. She had been gathering them for years before the plague, visiting different parts of the world, and she still had lots left. After the outbreak she somehow got some seeds and brought them to Limea, demanding that she plant them in her garden. Now Limea was her friend's only supplier of fresh herbs.

Bialta made her own herbal mixtures for different occasions, and Limea was sure this one was going to soothe her.

"Are you okay?" Bialta asked after about five minutes of drinking tea in silence.

"As much as I can be," Limea answered. She actually felt much better. The tea took away the edge, and she was able to think more clearly, looking at things from a perspective.

"Now we can discuss it like adults," Bialta nodded. "Will you drop this stupid idea?"

"No. Sorry, Bialta, I can't. I know that you are right, but I can't just do nothing. I'll go mad. I have to try."

"Shit," Bialta closed her eyes. "I knew I shouldn't have told you about them. I shouldn't have told you anything at all. Just that I couldn't find Cay. But it's too late now, isn't it?" she opened her eyes and looked at Limea with a tormented expression on her face. "You'll never get to the Orchids by yourself. You'll end up arrested, or killed, or fixed. Even if some miracle led you to them, you'd die anyway. You need a good plan. I'll have to help you. Fuck!"

Limea couldn't believe her ears. She thought Bialta was going to kick her out.

"Thanks, Bialta. You are doing so much for me," she said.

"There is nothing to thank me for," Bialta rose to her feet and shook her head.

"I'm sorry for doing it to you. But you are the only person I can count on right now."

"Sometimes I hate my skills. It would be so nice if the only thing I could do for you was tea," Bialta sighed. "Anyway, let's get down to work."

CHAPTER 11

Vietra was walking along the bridge connecting twenty-three buildings. It was the longest bridge in the city, and it was nice to be able to walk for such a long time. There were lots of sculptures and installations on it, some wild colors and holographic projections. It was an artistic and cultural part of the city with a great variety of galleries, sim-theaters, restaurants and other vibrant spots. It was quite windy, and she could feel the bridge vibrate, but she knew it was solid. She thought about the wind being molecules of air, traveling around the planet because of pressure differences. She was happy to feel this movement on her face and in her hair. She thought there was something magical about it.

Suddenly, something unusual captured her attention. Vietra didn't understand what it was at first, her brain just registered some irregularity in the environment. It looked as if space-time was distorted and curved. People closer to it took peculiar shapes and froze in weird poses. All the movement stopped, and the wind disappeared. The color of the sky changed to yellow so bright that it hurt her eyes. The rest of the surroundings started fading, as if the sky was sucking color out of them, feeding on them. Soon everything became grey, with something like a frozen whirlpool made of people and buildings mixed together in front of her.

Vietra turned around just to see the same picture behind her. Nothing and no one moved, it was just her. She was perplexed and scared. Her first thought when she urged herself to be logical was that she was hallucinating. It was possible, the sensory deprivation room and other experiences in the Nest could have messed her head. But what could she do?

Ignoring it wouldn't solve the problem, going to the fixers wasn't an option either. They'd rewrite and rewire her brain to make it "normal", but they'd also erase her personality by doing so. They'd make her who they wanted her to be, take her free will from her, turn her into their puppet. Their facilities were set up around the world by international corporations who wanted to turn people into obedient consumers and employees without critical thinking or ethical concerns. The world didn't need more of those zombies.

What if she came back to the Master? Would he be able to help? No! Whatever happened, she was not going back. Vietra sighed and continued her way forward. She had nowhere else to go anyway. She reached the spiral of frozen space-time and realized she couldn't move any farther. There was an invisible wall blocking her way. It wasn't any material she knew, she couldn't hit it, and she didn't feel anything when she tried to touch it, yet, moving forward was impossible. Vietra went backward but soon reached the same invisible obstacle. She was trapped there, and the only option she seemed to have was to jump off the bridge. She didn't want to kill herself though. It would mean giving up too easily and quickly. Maybe she had to explore the spirals once again or just wait for the hallucination to stop.

As if responding to her thoughts, the world unfroze, and Vietra found herself gasping, holding to the railing. Several people were eyeing her suspiciously, others continued their way without paying attention. Vietra pulled herself together and continued her way. She was trying to calm down when the bridge in front of her began collapsing, people and parts of it falling silently into the green chasm below. Before she could think it over, Vietra was already running away, but she couldn't outrun the destruction of the bridge, and she soon felt it breaking beneath her feet. She made a couple of more steps and found herself in the air. But she wasn't falling. She was just hanging there instead, watching the bridge collapse. Then everything turned black, and she found herself in the sensory deprivation room.

She had never actually left. It was all a hallucination.

Vietra didn't know how much time had passed before the door opened and the light jabbed at her eyes again.

"So, I gather you are planning on leaving us," the Master's voice said.

Vietra didn't answer. What was the point?

"You can't leave," the Master continued. "You are important to us. You have to complete your mission."

"I don't care," Vietra said. "What's my mission anyway?"

"You don't need to know yet."

"In this case I don't want any part of it."

"Don't you trust me?"

"Of course I don't. After everything you've done and continue doing to me! I'm surprised and disappointed I've only realized how fucked up you are now. But you know what they say, better late than never, right?"

"You can't leave, Vietra, there is no point in trying."

"I don't believe you. In fact, I'm leaving right now. Watch me."

This time reality began to break much earlier. She had barely set foot out of the Nest when thin cracks covered all the landscape around her, as if it was made of glass. The cracks were becoming wider until everything fell into pieces, leaving Vietra in the darkness of the sensory deprivation room.

She understood what the Master was doing. He wanted her to break down and give up on the idea of leaving. Vietra was furious. The door opened, the light sliced through her retina, the Master's voice sounded impartial as always.

"Are you ready to admit you can't leave us?"

"What are you going to do? Repeat the scenario over and over again? Well, let me tell you something: you can go on for as long as you like, I'll still be leaving you in a year or twenty years and until the moment I die!" Vietra screamed.

"You are expressing emotions."

"You are so perceptive, I'm impressed. In case you haven't figured it out: I'm not following your stupid rules anymore. I express whatever I want and go wherever I want. Think you can stop me? Well, you can try, but I'll never submit to you."

"You can't leave."

"You are repeating yourself."

Vietra headed out and experienced the break of reality again. And then it happened again. And again. And again. And again. She stopped counting after about twenty repetitions. It might have happened fifty or two hundred times when it began to feel as if she was losing her mind. It seemed equally likely that she had a thousand or ten thousand repetitions, but it could have been just three. Vietra knew one thing though: she wasn't going to let it break her.

The fact that she was being manipulated outraged her, and rage gave her strength to go on through the dizziness and fogginess of her mind, through the fear and blackness of despair. She was hoping that the time for action would pass, and it would be too late for the Master to use her, so he'd have to leave her alone. No matter how long it would take, she wasn't going to give him the pleasure of winning.

"Vietra, you have to listen to me," a voice spoke through the haze. At first, she didn't recognize it, as it didn't belong to the Master, and he was the only person she'd been talking to lately. "Can you hear me?"

"Yes," she answered and was surprised to hear herself. It had always been impossible in the room. "Who is it?"

"You really don't remember me?" the voice sounded worried.

"I..." she had a bad headache, and it was hard to concentrate. The voice seemed familiar and reminded her of something good.

"I'm Tyss. Tyssdin."

"Right, Tyss, you are the good guy."

There was a pause, then Tyss said with a note of despair in his voice:

"You have to give up!"

"Never."

"You don't understand."

"I don't want to. One thing is enough for me to know: the Master is trying to make me do something I don't want to, and I'm not going to do it. He can't make me, whatever he does."

"Except that he can, Vietra. You have no idea about the means in his hands."

"I don't care."

"You have to. Do you know how much time has passed since you first attempted to leave the Nest?"

"No idea."

"One-tenth of a second."

Vietra didn't say anything. She didn't want to give away how much it terrified her. She hoped Tyss was lying. It couldn't be true. Or could it?

"The Master can manipulate time in here. You understand what this means, right? For you it has probably felt like days, but it can go on for hundreds and even thousands of years until you lose your mind completely."

"Well… so be it."

"So be it!? Come on, V, you can't do it to yourself! You once told me you respected me, remember?"

"Vaguely."

"But you did, and I told you I respected you too. You know why? For your mind. It's… beautiful. You can't just destroy it like that."

"I'm not giving up."

"You are being stubborn!"

"I guess I am stubborn and have always been. So, you can go tell the Master I won't change my mind. He can let me go or watch me go mad here. There is no way for him to make me participate in whatever plans he has for me."

"I'm not here because of him, I'm here because of you! He won't let you go. He's stubborn just like you and will never admit to another failure. If you don't submit, he'll destroy you."

"So be it then. I'm not submitting, but thanks for your concern, Tyss. You are a good person."

"Shit, Vietra, why do you have to do this?"

Tyss seemed to continue cursing, but his voice sounded distant and vague. Soon all sounds disappeared, but the silence and the darkness acquired a new quality. Vietra realized she couldn't move. Now it felt more like lying in a coffin, and it was terrifying. What if she had to stay there motionless for what felt like years? Maybe Tyss was right, and she just had to give up. Maybe there was no point in fighting the Master.

"Okay, listen to me, we don't have much time," Tyss's voice was loud and clear now. "You are going to wake up soon. Everything that you've experienced in the Nest was a simulation. That's why you would never be able to leave. You've been in stasis for 10 days now, and everything you believe to be your life is just a construct of the sim.

"The good news is that it's a 100% accurate representation of reality, made to prepare you for it in the best possible way. The Nest and the city are exactly the way you know them, and everything you've learned about the outside world is correct. The skills that you've acquired while in stasis are going to stay with you. Your body is in a perfectly good condition, you are healthy and strong.

"The Master and the other Nestlings are real. They are all in stasis just like you, sharing a common sim. But as soon as the Master finds out you've escaped, I believe he's going to emerge from stasis to stop you, and he's really powerful. I'll stall him, but you've got to get as far away from here as possible, as quickly as you can. You'll need a new identity and a good hiding place. Lay low. You don't have an implant, but that's actually good, because you'd have to get rid of it anyway. Find the Orchids, they'll help you with that."

"What is it, Tyss? Another hallucination?"

"No, this is the reality, like it or not. The one you'll have to face very soon."

"How do you know all this?"

"I guess I shouldn't say it, but we are never going to see each other again anyway, so what the hell. I'm the one who created the simulation and was running it all along. I'm responsible for all your experiences in the sensory deprivation room, and I'm genuinely sorry. I was following the Master's orders."

Speechless for a moment, Vietra tried to process all the information that suddenly flooded her head.

"That's so cruel," she finally said. "That's not you. I know you are better than that. You should have disobeyed."

"I know and I'm sorry, but I didn't think I could until now. Maybe it won't be much of a consolation, but it was me who stopped the sim with your mother. I prepared it a while ago as one of the punishment scenarios. I didn't know you back then, and I didn't understand much. But when I saw you in there, I realized my mistake. I couldn't do it to you, so I ended it. And now I'm getting you out of here, so I hope it can make up for the damage a little, and one day you might forgive me. Now, there is one more important thing you should know before you wake up... "

CHAPTER 12

They hadn't slept for too long now, and Limea's perception acquired a dreamy and unreal quality. She was fascinated by Bialta's work. She'd never had a chance to actually watch her friend do her thing.

Bialta put her helmet on, stepped on the treadmill and immersed herself in the virtual world eleven hours earlier. She hadn't come out since then. It was her natural environment that she knew like the back of her hand. All the shortcuts and hidden pathways, all the dangers and pitfalls, all the connections leading to one another. She was walking, ducking, crawling, waving her hands, and Limea could only imagine what kind of deep corridors of data she was navigating. She saw Bialta's lips moving, giving commands, talking to someone, but the helmet muffled her words. Six hours into the experience, she turned the treadmill off and lay down on the floor. Limea knew her friend could navigate her way through virtual spaces with eye movements and voice commands; her helmet was an advanced tech that allowed that. After an hour or so, Bialta stepped on the treadmill again. Her body language betrayed her fatigue.

Bialta was a short and stocky woman with beautiful features of international origin. Her skin was light brown, her hair black and shiny, flowing down her back freely, her nails long, always done perfectly and painted in bright colors. She loved wearing makeup, cheap, shiny trinkets, high heels and tight clothes. Now, in the comfort of her home she was wearing shorts and a long, baggy sweatshirt that almost hid them.

Limea had no doubt that Bialta would find her a relatively safe way into one of the most well protected and serious criminal organizations because there were no barriers that could contain her inside the common boundaries of the virtual world. She'd always been curious and liked finding her way through restricted areas of knowledge and data.

Limea wanted to help, but the best she could do was stay away and let Bialta work. She tried to make tea according to the recipes handwritten in her friend's notebook, but every time she offered it to Bialta, putting a straw under the helmet, the woman winced and refused to continue drinking after the first sip. She was very picky when it came to tea. Limea also cleaned her apartment and made some order with the things, but she knew it wouldn't stay that way for long. Bialta was pretty messy. As much as she liked order when it came to organizing data, she despised it in her personal life.

Limea napped a couple of times, but her sleep didn't last long, and she didn't feel rested. She was uneasy, impatient, she needed to act.

She turned to the moments with Cay again to keep herself from bothering Bialta. The way they laughed and talked and joked. Their own little games, familiar frowns and turns of the head, an easily recognizable look in the eye, a slightly raised eyebrow and three thousand seven hundred eighteen shades of smile. Sincere talks, ripping the heart off and putting the shreds on display for each other to examine. That touch, wind in the hair and hand in hand, exploring. Mind exploding into infinity in a shared eternity of a moment. His inability to wake up with just one alarm and lying together half awake, talking dreamy talk, starting the day with a kiss and a smile from behind of narrowed eyes, cracks into other dimensions.

Limea thought about their bonding ritual. They were calm preparing for it, just doing the necessary things, organizing them one at a time, sometimes too late. There was no trepidation and rush she'd heard of from other people. The ceremony was small, just the closest people sharing the love.

It was difficult to prepare a secret that Cay hadn't already known. It seemed like they'd talked about everything. She had to think hard to recall something, but eventually she did. A thing she'd never told to anyone, a thing that made her feel vulnerable, small and stupid.

It happened when she was 19. She saw herself as an independent thinker with a strong personality who was unlike everyone else. Of course, she couldn't have been further from the truth.

There was one guy in her study group–Gasloo–who was a bit weird and awkward. He was different: his views on everything were unlike everyone else's, and he always spoke about them without any concern for the fact that no one agreed with him. He managed to find unusual angles to simple problems. He made his clothes himself from used materials and had a strange haircut.

Recalling him Limea thought that if she'd met him a couple of years later, she would have liked him a lot. She'd be interested in him and, if nothing else, she would definitely like to be his friend. A person like him could teach her new ways of thinking. He would have been a creative and entertaining companion who could help her broaden her horizons.

But he wasn't considered "cool" in her group. And even though somewhere beneath the masks and layers she felt sort of intrigued by him, Limea couldn't admit it even to herself. The strong need to belong to the group drove her decisions and shaped her behavior.

It was funny to think how much she wanted to be liked, how much her image in the eyes of others mattered to her, how hard she tried to build the right one and how oblivious she was to all that. How different the version of herself that existed in her head was from the real her.

She just knew that her group always made fun of Gasloo. They referred to him as "the weird guy" and never took anything he said or did seriously. For the young Limea it meant that she couldn't get too close to him, as it might lead to losing her status within the group.

However, she didn't want to be rude either. She couldn't just laugh in his face like the rest of them did. So, she was one of the few people who talked to Gasloo and discussed his understanding of the world with him, but she made fun of him with her friends behind his back later.

She thought that she had to because they always asked her what she and the weird guy talked about, and she couldn't just repeat what he said without making fun of it for the fear that her group would think that she agreed with him on anything. She couldn't let the fact that talking to him was actually interesting be known to her friends. She couldn't even admit it to herself because that would mean that her behavior was hypocritical, and she didn't consider herself a hypocrite.

The truth was that Gasloo often made her laugh, as he had original sense of humor, and his jokes were always unexpected and fresh. But when she was seen laughing with him, she later explained to her friends that, in fact, she'd been laughing at how stupid the jokes were.

One day, he came up to her and asked her out. He was sweet and shy, he blushed and looked at his feet when he said it. Then he looked up at her, his eyes inquisitive and hopeful. Even all these years later, Limea could still remember his look. And something moved in her chest, something big and warm when she saw him looking at her that way. Some part of her appreciated his courage. He knew she was friends with the people who openly made fun of him, and yet he found the strength to ask.

Limea suddenly saw him in a new light. It occurred to her how he never seemed to care what others thought of him, how he wasn't bothered or offended by their comments and jokes, how he just kept doing what he thought was right. Something shifted in Limea's view of him. And Gasloo must have seen it because his eyes brightened, and he grinned and lifted his chin. That scared her. She couldn't go out with someone like him: everyone would make fun of her. So, she laughed in his face and said: "Are you kidding me?"

She watched confusion, embarrassment, pain of rejection, sadness and anger all pass in his face quickly to settle into coldness. He kept looking at her silently, but his gaze hardened, and it seemed to Limea that he saw through her and was disappointed in her. His eyes seemed to say: "I thought you were different." Limea couldn't handle it.

114

She turned away and went to her friends to make fun of it. She kept laughing, but something in her chest hurt.

Gasloo didn't look at her anymore and didn't try to talk to her. When they had to work together on a project, he would treat her just like everyone else, and Limea felt that she missed his attention, his humor and the conversations that always led to unexpected places. She couldn't admit it to herself, so she settled on being mean and sarcastic with him. He didn't seem to be bothered.

A week later, a new girl joined the group, and two weeks later, she was going out with Gasloo. They seemed happy and in love. The girl, Aki, was weird just like him, and as Limea was watching them laugh and kiss, she was burning on the inside. Mocking the couple was her way of dealing with it, and she became the most vicious one in her group.

The new girl seemed surprised but not hurt. One evening, she came up to their group and said she wanted to talk to them. She said she didn't understand why they were so mean to her and Gasloo. She told them that it made her feel vulnerable and uncomfortable. She asked them to stop and said that if they had some problem with her, she was ready to discuss it. She was so sincere and calm that it was difficult to laugh it off. It made all of them feel stupid, especially Limea. She tried to mock Aki for it, but no one supported her, which made her feel small and irrelevant.

Aki soon became one of the leaders of the group, and Limea hated her even more for it. She hated seeing Gasloo look at her the way he used to look at Limea before. She hated her own stupidity and weakness. And most of all, she hated the way she must have looked in Gasloo's eyes, especially compared to Aki.

The dissonance between her image of herself and the truth was tearing her apart, but she still couldn't be honest with herself. She thought she had a genuine reason for her hatred, that it was all their fault and none of hers. She soon became the outsider of the group because she failed to adjust to the new rules imposed by Aki's leadership that valued mutual respect and handling problems in a mature way. Her friends turned away from her because being sarcastic and mean wasn't cool anymore. She was in Gasloo's position now, only, unlike him, she very much cared. She soon left the group under the pretext of finding new interests, but the truth was she couldn't handle her failure and the destruction of her image.

Well, that was a story that made Limea feel ashamed of herself. She didn't think it would change Cay's opinion of her because he knew her now, and she had changed a lot since then. Still, it was something that caused an acute feeling of embarrassment in her abdomen.

She encoded it into a painting of a flower opening its petals to the sun, dew shining in the light. Inside the flower was her ugly secret in the form of animation for Cay to see.

They got bonded before the plague, and their ceremony had the authenticity and charm the post-plague ones lacked. It was late summer. They were sitting on a meadow amidst hills, facing each other, their closest family and friends standing in a circle around them, holding hands. There were just about thirty people. It was windy, and the air smelled of coming rain. The clouds were moving fast in the sky, and the grass around them was rippling like water. Lime's hair was dancing around her face, and her skin was covered with goosebumps. She was wearing a simple yellow dress that complemented the color of her hair. Cay looked handsome and serious, his hair messy and playful. He was wearing a dark blue shirt and grey jeans. They were both barefoot according to the tradition. The sun appeared for a moment, painting everything gold. The ambinera was dressed in a traditional green dress that was long and loose, and she had a circlet of white flowers on her head. She downloaded their secrets into temporary, encoded virtual rooms keyed to their biometric data and put VR helmets onto their heads. Each of them was now alone with the other one's secret. They had 20 minutes before the secrets got destroyed. Limea's heart was racing.

She found herself in a generic living room. There was an envelope waiting for her on the table, it's edges slightly glowing. Cay's secret. Time was counted down on a large display. When Limea came up to the table and took the envelope in her hand, she had 19 minutes and 27 seconds left. She exhaled slowly, hesitating for a moment before opening it. Cay's story was handwritten on cream paper.

"I know I should have told you earlier, but I didn't have the courage. There never seemed to be the right moment, though it's just an excuse, I know. I would convince myself it didn't matter, but sometimes I would wake up in the middle of the night thinking about it, thinking how knowing it could change the way you felt about me. So, I couldn't tell you, but I also couldn't keep it a secret from you," the letter began.

"This is the reason I always tell everyone that I don't remember my childhood. It's a lie. You know that my father died when I was 5, and it was really hard on my mother, even though I didn't have the empathy to understand it back then. I guess her way of coping with it was trying to find new love, but it wasn't working. None of her relationships lasted more than a couple of months, and her choice of partners was questionable at best.

I don't really remember my father, but I know he died in an accident caused by him driving drunk. You know that, but what I have never told you, because I've always been ashamed, was that he also killed two people in this accident. So, it tells me something about him and something about what kind of partner my mother chose to create a family with.

After his death, Acrisha and I were watching this parade of men coming and going for a couple of years. All of them loved drinking, and my mother would always join them. It wasn't that bad most of the time, we kind of got used to seeing our mother drunk with these people, to occasional scandals with shouting and breaking things, to drama and tears when mother kicked one of them out just to welcome him back a couple of days later or to bring home someone new, someone similar. But most of them were nice to us. Some would bring us toys and sweets or would play with us and take us out once in a while. Others would just ignore us like we didn't exist. We didn't mind that either because we knew they would be gone soon, replaced by someone else.

This guy was different. His name was Gabor. We couldn't quite understand what exactly it was, being children, but we always felt uneasy around him and tried to stay away as much as possible, even though he played nice in the beginning. Drinking wasn't his only passion. He brought something new.

I remember first seeing my mother completely motionless on the couch. Her eyes were open, but she didn't see or react to anything. Acrisha and I tried to wake her up, tugged at her clothes, screamed and cried, but she didn't move. We thought she was dead, and we were left absolutely alone in the world. I still remember the overwhelming feeling of helplessness and fear. But she wasn't dead. You might remember stories about amathadon, a powerful drug that was invented to deal with acute pain, but turned out to be highly addictive, causing an epidemic before it was banned and replaced with a more benign version. This was what Gabor brought to our house. And my mother got hooked surely enough, so we had to get used to seeing her unconscious.

Over the next few months the guy became violent. He would abuse her verbally and occasionally hit her. Acrisha and I used to hide in the closet when he got home because we were so afraid. I know there was nothing I could do, but I still feel guilty sometimes for not even trying to protect her. It's wrong, I know. And yet...

We would sit in the closet for hours, listening to her cry and beg, and to him shout, until everything got quiet, and we would come out looking for food that often wasn't there, and they would both be unconscious. Weird as it was, this was the most peaceful time of the day for us, when we played and learned and were being children.

It got worse over time. Mother would take the drug more and more often, completely neglecting us. We begged her to kick the guy out in short moments of sobriety that she had, and she cried and promised us she would, but she never did. I think it was her addiction, knowing she wouldn't be able to get the drug without him. She was also afraid of him, as he was getting more and more aggressive.

He broke her arm once, and she didn't go to the hospital for two weeks, as she was numbing the pain with the drug. Her arm got really swollen, all red and bluish. It was a neighbor bringing us some food who saw it and finally made her go. She had to stay in the hospital for three weeks just to deal with complications, and then an additional month to be treated for her addiction.

There was a family of three who took care of us: a man and a woman in their forties and a younger man, probably in his late twenties. Even though a lot of our neighbors helped us out back then, they were the most caring ones, the ones we considered our friends. The man and woman had children of their own who weren't living with them anymore, so maybe they had some parental feelings to us, and their lover, well, he was just a sweet guy full of love to everyone. As soon as our mother was taken to the hospital, they kicked the guy out of our apartment, making sure he understood that he would have to face serious consequences if he ever came back. They took us to their home and surrounded us with love and support. I remember this time as a bright spot in the overall darkness, the time when I felt warm and safe, and when Acrisha laughed a lot and made silly jokes.

Our mother came out of the hospital clean and grim. When she didn't find the guy in our apartment, she got furious. She never said anything, but it seems to me that she was blaming us for his disappearance. Acrisha and I were spending more time with our neighbors than at home, as the atmosphere was always tense there.

Our mother wasn't handling it well, so one day she just turned to fixers. I understand her, but I think I haven't completely forgiven her to this day. She returned smiling and happy, but she just wasn't our mother anymore. All her choices, all the things she did for fun or bought for us, everything she did was dictated by someone's profits and market forces. We were too young to understand it back then, but we felt that our mother was gone, replaced by a simpler version of herself who didn't have this crippling emotional baggage, but who lacked the depth and messiness of a real human. We felt betrayed and abandoned.

As a teenager, I went through a violent phase when I would start fights with anyone who I thought looked at me the wrong way. I also tried bullying a couple of kids at school, but it left me feeling disgusted with myself. Fighting, on the other hand, gave me a momentary relieve from my fury. I was so angry at the whole world at that time that I would walk mindlessly along the streets kicking trash cans.

I got over it when I was sixteen. I went to a retreat where a real kalumi healer from a tribe still living as if civilization had never happened held a ceremony for about fifteen people. We fasted and meditated for three days, only drinking water. Each of us talked to the healer before the ceremony privately, telling her about our pain. On the fourth day, we drank entheogenic brew prepared from the plants collected by the tribe. It was brutal, it was painful, it was scary, and it was my first experience with mind-altering substances. It lasted about 20 hours, but the kalumi guided me through it and out of it. When it ended, I was free. I was able to accept what had happened to me and leave it behind. The anger was gone. My mind was clear. The world gained colors. I could feel joy again! People suddenly seemed much friendlier. I wasn't surrounded by enemies anymore. My body relaxed. I started feeling good in it. It was as if I'd dumped a huge burden that I'd been carrying on my shoulders.

I wanted to get Acrisha to try it too, but she was in a dark place, in bad company, and she tried to exclude me from her life. She got addicted to drugs and stimulations that were just emerging at the time and was completely neglecting her life and health. I tried to reach her many times. Every time, she lied and manipulated to get the money that she needed for the stims. When I stopped believing her, she stole from me. But there was one moment of clarity when she realized her body was falling apart, even though she was in her early twenties, she'd lost all her friends and was constantly deceiving and rejecting the only person who still cared about her. She called me in tears and begged to help. She didn't want to go to the kalumi since it involved mind-altering substances, and she didn't want any of those in her life anymore. So, I found her a good rehab and supported her through the process. When she told you once that I saved her life, this is what she meant. She was too ashamed of herself to tell you the whole story, but I think if she had more time to get to know you, she would. I guess because of our past trusting someone wasn't easy for her. It's not easy for me as well. You know she became a rescuer and died a hero, trying to evacuate a village that was being taken over by the plague, so there was not enough time for you two, but she really liked you.

Now you know the secret that no one else knows about me. Even though I feel healed, I want you to be aware that I'm still more likely to get addicted or become violent than others because of my past. I want you to make this decision knowing all the facts. If you want to leave now, I'll understand and won't hold it against you. I want you to be safe and happy.

Love you,

Cay"

Tears were running down Limea's cheeks. How could he have doubted her love? If anything, she loved him even more now. Her own story seemed stupid in comparison to this. She knew Cay had been through some rough times in his life, but he preferred not to talk about that, and she never insisted. Now that she knew, what Limea wanted to do most was hug him and tell him how much she loved him. She hated that he had been dealing with this alone, but now he didn't have to anymore.

She wanted to exit the virtual room immediately, but she had to wait for the time to end. She was counting minutes impatiently, glancing at the letter. She thought about picking it up and reading it again, but she couldn't bring herself to do it.

When the time stopped, the letter turned to ash, Cay's secret erased.

Limea took her helmet off, searching for Cay's eyes. There was a silent question in his gaze, and when he saw the answer, he smiled.

"Now that you know each other's secrets," the ambinera said, "do you still want to bond?"

"Yes!" they said simultaneously, and their loved ones cheered. Limea had completely forgotten they were there.

They stood up and held each other.

"I've never loved you more", Cay whispered into Limea's ear.

"You are the love of my life," Limea whispered into his.

The ambinera tied their wrists together with a soft, blue ribbon.

"You are now bonded to stand together as one against all challenges and troubles, to support and love each other in the darkness and the light, to multiply each other's joy and to lift each other up, to be there for each other for the best, the worst and the mediocre, to help each other grow and be happy, to take care of each other and be each other's strength," the ambinera said.

Just thinking about that moment brought chills and tears.

Limea let her mind flow. She thought about a couple of trips to the mountains they managed to take before the plague. The open space and ancient rock that watched the birth of the planet. Deep water streams that found their way to the surface, gathering in crystal clear lakes. Nature untamed. It protected itself so well from human violation, only allowing those who didn't have to bring civilization with them to enjoy the silent tranquility of its vastness. It freed the mind from boundaries, from rules and restrictions imposed by the outer world. Made it more spacious, airier, more graceful. More flexible, until almost unnoticeable behind the ancient truth that can't be expressed in words. A wave of gratitude rose in her chest and found a way out through her eyes. How incredible that they had a chance to experience that together before the plague. And how precious, how stunningly rare their love was.

As her mind kept rushing through associations, Limea smiled thinking about riding a bicycle in a spring forest, a little high, listening to the birds, sitting by the lake and watching the water flow. Blissful, carefree moments.

It wasn't that the experience was completely lost after the plague. People made incredible bicycle tracks connecting buildings, encircling them, running on top of the world. Some of them were made of a new type of glass, extremely thin and solid at the same time. Riding there was like flying on your bike in the sky, watching the lights of the lower dimensions of the city, usually invisible from public roofs. Sometimes they ran through buildings with illusions of parks, oceans, forests and other marvelous views created within. There was one of space with galaxies floating around that she helped create. Some of them were fantasy worlds filled with curious creatures and magic. And then you flew out of them right into the sky. Limea admired the creativity of those who flavored the new world with a bit of adventure.

Suddenly, Bialta dropped her helmet on the floor and stretched like a cat, pulling Limea back into the present moment with her. She looked completely mad. Her eyes were scary and outlandish. She needed time to adjust to reality, and she made a couple of circles around her apartment in silence. Her voice was hoarse when she could finally speak.

"I did it," she said.

"Shit!" she added after a moment and galloped to the toilet.

"You are lucky that I happen to have some connections in the criminal world, and that some favors are owned to me. I wouldn't have got to them otherwise," Bialta continued when she was back.

"Thank you!" Limea wanted to hug her friend, but the look on Bialta's face warned her against it. "I've recalled something while you were in, a map Cay and I got from a stranger one night. He told us we could use it if we ever needed to change our identities. Cay might have taken it."

"Well, maps used to be a way of getting to the Orchids, but only a number of trusted individuals got them. They were distributed about twice a year, as the route to their facility was ever changing. They don't do it anymore, and it's suspicious that you got the map from a random guy, it might be a trap. Anyway, now you can get to the Orchids if you are referred by someone they trust. I've got you referred through their client. They are waiting for a confirmation to start a background check on you. If you pass it, meaning if they find you trustworthy enough, you can visit them."

This time Limea couldn't contain her emotions and gave Bialta an affectionate hug. She knew no one else could have done it for her.

"You'll have to go through more checks though, and you need to have a good legend of why you are changing your identity," Bialta continued, gently pushing Limea away. She didn't want to hug, not yet, as she still had important information to relate, and she wanted Limea's full focus. She was also still angry.

126

"Here Cay's disappearance works in your favor," Bialta continued. "It's a good reason for you to want a new implant."

"But I don't want one."

"Firstly, you won't get to them if you don't want one. This is what they do, so they won't let you anywhere near if they don't think you are another client. Secondly, you are going to need one, because you can't get there with an implant–the risk of being tracked down and found is too high for the Orchids. You'll lose your implant way before you meet them."

Limea needed some time to process this. She was ready to risk her life if it gave her the slightest chance of finding Cay and helping him. But she was always hoping they'd be able to return home together afterwards. It was the first time it dawned on her that even if she found him, their lives would change forever. If Cay got rid of his implant, he would never be able to come home, otherwise he'd end up in fixers' hands, which he considered to be worse than death. They'd have to start a new life somewhere else and never see their friends and families again.

Limea had never thought she would have to make a choice between him and everyone else she cared about. Cay or her whole life. She could see now why Bialta was so mad at her.

This shouldn't be a choice anyone should ever make, Limea thought. Her consciousness split into two distinct parts. The logical one told her with cold clarity that she should give up on this crazy idea and go back to her life. The chance of finding Cay was minuscule against a very palpable probability of losing everything. The emotional one sang into her ear that she couldn't just back down now, when she was so close. It splashed the colors of devotion and longing, painting the portrait of their love.

It wrapped Limea into the warmth of the hug she was so yearning for. It ruffled her hair with the sense of adventure and put the taste of new life onto her tongue.

"Can I ask the Orchids to restore my old implant in case I don't find Cay?" Limea asked.

"I have no idea," Bialta shrugged. "I don't think it's what anyone ever does. But I guess it's technically possible, must be even easier than creating a new identity. They may find it suspicious though. It can be dangerous."

"I'm doing this," Limea said looking her friend in the eye and knowing with absolute certainty she'd made the wrong choice. "I'm sorry."

"Okay," Bialta said. "I'm sending the request right now. It's done. You are under the background check."

Limea saw revulsion on her friend's face. She was hurt. She was hoping Limea wouldn't give up on her. But somewhere behind the wound there was understanding. Deep inside, Bialta already knew that was what Limea was going to do. She'd been expecting it.

"I need to sleep," Bialta finally said.

"Troy will wake me up when we get word from the Orchids. You must have the equivalent of 50,000 birkles in one of these cryptocurrencies here," she showed Limea a rather short list. "Do you have an account?"

"Yes," Limea said. Some of their savings were in cryptocurrencies. She'd just have to make a couple of transfers to have all the money in one wallet.

"Okay. Get it done and get some sleep, too."

It was probably a good idea, but Limea couldn't. Her mind was too active and her body too restless. She was pacing around the apartment, when six hours later Bialta came out of her bedroom.

"You are in," she whispered. Her face was pale and her hair unkempt from sleep. She blinked a couple of times, looked around, found a glass of water and emptied it.

They spent about half an hour preparing, packing and rehearsing the legend. In short, Limea had to say she was worried for her life because Cay had disappeared. He'd been acting weird lately, and since he disappeared, she felt like she was in danger as well. She needed a new identity to start a new life somewhere safe.

If everything went well, she could try to inquire about Cay, asking the Orchids to get a message through to him, but Bialta was sure this wasn't going to work and warned Limea against it multiple times. She was instructing Limea on her upcoming journey. It was hasty and fervent, and Limea regretted not having had a proper talk with her friend. It was part of the arrangement that everything had to happen immediately after receiving the confirmation, otherwise the deal was off the table. Their last hug was long and firm. Bitter and painful.

"Good luck," Bialta whispered and turned away.

And there she was, following the instructions she'd got from the Orchids. Since they were erased immediately after she listened to them, Limea was continuously repeating them in her head, scared of forgetting a significant detail.

She got to a hospital and uttered the symptoms she memorized from the recording. She was referred to a doctor, whose face was covered with a mask. He didn't meet her gaze and didn't say anything. He showed her to the chair with a gesture, injected something into her hand, removed the implant, covered the wound with a healing invisible bandage and nodded at the door. It happened so quickly, Limea barely had time to process it. She stared at her palm and didn't believe she didn't have an implant anymore. She didn't even feel anything. It seemed unreal.

She continued her way according to the instructions and met a girl of about ten years old who took her hand and led her to a large toy store. They walked through it, with the girl stopping and examining a toy once in a while, and exited through the back door. They went down a couple of floors by stairs and reached the elevator with a warning sign according to which sure death was waiting below. The girl pressed the button, and as the elevator arrived, she showed Limea in, handed her a blindfold, pressed the ground floor button and turned away.

Limea was all tense. She didn't know what would happen next, her last instruction was to follow the girl, so she had no idea of what to expect when the elevator doors opened. She put the blindfold on and stepped out as the lift reached its destination. There was someone waiting for her. He scanned her and searched her, took her hand and led her somewhere. They were walking for about 15 minutes and made about 20 turns. Limea was trying to keep track of them to maintain a sense of direction, but she gave up. Then her guide let go of her hand, and for a moment, she was standing there, blind, waiting.

"What is the purpose of your visit?" a voice asked. It was distorted, somewhat metallic, changed so that she couldn't recognize it later.

She replied just like she'd rehearsed that she was in need of a new implant and answered a couple of questions regarding her personality and the nature of her problem. Then someone took her hand again and led her to a subway station. According to the public knowledge the subway was no longer operational, it had been impossible to get underground without being killed by the plants for a couple of years now. But there she was, waiting for a carriage to arrive, alone. She was instructed to get on the train and get off when it stopped. She took the blindfold off and looked around. There were no plants, so Limea guessed the station was protected by modern experimental materials capable of keeping the greenery away for several years. The train arrived.

Limea was passing by deserted stations which reminded her of post-apocalyptic movies. There was a certain atmosphere about them, some special vibe that only places built by humans and abandoned by them could emit. They were creepy and appealing at the same time. She couldn't take her eyes off them, especially when she saw plants breaking through, reaching out to her. Some stations drowned in verdancy and looked more like a dreamy jungle. Limea came up to the door and touched it. There was only thin glass between her palm and the leaves, and if the train stopped there, the plants would destroy this barrier in a couple of days. So close, yet so far. Streams of tears ran down her cheeks.

She'd lost contact with the nature in the new world, and there was nothing that could fill this void. She could touch the plants in her apartment, but there were just a few of them in a closed space. She could have all the space and air high up the city's roofs, unobstructed and open, but she couldn't touch the plants luring her from below. And she longed for the wilderness of the mountains and the calm of the forests, for being part of the nature, for connecting to it through all of her senses and the very essence of her being that some people called melana.

Tears washed away the barrier of the glass separating Limea from the plants, and for a moment, it felt like she was actually touching them. As if the leaves were tickling her palm and warm wind was fluttering her hair. The illusion took her pain away, and tears of joy replaced the painful yearning.

It was over soon. The train stopped at another sterile station well protected from the greenery. Limea got off as instructed and put a blindfold back on her eyes. Someone took her hand and led her on. Behind closed eyelids she still saw untamed and diverse vegetation as if walking through a rainforest.

CHAPTER 13

When the woman returned to the room, Cay was lost in thought. He hadn't come up with anything, and at some point, his tired mind just went on a journey of its own. He didn't expect that the hour she'd given him would end so quickly.

"What's your decision?" the woman asked taking a seat opposite him.

Cay wasn't ready. He felt scared, something was stirring in his stomach uneasily. His thoughts were bouncing off empty walls, and he was completely unable to produce anything meaningful. He let out a breath and gave up.

"Fuck it," he said. "I'll tell you what happened, but I'm warning you that it will sound crazy."

"Let me be the judge of that."

"Yeah, right. It's about my bonding partner."

"Limea," the woman nodded.

"Yes," Cay brushed off the annoyance he felt at the reminder of his lack of privacy.

"I love her. She's the most important person to me. We are very close. I think way closer than most people. She's... my best friend, my partner, someone I can always rely on, someone I can trust. We've been together for over ten years now, and I know her really well. I know her... melana, for the lack of a better word. And I think..." Cay sighed and braced himself. "I think she's been replaced by someone else."

"What do you mean?" slightly raised eyebrows were the only indicator that the statement surprised his interrogator in any way.

"I mean it's not her. She went away to her parents one day, and someone else returned instead of her. It's in her eyes. She looks exactly the same, talks the same and does the same things, but something is missing from her eyes that has always been there. Look, I'm not too good with words, and I don't know how to explain it because I don't understand it myself. It's like a great copy, and I know it's impossible to do, there is no technology to do it. The only thing I know is that whatever or whoever she is, she's not Limea. I had to get away from her, and now I have to find out what's happened to the real Limea."

The woman was staring at him for about ten seconds without blinking. It was the first time Cay shared those thoughts with anyone, and he felt great relief wash over him, as if his system was cleared of a disease that had been tormenting him all along. The tension he wasn't even aware of suddenly left his muscles and was replaced by exhaustion. His whole body relaxed, his limbs and eyelids became heavy, and his mind was blissfully empty.

"You look tired," the woman finally said. "I'll have to discuss it with my colleagues, as I'm sure you understand that all of it sounds very strange. How about you get some sleep, and we'll let you know?"

Cay managed to nod, feeling grateful for the offer. He felt that it would probably be the first time he could sleep well since all the weirdness started. He was led to another generic room with grey walls that had nothing in it but an empty white cupboard and a grey couch. Cay fell on it and was immediately out.

When he was awoken several hours later, there were three people in the room: the woman who had talked to him before and two unfamiliar men. Cay sat up and rubbed his eyes. The light was too bright. His mind was hazy, and he felt like he would fall back asleep immediately if he lay down and closed his eyes.

"Olonda", the woman finally introduced herself, offering him a hand. Her handshake was firm. "Welcome on board. We are the Orchids. This is Jam and that's Saki".

Cay got two more handshakes from the men. Jam was a short, chubby, friendly-looking, dark-skinned guy in his mid-twenties, who had a big Afro and was wearing an old-fashioned colorful tracksuit. Saki was a tall, skinny man in his fifties with attentive eyes and an epicanthic fold. He was reserved and serious and was wearing a formal black suit that was slightly baggy for his figure.

"They are two of our best technicians. They will get you a new implant and take care of the records of your deal with Sunny. Then they will help you assemble a team that will work with you on creating a solar system of your design for this facility. We want it to cover all of our energy needs, and we want batteries to store excess energy. Sern and Milsa let me believe that this is possible, is that so?"

"I'll need to know more about your energy needs, but I don't see why that would be impossible if I have access to the necessary materials and equipment," Cay said.

"Of course, we'll provide you with everything. My colleagues here will also show you around and will help you with your temporary relocation."

"I don't have time for that," Saki remarked.

"No worries man, I'll take care of you," Jam winked and patted Cay on the shoulder with a broad smile. Cay smiled back absent-mindedly and turned his gaze back to Olonda.

"You'll have to stay with us while working on the project," Olonda continued. "This is the safest way. You'll get everything you need while you are here."

"So…" Cay cleared his throat. "You believe me?"

After a small pause, Olonda said, "Jam, Saki, thank you, this will be all for now"

When the men left, she sat on the couch next to Cay and looked him in the eye with a degree of sympathy.

"We have a policy of honesty here, so I'll be frank with you. We don't believe you. It sounds like a delusion, and we know you have a history with mind-altering substances and technologies. Besides, the plague hasn't been easy on any of us, sooner or later it breaks a lot of people. Still, we've seen your ability to work and deliver, and after weighing the pros and cons we decided that having the technology will be extremely beneficial for us, and our team can learn a lot from you. You will also be free to begin mass production for the market after you finish here, and, if you want, we'll be able to invest, but that's a conversation for later.

"We can find you a good specialist that will help you deal with your delusions," Olonda added more quietly. "You could stay here and keep working with us too, we are always looking

136

for good specialists. But don't let that overwhelm you, we'll take one step at a time, and you'll be able to make all the decisions as you see fit. For now, I just want you to know that you have options."

"Thanks for being honest," Cay replied. "I see why you'd think that. I'd be happy if it were true. But you are right, let's take it one step at a time. I don't really know what's real anymore."

"No one does. The world has become too strange too fast, and the simulations are indistinguishable from reality, so how can you expect anyone to know what's real? I often find myself wondering if what I'm experiencing is just a sim, and I'll come out of it soon to a world with no plague and my plants on the windowsill," she chuckled somewhat bitterly and rose. "You'll be fine."

Cay got an implant with a record of a law-abiding citizen the very same day. With it, he got access to some parts of the building that were only accessible to the members of the Orchids. Of course, large sections of it were still out of bounds for him, and some doors just wouldn't open, but Jam showed him around, and he now knew where the kitchen was and where to leave his requests for products. He also got a small apartment with a shower, a toilet and a bedroom that, quite annoyingly, had red walls.

The next day, Cay got to know several new people who wanted to work on the solar system with him. He outlined his needs for them, explaining what materials and skills he required. By the end of the day a team of ten was formed, and he was shown to a workshop where they could start building his product. Jam came and announced excitedly that the records of the deal Broon had made with Sunny were deleted. The next day, most of the materials arrived, and two more people joined the team. One of them was Sern, the boy who examined his battery initially, and Cay was happy to see a familiar face. The team showed him building plans and established their energy needs, making the first drafts. The work started to gain tempo, and Cay found himself pulled into it.

It was a bit too perfect. He was almost convinced now that he was in a sim. Somehow having a map that lead him to the Orchids without remembering a clear back story? Managing to pass through all the obstacles, surviving an encounter with the plants, killing a man? And now becoming part of an underground criminal organization and suddenly having his project back?

Cay chuckled. If he had chosen this scenario, he should have known that he'd guess it was a sim. Maybe he wanted to. More likely, this sim was playing on his subconscious, making his dreams come true in a sort of a backward way. These types of sims were sometimes used in psychotherapy. Anyway, the things that were happening to him weren't something he would expect to experience in real life.

Cay dared himself to do something crazy, maybe unlock an easter egg? Or he could kill himself, and the show would be over, he would wake up and go home. He seriously considered it for a moment.

No, he couldn't do it. Cay sighed, feeling a bit disappointed. He couldn't be sure. The events playing out didn't seem plausible, but they weren't impossible either. There was nothing so out of place that he could state with absolute certainty that it wasn't real. And he was looking. Searching for the smallest details that would give away the truth. Little shortcomings, almost imperceptible inconsistencies and glitches. So far, there had been none. The plot had been weird, but he wouldn't put his life on it. Not yet.

He decided the best thing to do was to play along with it and try to find out what had happened to Limea. If that was a sim, maybe there was some logical conclusion there, and it would just end. If it wasn't... who knew? He couldn't stop or change it, so he might as well enjoy it.

Cay thought that he should bring the Orchids into his search for Limea. If anyone could help, it was them. Of course, the fact that they thought he was delusional could interfere with this plan, but maybe they'd trust him more after he'd complete his revolutionary system for them. For now, he decided to focus on the task at hand, pushing his doubts about the nature of reality aside. It was easy to forget them when so much needed to be done. He immersed himself in work and enjoyed the electrical currents of motivation flowing through his body.

He was in the workshop with Sern, crafting the solar fabric for the building. He liked the workshop for its spaciousness and design. Everything was thought through here, organized in the most convenient and optimal way. The workbenches, the holoscreens and computers, the best VR helmets, the tools signed and sorted according to their utility, the high ceilings and large windows all around that let a lot of light through. It was also decorated with graffiti in the cyberpunk style that depicted the world after the plague and people making strange machinery. It was a sunny day, and Cay felt excited. He was finally doing it! His project was brought back to life, and it illuminated everything. He was in work fever.

"We have a situation here," a guy, whose face Cay recognized without being able to place a name to it, peered through the door. "Come with me, Cay."

Cay put down his tools and followed him, somewhat annoyed at being interrupted.

"What is it?" he asked.

"I guess you just have to see," the guy said, making a helpless gesture with his hands.

CHAPTER 14

Vietra was walking along the familiar bridge connecting 23 buildings again. She was expecting the world around her to collapse any moment, but it didn't. Every step gave her a bit more confidence and hope. Was she really free this time?

Tyss hadn't lied, the city was exactly as she remembered it from the sim, but the other things he'd said were too bizarre to make any sense. Vietra pushed these thoughts aside. She had more important things to worry about. She didn't have an implant, which meant that she couldn't use any of the publicly available services, get food or find a place to stay. Technically, there were shelters for people without implants, but those were shady places regularly raided by fixers. There were even rumors that fixers set them up to get easy access to misfits. Vietra didn't need any more headache than she already had.

She also had to get to the Orchids, but she didn't know where they were, and even if she found them, she wouldn't have any way of paying them. Given enough time, she would gather the information on the streets, steal the money and build a network of criminal contacts eventually leading her to the Orchids, but she couldn't afford that luxury without an implant. So how could she get to the criminals?

Vietra stopped for a moment and leaned against the railing of the bridge. Here the reality collapsed the first time she decided to leave the Nest, unaware that she was in a sim. She looked down at the deadly sea of plants below. It would look almost innocent from the height of about 300 meters if she allowed herself to forget that it was slowly devouring the buildings and getting a bit closer to humans every hour. Vietra inhaled the brisk morning air and closed her eyes, giving herself a moment to enjoy the warmth of the sun on her skin. It would feel peaceful if it wasn't for the buzzing of drones overhead.

It suddenly dawned on Vietra that if anyone had enough information about the Orchids and a way to access them quickly, it would be the police. She felt a tingle of excitement at the idea of infiltrating the law enforcement and smiled with her eyes still closed. Lucky for her, she had all the skills she'd learned while being in the Master's sim. In comparison to other humans, she was like an efficient machine. She was so much faster and stronger than them, so much more precise that she would have no trouble winning any fight. Of course, she could be hurt by their weapons, but her vigilance and alertness would allow her to take action way before they even had a chance of recognizing her as a threat. She was confident in her skills.

Vietra opened her eyes with the smile still on her lips. She knew the city and all the key buildings in it well—another courtesy of the Master's training. In her mind's eye, she immediately saw a map with the police department holding the organized crime unit highlighted with soft glow. The bad news was that her destination lay about 20 kilometers away, and drones weren't an option. The good news was that she could reach it by bike. She would have to make quite a detour, taking the bridges and passages to get there, extending her journey to slightly over 100 kilometers, but that was manageable.

She could have just kicked someone off a bike and take it, but that would attract attention, so Vietra decided to look for one that she could get quietly. She found it on the next roof. It was pink, with yellow and green ribbons on the handlebars. Vietra identified the boy who had ridden it there: he had a pink helmet under his elbow, a yellow T-shirt and green shorts. It looked like he had run into someone he knew and just stopped for a moment to talk without bothering to secure his bike. There was a lot of movement on the roof since a morning stretching workout was about to begin, so they drifted away from the bike to let others pass and were now both quite invested in their conversation. Vietra strolled to the bike like it was hers and got on top of it. There was a moment of thrill when she thought she might get caught and childish triumph when she realized that she was out of the boy's reach. She let herself enjoy the excitement and the sensation of riding for a little longer, but it was time to devise a plan.

It would be easy to disarm and question the police officers one after another, forging through the boscage of ranks, getting to the person who was in charge of top-level operations. Vietra knew she could have total control over those people. She knew hundreds of ways to kill them. She could make them suffer intolerably or pass away peacefully in their sleep. She knew how to make their memories hazy and unreal. And she definitely knew how to make them speak.

She had to make an effort of will to stay reasonable. That wasn't the most viable plan as it could make the police take a hasty action before she got her implant. Vietra admitted with regret that she had to use another set of skills: manipulation and deception. One of the Nestlings was a qualified psychologist who taught them various tricks and behavioral techniques.

By the time she got to the police station, Vietra had a rough idea of what she was going to do. She walked around to get familiar with the layout of the building and talked to some people pretending to be an intern, a victim, a technician and a former employee. It was just as easy as the games they'd played in the Nest for practice. She covered her hair with a hat someone had left on a bench and changed her mannerisms and accent every time she spoke with someone. She was behaving in a way that would make them like her and then immediately forget her. A nice person without anything that would stand out or capture one's interest.

This way she gathered enough information and found out that she had to talk to major Dre. The plan was becoming clearer in her head. She ate some tasteless mush she had found in the fridge, thinking she probably needed a uniform to help her build credibility in major Dre's eyes. All the Nestlings were wearing simple black T-shirts and pants that allowed freedom of movement. Vietra felt it was something that police officers could wear in unofficial settings, but it wasn't good enough for her performance. She pondered stealing a uniform but dismissed the idea: it would be missed and surely wouldn't fit well. As most clothes were now 3D printed, and she'd noticed a printing lab in the police station, Vietra was fairly sure they were making their uniforms right here. Of course, she wouldn't be able to get access without an implant and a police officer's ID. She needed help, and after having spent half a day in the police station, Vietra knew just the right person.

"Oiku," she said, coming up to the secretary. "I'm Chief Andante. I was directed to you."

Oiku was a short, middle-aged woman with red cheeks and blond hair, who, as Vietra had learned, was extremely agreeable and friendly. She almost jumped to her feet looking up at Vietra.

"Chief Andante, I wasn't aware... how can I help?" she was clearly confused, and that was what Vietra needed.

"I've just arrived today to oversee an important operation, but my uniform was lost in transit. I have an appointment with major Dre..."

"Oh," Oiku was visibly uncomfortable. "Major Dre has just left."

"Of course, our meeting is tomorrow. But I need a new uniform, and I've been told you could manufacture one for me. You see, I've got important work to do before my meeting with the major, so I'd like you to record my measurements and get the uniform ready for me."

"Yes, of course," Oiku clasped her hands and raised them to her chest earnestly. "We'll have to go to the lab to take the measurements, but I can oversee the whole process after it, you won't have to do anything at all."

"Fine," Vietra nodded curtly and followed Oiku to the lab.

She showed just enough impatience to prevent Oiku from asking questions and keep her occupied with trying to please the "chief". As soon as the measurements were taken, she took several steps to leave the lab but turned around at the door.

"What time does Major Dre arrive tomorrow?" she asked.

"I'm awfully sorry, I don't know for sure, but he usually comes to the office about 7:30, so..."

"Good. I'll be back in an hour for my uniform," Vietra said and left.

She spent the hour stealing makeup from one of the lockers and trying it out to look older. She doubted it was common for the police officers to become chiefs in their early thirties. Of course, the seriousness of her face, lines she made sure were visible on her forehead and the overall gravitas she was projecting had already helped Vietra look older. But she needed to get it right for her meeting with the major. After she achieved satisfactory results, Vietra washed the makeup off and went back for her uniform. She waited for everyone to leave the station and opened a jar of soup someone had forgotten in the fridge. The stench made her eyes water. It must have been there for months, and it was alive now. She put the lid back on and returned the jar into the fridge. Luckily, there was more artificial mush, tasteless but full of nutrients.

Vietra slept on the couch in someone's office, woke up at 6, washed herself as best she could in a sink, ate some more mush, thinking if someone was going to miss their lunch because of that, applied the makeup that helped her gain about ten years, put the new uniform on and entered major Dre's office decisively at 7:35 a.m.

"Major Dre," she said, shaking his hand firmly with an air of respectful, yet slightly impatient superiority. "Chief Andante. I oversee organized crime investigations."

"What happened to Chief Umi?" Dre blinked, looking confused and shook her hand automatically.

"Dead," Vietra said without hesitation. "You have to deal with me now. Your department's results have been quite disappointing lately."

"But the numbers..."

Vietra raised her hand stopping him, "What's going on with the Orchids? Why don't we have a breakthrough? What's with your informant?"

"It's a delicate matter, chief, as I've explained to Chief Umi. They are very cautious, and it's almost impossible to get to them without someone on the inside. It's the first time that we've managed to put an informant among them, and it's critical that we let her do her job without compromising her position. We want her to get enough evidence before we act."

Vietra was gambling when she mentioned the informant. She thought that it was a possibility based on what she'd learned at the station, but she couldn't be sure. Excitement rushed through her body, but Vietra contained it.

"Do you have a way of contacting her?"

"Yes, but we agreed to use it only in case of emergency."

"I need you to do it now. I need her to find a way in for me."

"You?" Major Dre's eyes widened, and he stared at Vietra in disbelief. Probably it wasn't common for police chiefs to risk their lives like that.

"Major," Vietra's voice and gaze were hard. "I'll be honest with you, it's been too long. We're being pressured from above," she made a face and pointed her finger up. "We need to show them some results, otherwise we'll both lose our jobs."

"Just give her a month or two, and we'll have them!"

"I have some instructions for her that I have to pass personally, and a couple of things I need to do in their facility that I can't share with you for reasons I'm sure you understand. She only has to refer me as a client requiring a new identity. She won't be compromised."

"It's too risky," Dre said, eyeing her with a strange expression on his face. Was he beginning to suspect something?

"Major," Vietra let irritation slip through her professionalism. "This decision is not mine alone. It's come right from above, and the orders were clear. I'm not debating you. I'm merely passing the orders down to you. You are to organize my way in."

As Dre was studying her without movement, Vietra found herself hoping he wouldn't obey and give her an excuse to use her physical arsenal on him. There was a lot of evil in her, she realized. Violence was so tempting. She was almost sure that if she let it out, she would never be able to cage it again.

"This is a mistake," Dre said but did as he was told.

It took a couple of days to get everything ready. Vietra kept sleeping and eating at the station without getting caught. She witnessed a couple of arguments as people accused each other of stealing their food. It was hard for her to keep a straight face. She was still secretly hoping something would go wrong, and she'd have to unleash her powers, but everything was extremely smooth. The price for her implant was paid by the police. She was sure she hadn't left any DNA or other traces she could be identified with. Her appearance and voice were changed. She was consciously controlling her movements and gestures to make them different from her usual patterns. Most of the time she managed to avoid the cameras, but even when it was impossible, she made sure her face wasn't captured. She even felt grateful to the Master for the skills that allowed her to do that, as it amused her how in the dark people were, how easily they could be manipulated. Of course, they'd find out they were tricked soon enough, but she'd have her implant and be long gone by then.

It was time to meet the Orchids.

CHAPTER 15

Cay was led into a dark room presenting a hologram of two women standing opposite each other in obvious shock.

"They arrived here one shortly after another, through different routes," the guy who brought him in said while Cay's heart was skipping a couple of beats. If he was waiting for a confirmation he was in a sim, that was it.

Limea was staring at the other woman and couldn't believe her eyes. She looked exactly like her, up to the tiniest detail: the same thick, red curls and green eyes, the same porcelain skin and freckles, the same tall, slim figure, the same sharp, slightly upturned nose. She had bigger muscles though and looked like a person who'd been through a lot. Limea didn't remember having a twin sister, and she suspected she was hallucinating. It wasn't real. It couldn't be.

Vietra was looking at her double with awe. So, it was true then, what Tyss had told her. She didn't expect to meet her, not by accident anyway. What were the odds? She inspected the double with scrutiny: she looked like a good but desperate person, who clearly had no idea what was going on. Vietra felt sorry for her. It was strange to see her, like looking at a version of herself from a parallel Universe. In a way, she was.

A man entered the room hastily. He looked bewildered. Vietra was sure she had no memories of him, yet, something in her clicked. She felt an impulse, a drive, a sort of a tickle inside. It ran through her entire body, it changed the way reality looked. It was such a strong kick that it knocked all air out of her lungs.

It scared her, and she gasped for clear thought. With an effort of will Vietra stopped it. Restoring her breath, restoring logical thinking.

"Cay!" Limea exclaimed and ran to him. She hugged him and started crying. He hugged her back with an insane gaze.

"Wait!" he said and then repeated more quietly, "Wait."

He took Limea by the shoulders and held her at arm's length, gawking into her eyes. For a moment, they stood frozen. Vietra suppressed the urge to swallow.

"No," Cay said and shook his head. "It's not you."

"Cay..." Limea whispered helplessly as he turned to Vietra and took several decisive steps towards her. She was getting ready to kick him when he stopped in front of her and locked his eyes on hers. It was almost physical. Vietra felt her eyes widening, unable to look away.

She was definitely not the person he remembered, but rather a version of herself she could have been if she had lived a different life. As if other experiences shaped her personality, other information entered her lungs with the air she breathed. But as he looked deeply into her eyes, Cay felt drawn to her as if there was a string attached to the truth within him, and someone pulled it abruptly. Her eyes were different, there was a lot in them he didn't recognize. But there it was, the inexplicable something that he had missed so much, the light that made her the woman he loved.

"Limea," he said and took Vietra's hand.

"What's going on?" Limea's voice rang with despair. She didn't understand how the person she loved could have mistaken whoever that other woman was for her.

Vietra struggled for words.

"It's complicated," she finally said in a low, hoarse voice, taking her hand from Cay. "And highly fucked up."

His touch felt good. He was no one to her, but there was a feeling scratching from behind thick walls, crying out for her attention. It was frightening.

Vietra realized immediately it was a mistake to speak. Now they both were looking at her with anticipation, expecting her to explain everything to them. She slapped herself across the forehead, contemplating her stupidity. She had no choice but to tell them. It was her duty, of course, but she knew they would take her for a loony anyway, so it would be nice to avoid the embarrassment.

"I guess we'll need some privacy," Vietra said with a sigh. She was surprised how quickly a room was organized for them.

"Well," Vietra said gazing briefly into Cay's and Limea's eyes and hastily looking away, "it's not going to become easier or less insane, so let's get this over with".

They were sitting in a small room with white walls and a round white table with four black chairs around it. There were no windows, and Vietra didn't like it.

"I don't remember ever having a family. My parents died when I was a baby, and I went to an orphanage. I was almost immediately adopted by a man who called himself the Master. It's funny, I never knew his real name, but it was just natural to call him that because I was used to it. There were also a lot of other kids he'd adopted. We lived in a house called the Nest, and we were called Nestlings. Since early childhood the Master taught us different skills. My main area of expertise was botany and plant genetics, and I worked on creating new species of plants and changing the properties of the existing ones. Just like you, I guess," she glanced at Limea.

"We were also trained in martial arts and other stuff. We were taught to obey the Master unquestioningly and were punished if we didn't. We were being trained and prepared to fulfill our purpose, but we were never told what it was going to be. We just knew that whenever the Master decided we were ready and the time was right, he would give us orders we were supposed to follow. We knew it would involve our skills, but that was basically it.

"It all seemed perfectly normal because I didn't know any other life, until one day after a cruel punishment when I began to question it. I tried to walk away, but strange things happened, and I couldn't. Then one guy from the Nest told me that the life that I knew was actually a simulation. That most of my memories weren't real. That my actual memories were overwritten by the fake ones about having no parents and living in the Nest for my entire life, while in reality I was only there for a couple of weeks, sleeping in a sim-casket.

"My only real memories were those of botany and genetics, as, for some reason, the Master considered them more reliable and stable than the overwritten ones, and he was going to need them. But I also still have the skills I've obtained in the simulation, my neural pathways have been changed accordingly as if I have actually been training for my entire life. Even my body has changed, though it seems impossible. I woke up with the help of the guy who had told me the story, unplugged myself from the sim-casket and walked out of there.

"Now comes the most fucked up part. As the Master wanted my knowledge of botany to be real, he had to take an actual person who was genuinely good at it. Apparently, he was searching for people with different skills that he required for his plan: the other Nestlings were just like me. I saw them sleeping in the caskets when I woke up. Anyway, I was a good candidate for a botanist, so he abducted me and put me through all these procedures, erasing my actual memories so that they didn't get in the way. But he couldn't just let me go missing, he didn't need unnecessary attention. That's why he replaced me with a..." Vietra stopped and glanced at Limea. She could only imagine how what she was saying sounded.

"A biologically engineered clone. According to what I gathered, he scanned my body and brain, took my DNA and kind of... 3D printed you."

"That's insane!" Limea jumped to her feet. "Let me get it straight: you are saying that I am your clone made to replace you after you were abducted by some Master to fulfill an unknown purpose related to botany? I think you need to see a doctor, and I'm not saying it to be mean."

"Look, I know how it sounds," Vietra sighed. "I wouldn't believe it either. Maybe that's bullshit, but this is what the only guy I trust in the world told me, and seeing you confirms that. I'm not going to try to convince you. I don't care if you believe it. I just figured I had to tell you."

"That's insane. She's crazy," Limea turned to Cay, and it took her a moment to realize with dread that he seemed to take it seriously.

154

"Come on, Cay, you are too intelligent for that," she said, but he looked at her and shook his head.

"I knew you weren't Limea."

"But that's!.." Limea slapped her hips angrily and scowled. "What about my memories? My childhood, our life together? Ask me anything, and I'll tell you!"

"I'm afraid those are my memories imprinted on your brain," Vietra said quietly.

Limea gasped for breath, unable to talk, but when air returned to her lungs and she opened her mouth to speak, she realized there was nothing she could say. How could she convince two crazy people they were delusional? She didn't think she could get help for them from the Orchids. Limea's world started crumbling. There was no ground beneath her feet anymore. There was nothing she could hold on to. She was being thrown into open space without instructions or equipment. A new life she didn't want, her personality cut out of her with the implant, all the people she knew gone. She was going to be absolutely alone despite having found Cay, and for the most idiotic of reasons. She knew now what real dread meant.

"It can't be happening," Limea shook her head. "It must be a bad sim, and I want it to end."

She turned around and left the room.

Cay and Vietra were looking at the door that was still closing behind her, listening to her hasty footsteps. They turned to each other and looked into each other's eyes. It scared both of them as they felt naked, with their deepest feelings on display. It was too intense.

"I have to…" Vietra interrupted herself, deciding there was no reason for her to explain her actions to that man. She went out into the corridor to look for Limea. It was a strange impulse, she realized, but she felt bad for the woman. Cay should have supported Limea, dismissing Vietra as a lunatic. Instead, he took her side. Vietra was angry with him for that, and trying to find a rational explanation for those feelings pissed her off even more. She couldn't find Limea. She might have taken one of the several turns, and Vietra didn't see her do it.

Cay followed her into the corridor. He stood near her, looking ahead for a couple of seconds, then turned around and said, "I'm glad I found you, Limea. I've come here to look for you."

That was one more awkward thing she had to deal with: a man from her past who apparently loved her, but whom she didn't remember at all.

"I know it must be my name, but it feels alien. I don't remember being Limea, I only know myself as Vietra. Call me that, please."

"Okay. Vietra. I guess I'll have to get used to it," Cay smiled.

"And you are Cay, I gather."

"Yes, Cayrony, Cay for short. You don't remember me at all?"

"Sorry. My brain was reshaped, and my memories overwritten. I'm afraid I'm not the person you used to know anymore."

"I can live with that."

She felt uncomfortable with the way he looked at her and with the feeling rising from her stomach into her chest. She could see deeply into him through his eyes, and he seemed to allow, maybe even encourage it. That was strange. It was un-wise of him to trust her so much.

"I'd like to be alone if you don't mind. And I need an im-plant, that's why I came here in the first place. Can we talk lat-er?" she asked.

"Of course," Cay said. "But promise me you won't leave. Give me a chance to get to know you again and help you. These people here are quite powerful, and I am on good terms with them. I'm sure we can find some information about this Master and his experiments."

"Okay," Vietra said.

"Promise," he insisted.

"I promise," she said wondering why it was so important for him to hear it, as if a word could shape reality.

***

While an implant was being prepared for her, Vietra was left alone and had some time to think. All of it was too bizarre. Not that she wasn't used to bizarre, but it had an absolutely new quality now.

Meeting Limea made a devastating impact on her. When Vietra first heard she was cloned, she was startled, but the news mingled with all the other shocking information and events, so it was just a part of a bigger creepy picture. She wasn't sure whether she was going to try to find out anything about her previous life and go back to it. She put this question aside and decided to deal with more vital problems. One step at a time. But even though she was curious about who she used to be, there was a thought at the back of Vietra's mind that she proba-bly should just start over. She knew she wasn't the same person anymore and suspected she wouldn't be able to go back to whatever life she'd had. How was she supposed to know that the life was going to jump at her like that? And now this clone.

She hadn't given it much thought before, but subconsciously she believed that it was some kind of a defected creature, only partially human. For some reason she imagined it more like a machine than anything else. No feelings, no original thoughts, just a copy. But what she saw was a person, emotional and unique, vulnerable and real. A person who had no idea what she was, having the truth strike her like that. It was strange to think that Limea was actually herself from before encountering the Master. Vietra sympathized with her. She seemed like a good person.

***

Limea ran out into the corridor, blinded by tears. The surroundings were blurry, as if seen from the inside of a drone caught in a downpour. She didn't know where she was going, it didn't matter. Nothing mattered, even when she found herself in the area where greenery was thriving. Limea would die if she was careless and got too close to the plants, but she was too tired to care. She was detached from the thought of her own possible death, as if it concerned some distant stranger.

Limea felt bruised on the inside. The feeling seemed too physical, and it was frightening her. She was weak, on the edge of collapse. She didn't know what to think. She didn't believe a single word Vietra had said, but she saw it was impossible to prove the absurdity of it to Cay, who had completely lost his mind.

On the other hand... On the other hand, Limea thought, she didn't know what was real anymore. She had lost the ability to see clearly quite some time ago. The post-plague world had made the already thin boundary between the real and imaginary even more elusive. It was difficult to distinguish between reality and elaborate, mind-altering simulations. And in this confusion the technological advance burst out, spurred by humanity's possible extinction. How could she actually know in the new world of hazard and opportunity whether what Vietra had said was true or not? She thought it was impossible, but maybe she was wrong. The irony was that there was no way to be sure. Limea felt exhausted.

A memory flashed in her mind. It was from the time she and Cay weren't yet together. There was something between them, a connection stretching thorough time and space that made their friendship stand out among all others. Limea didn't yet realize her feelings for Cay were the purest form of love. He was very important to her.

One night, in her dream she heard a song. The simple beauty of it pierced her chest and touched her heart. She could still remember the melody and a couple of words knocking against her waking mind. Something about lost souls in a fishbowl. Limea woke up with the aftersound floating around her head. She thought of Cay immediately. She felt like the song was about them somehow. Not completely awake, she got carried away by dreamy impressions, seeing them both as particles drifting through empty space. Sometimes they got closer and touched each other, turning into colorful sparkles, illuminating the darkness. As they moved away from each other, their glow gradually faded until they couldn't be distinguished from other particles. But they were drawn to each other, and it felt like everything was about getting close to light up again.

Even when they were far away, they seemed to be connected. Entangled. What happened to one of them appeared to be affecting the other. Similar ideas gleamed in their minds, and similar thoughts puzzled them independently. When Limea woke up completely, she knew she had always loved Cay. She also looked up the song and the mysterious word "soul" but found nothing of relevance. Nevertheless, the word was clear. She wouldn't be able to explain it, yet, she instinctively understood what it meant.

It was over now. The connection severed. Maybe it hadn't even been real in the first place. But it felt like Limea was alone for the first time in years.

Someone passed her by and said something. Limea didn't even bother to answer. Speaking seemed irrelevant and contact with another human too demanding to carry out. Limea hoped she could just stay there forever without ever having to do anything. *They must leave me alone*, she thought. *I'm no one to them, they shouldn't care.* A thought of suicide passed through her mind. She didn't consider it seriously, but she realized she could do it without hesitation if only she was capable of getting up. Not because she actually wanted to die, but because she didn't care about anything, including her own life. There would be no fear or moral dilemma, it would be an act like any other: meaningless.

Limea closed her eyes and watched colorful patterns dancing in front of her. She had no idea of passing time, she was out of its framework. She didn't have any thoughts or any aware-ness of who or where she was. She even had no idea of such concepts as "who" or "where", they were as alien to her as any notions creatures from outer space could come up with. There was no her anymore. There was nothing, but the eternal beauty of dancing patterns.

CHAPTER 16

"We have to find out who this Master actually is."

"Look," Vietra sighed and made a pause, trying to gather her chaotic thoughts into some logical structure. It wasn't easy, they were all in conflict with each other, but she felt she had to say it. It was the right thing to do. "I understand why you feel obliged. You think I am the woman you love, and technically I am. But I am, in fact, an absolutely different person who's had an absolutely different life, where there was no you. I don't know you, I don't remember you, and I am not the person you know. I am someone else. I only share genetic material with her. I am just the body, the contents of my head are different. You understand this, right? Limea, I mean the clone... shit, this sounds stupid... but the clone is actually the woman you love. She has all the memories and the experiences. The right personality. You understand? She is much more me than I am... Sorry, it sounds ridiculous, I don't know how to talk about this stuff."

"I understand what you mean," Cay said. "It's logical, as much as it can be anyway. But I don't care. I see you. I know who you are, even though you've changed. I can't love her because I know she's not you. I recognized you the moment I saw you, and in your eyes, I see your world."

"There is no world," Vietra felt annoyed. "There are just experiences, surroundings, knowledge, thoughts and chemical reactions."

"Do you believe in it?"

"I don't know what I believe. When I look deep inside myself, I see emptiness. There is nothing there. There are layers and layers of something that others can take for a personality, but there is nothing beneath them."

"There is light."

"No."

Vietra didn't know why they were discussing this. She wasn't used to talking about such things, and it felt strange. It was making her vulnerable. Why would she want to be vulnerable?

"Anyway," she said. "It's dangerous. The technology the Master has—even these geeks here can't compete with that. I'm just saying, you shouldn't be risking your life for someone you don't know. I am a stranger to you."

"I agree. And I want to know you."

"I might disappoint you."

"Then our problem will be solved, won't it?" Cay smiled. "I'll finally leave you alone."

Vietra didn't understand why she was getting even more annoyed.

"What if I don't want to know you?" she said angrily.

"I can't make you," Cay looked her straight in the eye with this exposed look of his that felt so inappropriately intimate. Too sincere, without protective shatters people usually wore on their eyes when looking at others. Showing the depth of what he was inside, showing that he was hurt. "But I'd like to help if you are willing to accept it. I expect nothing from you."

"I just... it's not right."

"What does right even mean?"

"Okay. So, you want to help me get to the Master. I want to do it because I have nothing else. No family, no friends, no life. But you have lots to lose. It's not worth it."

"It is."

"You are strange."

"Thanks."

Vietra chuckled despite herself.

"It wasn't a compliment."

"It seems that people rarely hear what others have to say anyway, so why don't I just perceive everything the way I want?" Cay shrugged. "It's a compliment to me."

***

Limea was facing enchanting space. She didn't remember how she got there, but after wondering mindlessly along deserted corridors, taking turns and stairways, she finally found herself on one of the lower stories, inside a large hall of about a hundred square meters across. One of the walls was almost completely ruined, with just a part of its structural frame left. It opened to a view of a vast forest, a piece of violet sky and feathers of the clouds lit by the flares of the setting sun. Greenery was rushing inside, seizing the walls and the floor, like a giant caught in the midst of trying to get into the building.

Limea looked at the vegetation, mesmerized. There was no better place for her to be right now. It was soothing to be so close to the plants, to have such a broad perspective from inside the building. It was beautiful.

She took a step closer to the gap and then another one. The plants didn't look like anything she had studied as a botanist. She'd give everything to be able to work with them. One

164

more step. It seemed they were within her reach. They sensed her too. There was a small, barely perceptible predatory tension. Limea knew she was too close, but she took another step. The plants leaned to her, trembling slightly. Was it fair that she loved them so much while they only craved her blood? Probably, it was. People deserved it for everything they did to the planet. Whether she wanted it or not, she was a part of it. No matter how hard she tried to reduce consumption and waste, she was incorporated in the system that abused the nature.

Limea missed her home plants, carefully selected, uninfected pre-plague species she guarded so passionately to be able to take them to spaceships and stations and, eventually, to other planets. She worked on their resilience, developing new properties in them, so that they could sustain unfavorable conditions. She tended to them every day, and it gave her peace. She dreamed of vast forests where people could walk again.

She took one more step forward mindlessly and had to jump back, as she found herself too close. It was an odd feeling. She was afraid of the plants and admired them at the same time. It felt good to be able to see greenery so abundant, so wild, so unstoppable. As a scientist, Limea had no rational explanation as to what might have happened to the flora. As an individual, she believed it was the planet's retaliation.

Being surrounded by the plants evoked something in her, some deep, ancient feeling that settled in her chest. It was like slight pressure, like something reaching out from within, but without urgency or aggression–the feeling was light and pleasant. As if some part of her was peering out after hiding in the shadows for a long time. She felt airy. Light. She realized it was the view. There were several visual stimuli that gave her such a physically intense feeling. Vast mountains surrounding her with a long path behind and ahead of her. Candles burning at dusk in slight mist rising from a cooling ground of a cemetery amongst trees. Both were lost in the pre-plague world, but there was another one in front of her, and it was pure beauty connecting to her inner light in spite of all the pain.

"You feel that too, huh?" she heard a quiet voice from behind. It was the other her. Limea wasn't sure who was the real one anymore. How could she know?

"Yes," she said quietly.

"I've never felt this way before," Vietra commented bemusedly. "It's like a visual orgasm."

"It's glory and bliss," Limea said. "Have you ever seen candles on a cemetery at dusk?"

"I don't seem to recall it," Vietra pondered upon it. "There are no cemeteries in my memories."

"It's a shame," Limea said. "Though, maybe that's for the best. Maybe you don't remember death either."

"There was enough death. But there was never grieving."

"How did you cope with it then?"

Vietra shrugged, "I guess we just moved on."

"No offense, but this community of yours sounds insane."

"None taken. It is. I'm only beginning to realize that now. I'm sorry," Vietra added after a pause.

"For what?"

"For showing up like that and ruining your life."

"It was ruined before you showed up, so I guess it's okay."

Vietra stayed quiet for a while. There were lots of thoughts running through her head, lots of feelings roaming in her chest, but she didn't know how to bring them out. No one ever taught her. She didn't know what had brought her here, but somehow, she had a feeling she would find her double when she set out for a walk. She didn't have a specific destination in mind, submitting to her heart to lead the way, and there she was, in the most magnificent place in the whole building.

Limea was silent, too. She didn't want to be hostile to Vietra; the other woman didn't deserve it. But she couldn't help feeling it anyway. Mostly because of Cay. She knew she'd lost him, and even though it was none of Vietra's fault, Limea couldn't but blame her.

"Look," Vietra said as if reading her thoughts. "I didn't want it to happen. That guy... Cay... I told him he should stick with you. I hope he'll see reason."

"He won't," Limea said.

"Then I'll just leave quietly and let you do the convincing."

"Don't do it to him. If you want to leave, tell him."

"Why? Don't you want him to stay with you?"

"Not if he doesn't want it. He clearly wants you, so there is nothing I can do. And I don't want him to suffer, especially now, when I know how it feels to be left behind."

"Not in the slightest?"

"Well, I guess part of me wants it, but I don't *really* want it to happen. I love him."

"I don't get it, but I respect your choice. You both seem like good people."

"Take care of him. Be honest with him. If you really are me... or I am you... you'll fall in love with him in no time."

"I don't think I want it."

"Have you ever been in love?"

"I don't think so. Though there was this guy in the Nest who was really nice to me, the one who helped me escape. I had some good feelings for him, not sure it was love though."

"Then it wasn't. When it's love, you know."

"How do you know?"

"You just know," Limea smiled for a moment, lit by memories. "This phrase doesn't make sense, I thought so too before I met Cay. And then I just knew it was him, and it had no rational ground beneath it. There was this certainty, even though I didn't properly know him. There will be no doubt. You'll recognize it when it comes."

"Will it be too strange..." Vietra paused. She realized what she was going to say was probably outrageous and even cruel, but she couldn't help it. "If I ask you to go with me?"

Limea looked at her with utter disbelief.

"Go where?"

"To deal with the Master. I know it's dangerous, and you probably have a life of your own, but... this motherfucker did it to us. I want him to look us in the eye and say he had a reason."

It wasn't the only reason Vietra wanted Limea to come. She'd never known her family, and she got used to being lonely, not attached to anyone, living under one roof with other Nestlings, and yet, never really bonding with them. It was forbidden. They had to watch their every step and avoid being emotional. They competed with each other for the Master's praise. For the first time, she could talk to someone so sincerely and openly, share emotions. Limea was wearing her vulnerability gracefully, and Vietra thought she could learn a lot from her. It felt like having a sister. She couldn't have guessed she would ever experience this type of connection, but she felt strangely comfortable with Limea, and she wanted to protect her and to share something with her.

Limea pondered upon it. No, she thought, she didn't have a life anymore. She'd lost it the moment she removed her implant. She hadn't yet got a new one though, so maybe she could ask the Orchids to give her old personality back to her. Did she want it? Could she just go back as if nothing had happened? Was there anything that could save her now? Her art?

Maybe she had to find out what had really happened before she could move on. Maybe all the people she'd have to leave behind weren't even her friends and family after all, so she didn't have to worry about hurting them. What would she tell them if she came back home? If she told the truth, she'd end up in the fixers' hands sooner or later. And she despised lying, so it would be a constant additional torment. If she went with Vietra, she wouldn't have to pretend, and she'd have a mission, at least for a while. The problem was that Cay would likely be there too. It would be extremely difficult and weird too see him in love with another woman. And the fact that the other woman looked exactly like her wouldn't make things easier.

Limea knew she had to get over her feelings now that Cay didn't love her anymore. Probably, the shock therapy of seeing him in love would be a faster way. Limea looked at Vietra, probing her patience in watching her double every day. It was hard. She twitched.

"I don't know," Limea said. "Let me think about it."

Vietra was standing in silence for quite some time, contemplating the nature. Then she slightly touched Limea by the shoulder and left her alone. She felt her sister needed it. Limea sat down on the floor without taking her eyes off the greenery.

Considering the possibility that nothing she knew about herself was true, Limea realized she didn't have to be the person she used to be. She didn't owe anything to the world that had hurt her so badly. She didn't owe anything to any of the people she thought she knew. Their faces flashed through her mind, causing a familiar tickle of emotions. None of this was real. Just neural patterns imprinted on her brain. Did it matter if it felt real? She couldn't decide yet.

Gazing into the opening of the collapsed wall, she wanted to get lost in the majestic nature. She felt an impulse persuading her to get up and merge with it. A calling. A whisper. And then something shimmered between the tree tanks deep down. Was she imagining it? Was she hallucinating? The shimmer repeated. The light seemed to touch the tip of her nose playfully. Limea rose to her feet, trying to see it from another angle, but it disappeared. What was it? She felt restless and couldn't sit down again. There was some energy pushing her from within. She started pacing along the opening in the wall, peering into the depths of the intertwined trunks and stalks, flowers and leaves. The absence of the mysterious light urged her to come closer to the edge. The closer she got to it, the more excited she felt, as if some part of her was screaming in joy from within.

She took another step closer and then another one. One more. She felt physically drawn to the forest, as if something was pulling her. Suddenly, she felt a touch on her face and halted, coldness of fear spreading from her stomach to the chest. She let a plant touch her! Time slowed down, stretching the moment into a protracted line. The acute realization she was going to die pierced Limea.

CHAPTER 17

Cay couldn't sleep at night. Too much had happened, and he was unable to grasp it. It turned out that he was right about Limea, but the story was too strange to accept. He found her again, but she was a different person. She had a different name. She didn't remember him. She didn't trust him. He was afraid she would take off without him, and he'd never see her again. And the woman who he thought was an imposter turned out to be an innocent victim who had no idea what was going on. She believed she was Limea. It must have broken her heart when he left, when he chose Vietra over her. It certainly did. He knew it wasn't his fault, he had nothing to blame himself for, yet, he couldn't but feel her pain. Could he do anything to make it up to her? It didn't seem so.

Cay got up and went to the kitchen along the corridor to get some water. He could get it in a sink in his apartment, but he wanted some movement to clear his head. It was dark, but Cay didn't turn the lights on. His eyes had adjusted to the darkness, and he could see the silhouettes of familiar objects. It was enough. It was good this way. The light would be too invasive. Everything looked somewhat surreal and mysterious in the dark.

He wished he could find some proof to be sure it was a sim. He could just jump out of the window. Wake up and go back to their cozy apartment, where Limea was waiting for him. There was nothing he wanted more than the peace and familiar smell of their old life. Turn on some calm music, lie on the couch and watch Limea tend to her plants. Take her hand and pull her near

172

him. Lie there for a while, cuddling, in silence. Make some tea. Listen to her voice.

He sighed and shook the thoughts off. They were no good. That life was most likely over. Even though his logical mind kept telling him this could be nothing but a sim, another part of him wasn't so sure. The events kept placing Cay right into the heart of every moment, making it so tangible and acute that he forgot to doubt the reality of it. Of course, everything had to feel genuine, this was how sims worked. But there was some obscure quality to reality that virtual experiences lacked. He couldn't capture or describe it, he actually had never thought of it before. When he used sims, he just enjoyed the scenario without analyzing much. But it seemed like reality felt a bit more real afterwards. He wasn't sure. Maybe he was making it up.

Cay thought about the new Limea. He had to get used to calling her Vietra now. When he first recognized her, happiness filled him. He found her! Even when he realized she had changed, it didn't matter much to him. It seemed fun: he would have a chance to get to know her from the very beginning. But as the first euphoria passed, he started worrying. Doubts began to cram his head. She was a different person with a very disturbing story. The things she'd been through—and Cay was sure she'd only revealed a small fraction of them—must have messed her head. He loved her, but if he had to be honest with himself, the love actually belonged to someone else. The person she used to be. He couldn't even be sure that she'd love him again, and for a second he thought, maybe it would be better if she didn't. The problem would be solved. He would just have to come back home and try to learn to live without her.

Cay imagined that and realized with sudden clarity he preferred to go through a million troubles with her than to never see her again. There was little rationality in it, but what does love have to do with rationality? He recognized her, the deepest truth about her that stayed the same in spite of everything that had happened to her. And he couldn't resist the light, just like a moth, he had no choice but to let it burn him. Every other decision would be a lie.

While pouring water into the glass in the dark kitchen, Cay suddenly felt someone standing behind his back and turned around quickly. He saw a silhouette, and before his brain formed a thought of recognition, his heart paused for a moment just to speed up again. He closed the tap and put his glass down.

"Limea," he said and immediately corrected himself, "Vietra. What are you doing here?"

"She's gone," Vietra replied in a hurt voice that made him uneasy.

"Who's gone?" Cay asked, moving closer to her and resisting the urge to hug her. She might not like it, he had to remind himself. He was just a stranger.

"Limea," she said. "I couldn't sleep, and I wanted to find her. I went to the place where I last saw her, but there was no sign of her. I was looking everywhere. I know she's gone. I'll never see her again."

"Maybe she's also wandering somewhere. You know, it's not easy for her. You'll see her tomorrow."

"She's gone. I know it," Vietra repeated with emphasis and slight irritation. Even though it was dark, Cay knew the look on her face.

He wanted to ask why she cared so much, but he sensed it could upset her. It was better to accept the way she felt.

"Can I hug you?" he asked.

Vietra hesitated for a little too long. Then she said "yes" quietly. Cay closed his arms around her, feeling the tension in her whole body. But as seconds were floating by, she began to relax. She exhaled and became softer. Cay took it as a sign of trust, and it made him feel better. He missed their intimacy.

"She was like a sister to me," Vietra said. "I know it sounds stupid. But she was the closest thing to a family I ever had."

"You actually have a family, and they love you," Cay said.

"They are not my family."

Even though she said it in a calm and even tone, Cay realized his words had upset her. She stepped back from him, breaking their hug.

"You refuse to acknowledge that I'm not that person. I don't know that family. They love someone else. And I don't know you," Vietra said firmly.

"I know. I'm sorry. But I feel like I know you. There is something in you I recognized the moment I saw you even though... Limea was also in the room. You are different because you've lived a different life... but you are also still you on the deepest level."

"I don't believe in the deepest level. I'm no one. An artificial persona created for someone's goals," Vietra shook her head. "Why am I even talking to you?"

Cay didn't know what to say. He stood there in silence and watched her silhouette dissolve in the dark. It hurt.

CHAPTER 18

Limea remembered her first encounter with the truth. She remembered the moment when a plant touched her, and how she waited for death to claim her. It never came. The plant didn't appear hostile. On the contrary, it was curious, trembling a little, as if it was sniffing and probing her. It wanted to know what she was, and, apparently, it didn't recognize her as the enemy.

She remembered the feeling of unrestrained happiness blast inside and spread in all directions around her. She could be part of the nature again! She could be in contact with it, and through it with her true self. There was no more fear, no more doubt and pain. Just freedom and joy beaming through her. She ran towards the opening in the wall, letting the plants touch her skin, spreading her arms, laughing. She jumped, confident there was nothing that could hurt her anymore. And she felt the tender arms of plants catch her in the air and lower her carefully onto the ground. Abundant verdancy around, species she'd never seen before, new inhabitants and rulers of the world, the ones who were going to defeat humans and start a new era.

It was a dream come true, being in the wild that looked so different from what Limea used to know that it felt alien. An ultimate adventure, a breathtaking experience. She wasn't sure where she was anymore. Maybe she went mad? Maybe she was dying, and all of it was a premortem hallucination? Maybe she was already dead?

But Limea discovered she wasn't when an unknown new species of animal, that reminded her somewhat of a huge panther colored by a crazy artist, attacked her. She had nothing to protect herself with and no time to react anyway. She felt sharp claws in her chest and deadly fangs in her neck. That's it, she thought. This time for sure. She felt grateful she could die this way though, in the wild, surrounded by magnificent trees. Become part of the food chain again, just like her ancestors, whom she suddenly felt connected with.

When Limea woke up for the first time after her encounter with the animal, she didn't understand where she was. She could barely see anything, and none of the vague shapes looming in the smoky air seemed familiar. Some of them were moving around and bending over her, which scared her, but she couldn't move or talk. Soon they dissolved in the clouds of smoke that became colorful and bloomed with patterns. Limea had no idea what was going on, but she had to admit it looked beautiful. She thought that, most likely, this time she was actually dying, and as much as the thought scared her, it also intrigued her. There was probably nothing she could do at that point, so she decided to follow the luminous flow and see where it would take her. She was grateful for feeling no pain. In fact, she didn't feel her body at all. She wasn't sure she had a body anymore. After all, the animal could have eaten her.

She felt vast and limitless. She forgot her name and who she used to be before. All concepts and knowledge faded, language vanished, and all that was left was pure emotion and sensations she couldn't comprehend. She was drowning in color and sound. She was light, floating in inconceivable space. Then she realized she wasn't alone there. She could see a creature, fluid and transient, changing its shape and multiple colors every moment. It was aware of her and was calling for her to merge with it and dissolve in it.

Limea was scared. She believed that merging with the creature would destroy her. On the other hand, there was no her anymore, her personality washed away by the experience. There was nothing she could come back to, so, after a moment of hesitation, she surrendered.

The experience took her on a magic journey that seemed to last for ages. Just like in the sim rooms she used to create, she visited distant planets and watched their mysterious inhabitants, only this time she was sure they were real. She became some of them for a while and got the chance to feel the world the way they felt it. Then she moved on to other planets, other creatures.

She got to know their planets from within their heads, through their perception. In those moments, her thinking was utterly changed as if her brain was rewired. She wouldn't be able to think those thoughts or feel those feelings if she were human. It relied on alien chemistry, biology and evolution.

Sometimes she just watched from the outside, reveling in endless variety of colors and shapes life took, inspired by nature's perfect creativity. Then she watched stars emerge and die, explode and slowly fade. She was one of those stars. She watched black holes devour light and matter. She was inside of them. She watched galaxies dance together in glittering clusters, forming a network of complex energy, a living organism functioning and interacting on multiple levels she could clearly see at that point. And all of it was a part of her, or maybe she was a part of it all, but it felt like she was looking inside herself, traveling within her own structure of life.

Thousands of years might have passed when she felt herself ripped apart from something big and cozy that she had come to love. She wasn't vast and complex anymore, and she felt all the knowledge she'd gained on the journey peeled off her, until what remained was a small, lonely consciousness, empty and pure. She didn't remember what she'd lost anymore, but a vague feeling of incompleteness shimmered inside. Then she saw the ever-changing creature again, who was looking at her with multiple eyes of Universal wisdom. The creature spoke to her. Its mouth wasn't moving, at times it didn't even have a mouth, but Limea heard the message clearly in her mind, even though it seemed to be conveyed through a much more exquisite and precise medium than words. It left no doubts as to the meaning of what was being said to her or how the creature felt about it. It was honest and sincere, pure and clear.

"Who are you?" the creature asked.

"I don't know," Limea answered. She found she could communicate through the medium perfectly well, in spite of having no understanding of what it was or how she was doing it.

"Remember," the creature said, and bright images flashed through Limea's mind.

Her whole life lined up into a neat sequence in front of her up to the moment of walking into the woods.

"Am I dead?" she asked, feeling surprisingly calm about it.

"No," the creature answered. "Do you remember who you are now?"

"I'm still not sure," Limea said. "The last thing I found out about myself was pretty confusing. It seemed like the whole life I'd lived wasn't mine after all. Seemed like I was some artificial being created for someone's perverted purposes. But it doesn't make sense. It's hard to believe."

"Do you want to know the truth?" the creature inquired.

Limea pondered upon it. Did she? She remembered being quite curious, but it might not even be her personality trait. She felt like the truth scared her when she was human, but at that point, she felt calm like water of a still forest lake. Did it matter? She didn't think so. But inside herself she found the wish to understand what had happened to her.

"Yes," she finally said.

The creature smiled. It wasn't a smile of the lips but a smile of the heart, shining through its eyes.

"Then so be it."

Limea saw herself manufactured from a couple of cells and a genetic code. She watched it from the outside, as an observer. She saw features of her face and peculiarities of her figure emerge slowly from a shapeless mass of matter. She also saw a brain forming inside her head. Folds and neural patterns were being imprinted on it, it was gaining its shape step by step, growing and becoming more complex along with her body. She knew the neural patterns belonged to someone else. She was getting a copy of somebody's mind. She was becoming a copy of another person.

She'd never thought it was possible, even with the advanced technology humanity possessed. She'd never heard of anything like this. When everything was ready, the fluid her body was floating in was gently removed, the tubes and cables she was connected to detached themselves, and she was left alone in a room filled with machines watching over her. She wasn't yet conscious, it seemed like she was in deep sleep. There was no one around. The whole manufacturing process was completely autonomous.

Was she the only one of her kind, Limea who was watching wondered? Were there others like her, manufactured the same way?

Slowly, Limea in the lab was beginning to gain consciousness. She woke up and looked around. She found herself alone in a transparent, oval tank. Sticky gel was clinging to her body and walls of the tank. She was naked, but as soon as she got up and out of the tank, she saw her clothes folded neatly on a shelf. She wanted to wipe the gel from herself, but there was nothing to do it with, so she got dressed, feeling unclean and cold. She looked around. She was in an oval room full of tanks like the one she got out of. They were all empty. There were small round windows close to the ceiling, about four meters high, and Limea could see nothing but the sky through them. The last thing she remembered was visiting her family. She hadn't had this memory before, but now, observing it from the outside, Limea recalled feeling completely confused. How did she get there? What was going on? She was terrified. She walked around and looked around but found nothing that could answer her questions. The door was locked.

Then someone entered the room. It was a middle-aged man, quite short, but wide in the shoulders. He looked sturdy and strong, standing steadily on his short, muscular legs. There seemed to be nothing special about him, he looked pretty ordinary, but Limea felt a shiver on her spine the moment she saw him. Maybe, it was the look in his cold grey eyes or something else, something elusive but tangible.

"Who are you? Where am I?" she asked.

"I'm the one asking questions here," he said with indisputable authority.

Limea didn't like to obey authority, but she realized with intuitive certainty that there was no point in arguing with him.

"So," the man continued. "Let's start with the easy things. What's your name?"

"I'm not telling you," Limea replied. She felt more and more frightened, and the man's stare made her freeze on the inside, but she wasn't going to play his game.

"Yes, you are," he said with a vile smile. The smile looked awkward on his face, as if he was familiar with the concept without quite understanding it. It made Limea even more uneasy and filled her with pity, intensifying her fear at the same time.

"You have to go first," she said despite the words clogging her throat. "I don't remember how I got here or what's happened to me. Why are you keeping me here? Who are you?"

"We don't have time for this," the man said with a sigh. "Look, I'm giving you a hand here. I can get all the information I want from you, but it might get slightly... unpleasant. Instead, I'm offering cooperation. You talk, and then you walk out of here, get a nice and cozy life."

Limea thought he was probably telling the truth. Answering his questions was a reasonable thing to do. And yet, something inside her resisted the idea of this stranger having total control over her. She shook her head.

"Not going to cooperate? Okay," the man sighed again. He made no gesture and uttered no word, but the machines suddenly sprang out of the walls, reached out for her with long robotic arms and locked her in their grip as if responding to his mere thought. Limea couldn't move. Something was injected into her neck, and for about a minute, there was silence. The man didn't speak. He was standing firmly without the slightest movement, his gaze locked on something invisible in front of him. Limea tried to control her breath in order not to give up her distress, but she was almost sure the man didn't care at all. He didn't see her as a person, she realized. In a couple of minutes, Limea started feeling different. Her breath slowed down, her body felt limp, her head became light. She was on the edge of falling asleep.

"Okay," the man said. "You are ready now. What's your name?"

"Limea Rebly," she said despite herself.

She still didn't want to talk. She still had the same feelings about the man, but she couldn't resist speaking. She felt the information pulled from her brain and put onto her tongue. It was physically unpleasant and tedious, she felt dizzy and helpless. Her head was spinning, and not being in control felt terribly confusing.

For a moment, she thought it might be a dream. She wanted to pinch her nose and try to inhale. It was a reality test she and Cay used to achieve lucid dreaming. Of course, it was impossible to breathe this way, but in a dream the air passed freely, betraying that she was sleeping. She couldn't raise her arm. She wanted to wake up desperately, but it didn't happen.

The man continued asking questions, and Limea continued replying. He started with trivial ones, like where she was born or what her job was, but he ended up with the most personal ones. He asked about her relationship with her parents and her worst sexual experience, about the things she was ashamed and proud of, about her fears and dreams, about her life with Cay and their fights. Limea felt robbed of the intimacy of the moments that shouldn't be shared with strangers. She felt humiliated. Eventually, the man was satisfied.

"Great," he said. "Everything works great. Now you can go and live a life."

Something else was injected into Limea's arm, and within seconds, she was soundly asleep. Then she was put into a drone, taken to the roof of her parents' house and left there. She came around remembering nothing of the encounter. For all she knew, she'd spent some nice time with her family and just walked out. She felt a slight headache and a vague disquiet that she couldn't explain to herself. Then she smiled. She was coming home to Cay, and thinking of him warmed her wounded heart.

The image froze and broke into pieces that reassembled themselves into the mysterious colorful creature.

"So, it's true," Limea whispered. "My memories are not real. Everyone I cared about are just strangers. I am... a clone."

"It's true," the creature confirmed. "Do you wish you haven't seen this?"

"I... I'm not sure," Limea answered, puzzled. "I'm glad I know and don't have to wonder anymore. But it makes me feel

184

sad and betrayed. Nothing that matters to me had actually happened. I'm… not real."

"But you are real. Regardless of how you've been created, you are here, you think and feel, you connect to others and care. Isn't that what being real means?"

"I don't know what it means. Who am I? Everything I know, all the experiences that have shaped me are a lie."

"Does it matter if they feel real?"

"I guess it does. They feel real, but now I know they are not. I don't know who I am, but I know I'm not who I thought I was."

"Do you want to forget? See a different story instead?"

"How can I be sure what I want? My mental processes and way of thinking are stolen from another woman. They aren't mine. Nothing I have is mine."

"This experience is entirely yours."

"But I'm not myself. I'm someone else, and I don't know how to be me. I don't exist as a personality. I'm an illusion. Even the things I'm saying now aren't mine. That's what she would have said."

"Your thoughts and words wouldn't be who you are anyway, even if this whole life was yours. You can forget everything if you wish. All Limea's memories will die."

"But her neural pathways and character made of her experience and genes will still be there."

"Do you want to start a life over? Have a chance to form your own mind?"

"Is that possible?"

"There's nothing impossible. Your tribe will guide you."

"My... tribe?"

"Yes. They are your family. They saved you from the animal that attacked you and healed you. They have brought you to me. You don't know them, but you will soon."

"Where am I?"

"Look."

Limea opened her eyes and saw warm light tangled in majestic tree crowns high above her head. The trees moved dreamily, whispering their secrets. Blue sky peeped through the branches, glittering in the light. Limea was lying on her back, and people were standing over her. She still couldn't see them clearly, shadows were playing on their faces, making them change just like the creature she'd been talking to. But she saw kindness, and kinship, and alertness, and a sort of confidence she seemed to have never experienced in her life, radiating from their eyes as beams of light. She trusted them instantly for the way they looked at her and the way she knew they treated each other. She could see colorful bonds connecting them. She knew they'd die for one another. She knew they cared. She wanted to be one of them.

Limea closed her eyes again to see the creature separating into several beings each of which looked unique. Then it reassembled itself into one and looked at Limea through a single eye filled with intergalactic beauty.

"What do you say?" the creature asked.

"Are they my tribe?" Limea asked hopefully.

"They are," the creature confirmed smiling with 6 eyes rotating slowly around it's face.

"What should I do to stay with them?"

186

"You should want to."

"I do!"

"Then you can. The question is who you want to be."

"I want to be me, but I don't know what it means."

"So how about starting your life over?"

"I'd love to."

"You can't be born again, but you can feel like you did. Have a whole life that'll shape your new personality that you'll live in a dream. And when you wake up, there will be a new you."

"No," Limea said firmly. "No more illusions. I want everything to be real from this moment on."

"You can do that, but your personality will stay the same."

"I'll have to rewire myself on my own then. I want to remember what happened to me, but I don't want to... be emotionally connected to it. Is that possible?"

"There is nothing impossible. You can be freed from Limea's feelings."

"Can I also be free from her beliefs and personality traits? I know they are in my head, but can I be... impartial? Like if I saw them from the outside, as if I was looking at another person?"

"This can be achieved, though it won't be easy. We'll have to create a new blank personality inside of you, who'll be able to connect with Limea's personality and be in control of it. But it will be somewhat like a dissociative identity disorder. And the problem is that your blank personality won't start as a baby to learn gradually but will be thrown right into adult life. It will have to learn in practice."

"That's the way I like it."

"It's settled then. Are you ready to be reborn?"

"As much as I can be."

"Then you have to die first," the creature said with the cold of open space flowing from its eyes.

"Wait... I..." Limea began to say, but it was too late. She felt she was dying. Again. This time it was really happening. The strangest feeling in the world. She remembered Cay saying he would like to be conscious during his death because he wanted to experience it. He believed it would be interesting. A unique experience indeed, Limea thought as the coldness of the Universe claimed her. She was becoming the coldness from within. The nothingness. She knew those were her last moments stretched out into the void she was merging with. She didn't want it.

"Goodbye, Limea," the creature said tenderly kissing her on the forehead, causing an explosion of whiteness.

She wanted to protest. To ask for more time or a chance to change her decision, but she couldn't speak to the creature anymore. It dissolved in smoke. They say you see your entire life flash in front of your dying eyes. It wasn't exactly how Limea experienced it. It was as if her whole life was pressed into one moment and she felt everything she'd been feeling during her life simultaneously. As if her life was given to her as a pill or an impulse that gave her a flavor of what it was like to be her. There was a sensation of movement, as if she was wind. As if she was rushing through her life instead of the other way around. Somewhere in the background there was awareness that none of it was real, none of it was hers. And then there was nothing.

Something emerged from the darkness. A cloud of clearing smoke, serious faces of people holding hands and standing in a circle around her, the last rays of the setting sun beaming through the trees. The people were singing, and around them was a wider circle of people dancing naked. The outer circle consisted of drummers banging a violent rhythm.

There was chaos in her head. Part of her knew something about the world, knew the names and purposes of things and living beings surrounding her, knew how to interact with them, but this part was distant and small. It consisted of Limea's memories. Her main personality though was like that of a newborn. She couldn't make any sense of what she was seeing. She had to draw knowledge from the part belonging to Limea and got the story behind what was going on, but it felt alien and weird. Yet, it was mesmerizing and fascinating at the same time. Her newborn personality was drinking the experience with the thirst of a desert touched by rain. She absorbed it and made it part of herself. She let the water turn the desert into fertile soil and bear the first plantlets of her own unique nature.

It was the first real-life experience that belonged to her, and she was enchanted by its beauty, its grace, its wildness. She heard whispers around her, repeating the same words over and over. She needed time to connect to Limea's memories and draw the meaning from them.

"Get up," the voices whispered. "Get up."

She obeyed and noticed three more people who were sitting on the ground around her. She couldn't see them while she was lying on her back before. They were holding strange round vessels made of intertwined tree branches, bark, flowers and leaves. The people in the circle closest to her began to move in the opposite direction of the dancers.

"Dance," the people sitting on the ground whispered. "Dance!"

And she started dancing to the rhythmic tribal music they were making with the drums, their voices, their hands and feet, and the people sitting on the ground were swaying and murmuring mantras. She lost control of her movements and felt like it was the music dancing her, rather than her dancing to the music. It controlled her movements making them violent and free. It felt good. She threw her head back and burst into laughing.

One of the men sitting on the ground rose to his feet and threw something from his vessel at her. It was a sticky liquid that covered her body. It was all the colors at once, and they were changing as she was moving. She continued dancing despite the shock. She couldn't stop: the music wouldn't let her. Then another man rose to his feet and threw something from his vessel at her. It was a colorful powder that stuck to her body, forming patterns as she continued her dance. She felt excited and lightened. Then a woman rose to her feet and threw something from her vessel at her. Those were flower petals, leaves and herbs that stuck to her hair and face and all over her body. She felt weightless and unrestrained. At that moment, everyone stopped. Only the drums were still beating a quiet rhythm of nature falling asleep. She stopped, too. It wasn't her decision, the dance stopped itself. Her arms were still raised, but they bent

190

slightly towards the setting sun. She couldn't help it, and she didn't want to. It was right.

"A new plant was born," the woman who had thrown leaves and petals said in a deep, melodic voice. The rest of the tribe made a sound resembling a sigh of delight.

"She grew from the remains of a plant destroyed by the people of the outer world," and there came a sigh of regret. "But the generous soil, the water of life and the energy of the sun healed her. The smoke of wisdom took her to the Mother's spirit, and the Mother found her worthy and gave her a new life."

"Aaah," the tribe exhaled, stretching the sound into the cooling air of approaching night. They bowed their heads and shook their risen hands.

"There she is, reborn, clear like morning dew, glowing, ready to grow and blossom again."

The woman looked her straight in the eye and asked, "What's your name?"

The drums stopped, and there was utter silence. Even the forest seemed to put all the sounds of its life on hold. All the eyes were locked on her, waiting. She knew the person she used to be was called Limea, but it wasn't her name or her real identity. She was scared for a moment, as she didn't know what to say. But from behind the tense silence within her mind, right from the inner source of her life a name came, and she knew it was hers.

"Aisami," she said.

"Aisami," everyone repeated, and then they reached out for her and touched her, leaving prints of their palms on her colored body.

"Aisami," the woman said, "you are now a root, a fiber, a branch, a leaf, a flower and a fruit of our tree. Our tree grows in harmony and peace with the fierce nature that has chosen to accept us unlike the others. From now on, you are never alone. Welcome home."

CHAPTER 19

Cay was afraid that Vietra would leave without him, and he struggled with the desire to try to explain everything to her once again. Their last conversation was awkward, and he felt that everything he'd said that night was wrong. But he had to let go, give her space to make her own decisions. He didn't want to seem needy. Criminal life wasn't so bad, after all. He was well protected, as the powers of the Orchids were limitless when it came to manipulating data and public records. He didn't know how they achieved such a level of expertise yet, but he hoped he would find out. Cay felt that he was beginning to earn their trust. Working on his project, he was admitted to some parts of the building that had been previously closed for him and was introduced to some of their innovative technologies that were unlike anything he knew. They were already integrating the solar fabric with the outer parts of the building and producing batteries of his design. Cay was overseeing the process in a small factory they turned out to have on sight. He was watching the parts 3D printed and put together by technicians into compact and beautiful batteries, but he was lost in thought.

There was an option for him to stay and keep working with the Orchids. It was something. There were a lot of exciting technologies and projects he could work on. That would keep his mind busy to prevent him from thinking about Limea, at least for some of the time. There would probably be periods when he'd totally forget about her. And maybe after several years he'd learn how to be happy again. Or at least not miserable. Not so miserable. He could also distribute his system around the world for free, as he wouldn't have to worry about money.

The Orchids were interested in the "twins". They wanted to understand what had happened, so they were keeping Vietra longer, trying to get some information from her. She wasn't co-operating. And no one could find Limea, so that was another mystery. Cay was worried about her. He was also worried about how the whole situation would reflect on him. On the one hand, there was proof for the Orchids that he wasn't delusional and something strange was actually going on. On the other hand, they might get suspicious and terminate their relationship.

"Cay, are you busy?" Sern asked, his voice breaking the walls of Cay's thought, making him start. He had a small device in his ear that allowed him to connect with anyone within the building, but he kept forgetting about it, so it took him a moment to realize that Sern wasn't actually near.

"I'm in the factory on the industrial floor. I'm supposed to oversee battery production, but it's going smoothly, and they don't really need me here. Why?"

"One of the twin ladies wants to see you."

"Where is she? Tell her I'll be there in a moment. Don't let her leave!"

Cay made himself walk slower in order not to appear too hasty, even though he wanted to run. He entered one of the faceless rooms that he remembered so well from his first en-counters with the Orchids. Now, having access to a larger seg-ment of their facility, he knew that those rooms were made this way deliberately. They were meant to be dull and unmemorable,

194

betraying nothing about the place the guests were brought to or their hosts. The rest of the building, unavailable to outsiders, was strikingly different. Cay saw loud colors, weirdly shaped furniture, graffiti and digital art, as well as functional and tasteful minimalism, beautiful paintings and pastel tones. The Orchids had freedom to shape their space the way the say fit, and various styles of different sectors, offices, floors and labs represented the diversity of the people comprising the organization.

"I was right," Vietra said as soon as she saw Cay. "She's gone. I knew it, but I let myself have stupid hope," she shook her head bitterly.

"Maybe she returned home," Cay said, realizing she was talking about Limea. The idea felt strange. A woman who believed she was Limea but was actually her clone living in their apartment. Was she waiting for him? Could he return to her and play along? No, that was impossible. But he wouldn't be able to just kick her out if he wanted to come back home either. After all, there was nowhere else she could go. Another reason for him to stay with the Orchids.

"I don't think she'd go there. You didn't make her feel welcome," there was a note of reproach in Vietra's voice. "She knew you didn't want her there."

"Would you want her in your apartment?"

"If I had one, I would. But it's too late."

"How do you know? If she didn't go there, maybe she went to her family? Or friends? She knows and loves them, she could use their help."

"And what would she tell them exactly?" there was no doubt now that Vietra was blaming him for whatever had hap-

195

pened to Limea. "Hi, I'm a clone of your daughter made in a lab by a psycho?"

"She wouldn't have to tell them anything. She could just pretend... I mean she could live like nothing had happened. She didn't even believe she was a clone. She thought you were crazy."

"Maybe at first, but later she at least took it as a possibility. And what about the implant? She had to get rid of hers to get here and, as far as I know, she didn't get a new one. What would she do out there without an implant? Go straight to the fixers?"

Cay had to admit he had completely forgotten about the implant. He also suddenly realized how exhausted he was. The weight of all the sleepless nights, all the worries and risks, all the shocking revelations and heartbreak fell on his tired shoulders. He didn't want to explain anything anymore.

"I don't understand why you are attacking me. What could I do? Don't you think it's tough for me, too? I don't know how to behave, I'm lost just like the two of you. And I feel for her, I really do. I'd help her if I could."

"I think she killed herself," Vietra whispered. "I saw her look into that forest... people don't look at it this way. People are aware of its danger. But she was hypnotized by it. She admired it. It was like... home to her. I think she just went there and let the plants do their thing."

"Admiring the nature sounds like her," Cay said. "But for all I know, Limea would never kill herself. No matter what. She is strong."

Vietra looked at him with a puzzled expression.

196

"I hope you are right, but I don't think so. I feel she's dead. Anyway, there is nothing here for me, so I'm going to leave. I'm going to deal with the Master and find out what his idiotic plan was. You said you wanted to come along, so..."

"I do!" the offer came as a surprise, and Cay's answer was too impulsive. He took a deep breath a continued slower, "I do... but I don't want to do it hastily. As far as I understand from your story, he is very powerful and possesses technology much more advanced than I can imagine. We can't just storm in there. We need a good plan."

Vietra looked at him grimly, waiting for continuation. She didn't want to agree with him, but she couldn't argue, as she saw his point.

"As I said before, I believe people from here can help. If someone has the technology and capabilities to match his, it's them."

"Are you sure they'll do it?"

"I hope so," Cay said, putting an encouraging smile on his face. He actually had much less confidence in that outcome than he showed. He saw no reason for them to take the risk and waste their resources on a project that looked like a bad movie, but he had to try to convince them.

CHAPTER 20

Aisami loved tribal life from the very first moment. It was difficult and full of dangers, but the kinship of the tribe and the nature around made up for it.

The animal that attacked her on the day she jumped into the forest left scars on her neck and chest, but she came to love them, too. They reminded her of where she was and who she was. Reminded her of the change she'd gone through.

She gradually learned about the forest, the tribal rituals and the beliefs of her new family. Nature was more than a god to the tribe. She was their mother, their sister, their friend and teacher. They saw themselves as an integral part of her. They were her, and she was them. They knew they wouldn't exist without her and practiced the deepest respect and tenderness for her in their every act. They believed they had been chosen and protected by her because they were different from the people on the outside. That their mother selected them to carry on the fire of human life, as she was going to exterminate most of the people who had been torturing and wounding her along with all the rest of her children for thousands of years.

Her tribe never damaged anything. They could only kill an animal if it attacked them, and there was no other choice. They could only use a part of a plant or a fruit if it didn't hurt the plant. The nature seemed to actually take care of them because they were immune to all the killing instruments it used on the rest of humanity. They could also digest absolutely anything from bark to mere grass, so food was not an issue. Of course, they had to forage for more nutritious and better tasting plants and mushrooms, but the forest was abundant, so they were healthy and strong.

There were about a hundred people in the tribe, and they knew there were more of them in other parts of the world. The nature could protect them neither from animals, nor from viruses and bacteria that were her children as well, but it could provide some means of healing and materials for tools meant to keep them safe. The tribe had to be inventive to discover them and find the use for them.

Their philosophy, as well as their deep affection for the nature was absolutely alien to anyone coming from the outside world. The world where humans saw themselves as the rulers of the planet, standing proudly apart from the rest of the living beings. Where everything belonged to them and served their needs. Where the goal always justified the means. Where it didn't occur to most people to think beyond their own comfort and pleasure. Where every attempt to be just towards the nature and other animals was mocked and ridiculed. Where profits, or good looks, or an opportunity to keep one's habits were valued higher than the tormented lives and deaths of billions of living creatures, the destruction of the environment and the lives of other humans. Where cruelty was considered strength, and empathy was seen as weakness. Well, it had to change when the nature struck back, but people only went along with it because they had no other options.

For Aisami, however, the tribal way of living and thinking was the most natural one. It was the first thing she felt when she got to know the forest dwellers. The sincerity and kindness of it touched her heart and shaped who she was. She could access Limea's memories of the outside world, but for a blank personality she'd got from the Mother's spirit it looked so absurd and cruel that she couldn't believe anyone would actually find it normal. She thought with ferocity that people deserved the plague. She even found herself wishing them dead for what they did to the Mother and all their siblings.

She also had to live with constant awareness that she and her family could die any moment, but it made living more vivid and sharp for her, more spicy and acute. She felt with her whole being there was nothing but the now, no guarantee for the future, and it made her freer than she had ever been in her previous, stolen life. It also made her happier, as together with the tribe she was praising every moment of her life, accepting it as the most precious gift. They took nothing for granted and held on to nothing, the ability that the people of the outer world had long lost. Aisami loved it.

She lived in perpetual awe and admiration. She was filled with sounds and smells, touch and smiles. She observed, listened and absorbed the marvelous world around her. Being alive made her tremble. Her new personality was that of an infant, so it didn't know how to think and analyze, it didn't predict and had no memories of its own. It was endlessly curious instead, taking the world in. When she needed to know something, Aisami drew information from Limea's memories, and she could easily connect the two personalities to be able to communicate or perform certain activities, but most of the time she just contemplated. She knew how much Limea used to think, and it seemed to be a natural condition for the people on the

200

outside, but it weakened their ability to perceive the world and be alive. Even the most magnificent things were ignored because of thoughts, and no one seemed to live in the present. Instead, they relived the moments long gone or speculated about the future. They didn't notice gorgeous sunsets and didn't hear the whispers of the ocean. They were always in some imaginary places inside their heads. Never here, never now.

Aisami compared her life to what she'd known before and missed none of it. Well, except for hot showers, perhaps. But the tribe lived in lovely tree houses, and climbing was what every day started and ended with, which Aisami adored. Their life, in spite of being tough and dangerous, was a play. They took nothing seriously. They had no duties. They didn't control neither each other, nor themselves. They laughed a lot.

It didn't mean they were careless or didn't get the necessary things done. It was rather in their attitude to those things. Nothing was tedious or monotonous, nothing was perceived as an obligation or imposed on anyone. They did everything with joy and attention of having it done for the first and the last time in their lives. They celebrated the most trivial acts, which became music, dance, art created by the Nature itself, for they were the Nature.

Dancing was a great part of their life. Losing themselves in wild tribal music, letting it take over and guide them. Connecting to each other and the world through the experience. Graceful and free from worries, troubles or thoughts, there they were, a single organism, a united cosmic consciousness in the eternal, mysterious now. Moving, breathing and floating as one. Beyond any boundaries, beyond any control. When they were dancing, there was nothing but them and the immense Universe existing as one untamed entity. There was magic and truth in it, there was freedom and light in vast space filled with love.

**

One day not long after she'd joined the tribe, Toobu, the woman who had thrown flowers and leaves at the ceremony of her rebirth asked Aisami to walk with her. She was the tribe's shaman. She was also the oldest woman, around 60 years old, who still remained irresistibly attractive. Her long grey hair had flowers and herbs in them, making her smell temptingly good. Her eyes were hypnotizing, it was enough to look into them to get pulled in and not be able to gaze away until she did it first. Aisami admired her and was happy to have a talk.

They were walking in silence for a while along a narrow path, Toobu leading the way. Aisami heard someone following them and saw the two other shamans who were guiding her ceremony together with Toobu.

Bomong was around Toobu's age, which made him the oldest man in the tribe. He was tall and handsome, with bright blue eyes that seemed to pierce others through, immediately seeing their deepest and most intimate thoughts. He and Toobu were lovers. In the tribe everyone loved one another, and most of the people chose to have sex with almost everyone else, but the relationship between the two of them was different. Aisami couldn't explain to herself what it was, but she could sense it. It was something magical that caused awe and respect. Something way deeper than the pure love others knew. It was as if they had a secret together, as if they were bonded by something special and unknown. Maybe it was because they were shamans, Aisami thought, and because they were older than the rest of the tribe.

The third shaman, Noki, was a 19-year-old man, already a father of 8 lovely children. He was of medium height, and there was nothing particularly attractive about his body or appearance in general. But he had the most sincere and magnetic smile Aisami had ever seen. When he smiled, even the darkest day became brighter, and even the deepest sorrow was lightened. His whole face was shining, and his eyes were releasing almost visible beams of joy. It was impossible not to smile back. And when he smiled, he became the most attractive person in the whole world. People were straining towards him like plants would strain towards light. They felt good with him, and he was never alone, always ready to share his happiness with the others.

The shamans performed a very important role in the tribe. They healed bodies and minds, held ceremonies and were the people everyone went to with every possible trouble or question. Even though every plant was edible for the tribe, some of them could be used for other purposes, like treating diseases or changing perception. The shamans studied the plants to learn as much as possible about them and collected the ones that could be useful. They made powerful mixtures and experimented all the time. They also studied animals and diseases to be able to deal with them. They often went to dangerous parts of the forest to forage for herbs or discover new ones. It was a difficult and risky role, but they never complained and did their best for the tribe.

They soon came to a small wooden hut hidden in the bush. It looked old and rickety. Plants were growing all over it, and

Aisami had a feeling it could collapse any moment. But Toobu opened the door and entered, so Aisami followed her, just like the two other shamans. Plants grew through the floor and walls, looking like a magical garden inside the hut. It made Aisami laugh. She touched the plants and sat on the floor with the others, ignoring the old wooden chairs that would probably fall apart if they tried to use them. She could only see greenery from the windows, which pleased Aisami. She looked at the walls that had faded pictures of a pre-plague family on them. There was a large wooden table, and she imagined that family having dinner at it. The image was so vivid and alive that Aisami got scared she was seeing spirits.

"We need to talk about your past," Toobu said breaking the illusion, bringing her back into the now.

"I don't have a past," Aisami answered. "I've just began my life here, with you."

"That's true," Toobu nodded with natural grace of a wild animal. "But we know there is more to your story. We observed your meeting with the Mother. We know that you've learned the truth about yourself."

"You don't think I belong because I was created artificially?" Aisami asked with overwhelming dread. She didn't know how to deal with emotions yet, and whatever she felt seized control of her entire being, leaving no room for anything else.

"No, dear, of course not," Toobu said with a reassuring smile, and all the shamans touched Aisami, letting her know she was still part of the family.

She felt relived and then cheerful. It was such a joy to be one of them.

204

"The truth is, all of us are like you. Everyone in the tribe was created the same way, except for the children born here."

Bewilderment and shock filled Aisami. How could that be possible? She stared at the two other shamans helplessly, but they nodded to confirm it was true.

"But we are the only people who know about it," Toobu continued. "We are the only ones who chose to learn and re-member the truth. The rest of us didn't want that. They pre-ferred to forget and start a life over. Some of them didn't want to keep the stolen personality, just like you, so they chose to be-lieve they were born in the tribe. The Mother guided them through the process of rebirth with our help, and inside their heads they lived a life from the very beginning and formed new identities. When they woke up, they remembered nothing of their previous lives and were sure they'd been born in the tribe. Others decided to keep the personalities they got from the Mas-ter, but they chose to forget how they were created, so when they woke up, they remembered the calling from the forest and entering it, they remembered some of the encounter with the Mother, but they didn't remember what they'd discovered about their creation. Some didn't even want to know the truth, so they remained in the dark."

"The... Master?" the word resonated with Aisami and brought a shiver onto her skin. She was sure it was the man who tormented her after she was created. She connected it to what Limea had learned from Vietra. Cold claws of fear clasped her throat.

"Yes, that's him," Bomong nodded, and in his eyes Aisami saw a reflection of her feelings.

The members of the tribe were fearless in the face of danger, and they fought bravely with whatever came their way. This was different. Aisami gazed at Noki and Toobu to find the same feeling.

"We can talk more about him later if you want," Bomong said, and his eyes returned to their normal feral beauty.

"Right now, we want to talk about the tribe's choices," Toobu continued. "We believe we have no right to take their innocence from them. They have free will and a right to live with the choice they've made. If Mother allows it, who are we to stand in her way? That's why we've created the legend about being chosen and protected by her.

"The truth is, the Master must have messed something in our... manufacturing process," she looked Aisami straight in the eye with the cruelty of the word gleaming in her gaze. She would never make anything sound better than it was just for the sake of the listener. Aisami appreciated the honor of being dealt with this way.

"Maybe it's something in our DNA. Maybe something humans have is missing, or maybe something was added to make us stronger. It might have been done deliberately, or it could be just a slip. Anyway, that's why we are accepted by the nature. She probably doesn't recognize us as humans. I believe it's also the reason why we can eat anything and why we age so slowly."

"How slowly?" Aisami asked.

"How old do you think we are?" Toobu demanded.

"About sixty."

Toobu and Bomong glanced at each other and laughed. There it was again, the mysterious connection that sparkled between them and fascinated both Aisami and Noki.

"We're 178, child," the woman said suddenly seizing to laugh. "Bomong and I were among the first Master's experiments, and we were the first ones to break free."

"I am what I look," Noki answered Aisami's inquiring look, laughing and raising his palms. "I just got here a year ago."

"Aging goes normally in the beginning, and you only notice it slowing down later in life if it comes to that. Most of the people in our tribe don't live long enough to find out.

"Back to our subject: the people have made their choices, so we want you to keep the information about your creation to yourself and stick to the common legend. Do you agree to do that?" Toobu inquired.

"Yes," Aisami said.

"Good. There is one more thing. As you know more than the rest of the tribe, we want to offer you to become a shaman. You don't have to if you don't want to, of course, that's up to you."

"Wow!" Aisami exclaimed with excitement. "Of course I do!"

The three shamans smiled to her and each other, then Bomong spoke, "It's not all that fun. That's a lot of responsibility and more danger than for the rest of the tribe. Shamans die pretty often. No one has lasted so long as Toobu and I, and we can be gone any moment. This is one of the reasons we need more people who we can share our knowledge and responsibility with. And we always prefer it to be the people who know the entire truth. They don't come so often."

"I still want it," Aisami said.

"Good. We'll teach you what we know. We also encourage you to seek knowledge yourself, and then, maybe, you'll be able to teach us something, too. We'll start tomorrow. Today is your last day to enjoy being a regular member of the tribe."

"Can I ask you something about the Master? Why do you call him that? What do you know about him?" Aisami inquired.

"Well," Toobu sighed, "it's what he called himself and what he told us to call him. He had a different approach in the beginning. We were manufactured from scratch, not copied from other humans. When we woke up, there were fifteen of us in the room. We were fully grown, about 20 years old. We were confused and didn't understand where we were. He was in the room with us, and he talked to us for a long time. He told us he was our maker and showed the recording of the manufacturing process to us. We didn't know anything about the world. Language and some generic thinking processes were imprinted on our brain, but there wasn't much knowledge. He was going to teach us everything on his own. Many of us thought he was god. Maybe that was his goal.

"He told us we had a purpose, that the meaning of our lives was to fulfill that purpose. He didn't tell us what it was. He said we would find out when we were ready. But we never got to that point. There were a lot of troubles with us. Not everyone learned the proper way. He tried to imprint ready-made knowledge from scientific books on our brain. It damaged some of us because that's not how brain works. Some lost their ability to talk, and walk, and take care of themselves. The Master destroyed them without mercy. There were only 9 of us left. He then tried to teach us in a sleep state: we were dreaming, but it seemed to us that we were living a life, learning the skills that he wanted us to have. Those were scientific and technical knowledge different for every one of us, as well as martial arts and general physical education for everyone.

"We all wanted to please him, but not everyone could. Learning was too difficult or too boring for some of us. We were punished for not doing well enough, but that didn't help much. More people began to show disturbing symptoms. They collapsed, had seizures, their internal organs failed, they lost control of their limbs... Some got paralyzed, some showed symptoms of mental illness. Two more people died. One girl tried to kill herself, but she couldn't do it because we were in a dream. She kept crying all the time. She was pulling her hair out and asking to let her go. We all tried to help and sooth her, but it didn't work. The Master got rid of her. He got angrier and angrier with us for disappointing him. We knew we could die any moment or be killed if we didn't do what he wanted properly. It was also a harsh truth to discover that our "god" didn't actually care about us. He had no compassion for us, we were just tools to fulfill his mysterious purpose.

"Those who had troubles with their bodies and minds tried to hide it from him to protect themselves, but he always knew. At a certain point, when there were only 4 of us left, we decided it was time to get out of there. We knew we were sleeping, he never hid it from us. We knew we were plugged to the machines that monitored our state and controlled our brain, feeding us with dreams that were supposed to teach us faster. I think you call it a simulation now? I've lived in the forest for too long, but I've seen the memories of the new members of the tribe. Back then the technology didn't exist in the outside world, and I don't know where the Master got it from.

"Anyway, we had to wake up somehow, so we first tried to convince him we knew enough and wanted to go back to real life to practice our skills. He said we still had a lot to learn, and we didn't have time to do it at a normal pace. We were afraid that if we waited long enough, he'd discover some flaws in us, and we'd be killed just like the others. He was going to replace us soon anyway, as he was making arrangements to produce the next batch. He thought we were his failure. We were going to die without ever seeing the real world.

"We had some concept of it from the books and the knowledge he'd imprinted, but it was flat and colorless. The world isn't something you can know in theory, you have to experience it. And we wanted it so badly. We craved to taste it and feel it at least for a moment before we died. So, we started experimenting with our states of mind to find out whether there was something that would make the machines wake us up.

"We all loved each other. We'd been together for so long, and we were the only people we knew," at this point Toobu stopped talking and looked at Bomong. There was such deep sadness in her eyes, such grief that Aisami had never seen there before. And there was also some absence, the type of emptiness that couldn't be filled. The same emotions flowed from Bomong's eyes, and they shared that moment of pain as if there were just the two of them. Then they closed their eyes for an instant, and when they opened them again, there was their usual vibrant and calm expression with no sign of grief.

"We learned how to be," Toobu continued, "together. It wasn't easy when our only teacher was apparently a psychopath, and our knowledge about the world so skewed. We were a family for each other, we've been through our best and our worst, the most confusing, delightful, agonizing and dull moments together. We discovered loss, love, desire, friendship and practiced all of it on each other. We discovered disappointment, fear and the dark abyss of madness and shared them to the last drop. There was no one else in the whole world but us.

"We couldn't break out. Then one of us, Ritvana, began to lose it. She had dreadful hallucinations. She was screaming for hours, and we couldn't stop it. We asked the Master to let her be, we promised to take care of her, we swore we would make her better, we begged, and we lied, and we tried to convince him that his plan was impossible to implement without her. He said she was damaged. The machines that were monitoring her brain predicted further decline of her mental abilities. We asked him to let her live with us. Even if she was of no use to him, it didn't mean he had to kill her. We promised it wouldn't impede our learning, we would take our turns tending to her, and we'd study twice as hard for her chance to live. The Master was surprised. It seemed that he truly couldn't comprehend the meaning of love. He didn't know what it was. He tried to make a logical explanation for it, but he couldn't find it. And I think it annoyed him. The fact that in some respect we were superior to him. That we could feel and bond while he was unable to do so.

"He killed her. But he didn't do it the usual way, when a person just disappeared from our virtual dream space. No, we had to be punished for questioning his judgment, so he made us see her die. And he made her experience it. She knew she was dying, and she was awfully scared, and we could do nothing about it. We saw the torment and fear in her eyes, her plea for help, but we couldn't move because the Master had control over us. We wanted to run to her and hug her, to share that last moment with her, but we were just standing there and watching her die alone, probably thinking we'd abandoned her. Gave up on her," Toobu suddenly broke into tears, and Bomong held her in his arms, hiding his face in her hair. There was silence for a while.

Now the roots of their connection became clear to Aisami. They'd been through too much together. They'd been through something no one else had. She looked at Noki. It seemed he was hearing the story for the first time as well. It occurred to her that it was probably the first time they were telling it to anyone.

"We were furious," Bomong continued. "We were also young and stupid. We couldn't cope with it, so we decided we'd better die than follow his rules. We refused to learn. We refused to do anything he wanted us to. We used our skills to break and destroy everything around us. We knew it was virtual, so there was no real damage, but we had to let our anger out somehow. We also knew he had some problems with creating our successors, some machinery apparently broke down, so he couldn't replace us yet. And we achieved what we wanted. The Master got mad and for some reason, instead of killing us in our sleep, he woke us up. I don't know why, and I don't think he had a rational reason for it. It must have frustrated him that he couldn't control us anymore."

"I don't think he actually understood what was going on with us," Toobu said. "Human emotions seemed to be alien to him. He didn't understand his own feelings either and got awfully confused by them. It looked like he knew about us the same way we knew about the world."

"Who is he?" Aisami exhaled.

"I don't know. But there was nothing human about him, except for his appearance. I think he learned more about control and power from his mistakes later. His other experiments were different from us. Anyway, whatever his reason was to wake us up, it was his biggest mistake, and I don't think he ever made it again."

"We were possessed by our anger and hatred. I think it was the only reason why we succeeded," Bomong continued. "When he woke us up, we acted so quickly and savagely that the machines didn't have time to react. I'm surprised they didn't predict it. The Master was with us in the room. All three of us, we didn't have to say anything to each other. We didn't even have to look at each other, we just jumped at him and started beating him. He didn't expect it. We kicked him down and beat him fiercely. I don't know if that's true, but I believe that he was somehow controlling the Nest, the doors and windows, because they began to open and close randomly. He must have been panicking. It was our chance. We ran for the door and then another one. And somehow, we were out! We kept running for half an hour at least, blinded by our emotions. When we finally stopped, there were just the two of us. Doro, the third survivor, must have stayed and continued beating the Master."

"I think we managed to escape thanks to him," Toobu said. "If we all ran, the Master would have regained control of the Nest faster, the doors would be closed, and we would be killed. I don't know if Doro did it on purpose, or if he just couldn't stop hitting the bastard, but he saved our lives. We've never heard from him again, and the Master is still out there. The simulation we lived in partially reflected the world as it was and taught us some basic things about it. Of course, it wasn't enough, so we had to learn a lot on our own, and we made many stupid mistakes. But it allowed us to survive.

"We found our place and tried to forget about the Master. But we never felt safe. It seemed like he was waiting for an opportunity to get to us, and the more digital the world became, the more difficult it was to stay unnoticed and leave no traces. Maybe it was just paranoia, but we changed our identities and moved around the globe quite often. Until we decided the only way for us was to get out of the civilized world. We started living in the forest long before the plague and joined an indigenous tribe. It was fun," Toobu smiled and Bomong nodded in agreement with naughty light shining from the corner of his eye.

"We learned a lot. Rituals, plant medicine, trusting other people," he continued. "When Toobu started having hallucinations, and I thought I was going to lose her, the shaman healed her. But then the plague hit and killed them all. We were the only ones who remained, and at first, we had no idea why. When we started foraging for new kinds of plants, there was another surprise: we could eat anything.

214

"We lived on our own for quite some time, but then others started coming. We modified the rituals and the belief system of our dead tribe to serve us in the new world. We became their shamans and leaders. And when we took them to the Mother, we learned they were like us, created by the Master. But not from scratch anymore. They were copies of living people now, just like you. None of the genuine humans has ever survived in the wild, none that we know of. When we connect to the Mother, we see there are more of us around the world. And all of us are attracted to the nature, we are drawn to it by irresistible force, we are thirsty for it, we see it in our dreams and feel it in our veins until we give up and come to it and discover it doesn't kill us."

"Why?" Aisami asked.

"We don't know," Toobu smiled sharing a look with Bomong. "Why is the worst question you can ask if you really want to know the world. Why requires logical reasoning that prevents you from feeling and understanding the reality."

"I don't get it."

"Words are bulky. There are only a number of things that can be described properly in words, but in many cases, they complicate everything and lead you away from the true nature of things. You can't describe the whole Universe in words, even with the help of the most advanced science. And even if you could, it would be too long and too sophisticated for anyone to have time and ability to understand. But you can feel the Universe, listen to it and taste it, interact and play with it. This is how you get to know it."

CHAPTER 21

It was the third conversation among the three of them in the last three days. Cay appreciated the equilibrium, but he was drained, as helping two stubborn women see each other's point was hard work. They were making progress though. Olonda seemed to believe that raiding the Nest could be beneficial for the Orchids. Vietra seemed to finally accept that the Orchids had useful means to offer.

Naturally, Olonda didn't believe Vietra's story at first, but Cay convinced her to investigate, and they discovered that the Nest actually existed. A weird domed building in an abandoned part of the city that gave him the chills. They also looked into Limea's family history and found out there had never been a twin. That made Olonda curious about the technology the Master possessed, but she still didn't trust Vietra and wanted to subject her to some psychological tests to assess her sanity. Vietra was very unenthusiastic about that.

"Look," Olonda was saying. "At this point the most plausible scenario is that your mother had twins, but someone has falsified the medical records. Probably the Master himself. He kidnapped you and other kids and trained you for this strange program of his. It surely had impact on your... mental health. I understand that and sympathize with you. I'm very interested in the facility itself and in some of the technologies you've described. I also believe that taking him down is the right thing to do. But I don't believe in the cloning story. We are on top of every cutting-edge technology out there, and this just doesn't exist."

216

"I don't care what you believe," Vietra crossed her arms and looked away. "If you want to help, let's do it. If you don't, I don't really need you. It was Cay's idea to bring you in, it doesn't matter to me."

"You have to understand me, Vietra. My priority is for this organization to thrive and for its members to be safe. I won't risk that without a significant gain that would outweigh the possible negative consequences. Studying the technology the Master possesses is something that would justify the risk. What we can offer in exchange is our expertise and everything you might need to get safely in and out of the Nest, which will increase your chances of survival and getting what you want. But I'm not going to take the risk if I'm not sure that you are sane, and that the things you've described exist in reality. You also claim your memory has been overwritten. It's impossible without a brain implant. So, either that's another delusion or you've got an implant you aren't aware of. We need to be able to trust you because in case we decide to cooperate, you'll work closely with our specialists and will see more than we usually show to our guests. Testing you is the only way to meet all these conditions."

Vietra was still looking away, clearly annoyed. She didn't need their help. They didn't realize what she was capable of. She regretted bringing Cay in on this instead of leaving quietly. However, she could also see the merit of not going alone. If the other Nestlings were awake by the time she arrived, she wouldn't be able to deal with them on her own. And if the Orchids were really capable of what Cay was telling her, they might prove to be useful.

"Vietra," Cay said softly. "It's a way for you to find out what the Master has really done, and what impact he's had on you. The better we understand what's going on, the better we'll be able to prepare."

Vietra looked at him angrily and turned to Olonda. She seemed to be burning the woman with her gaze, but the Orchid remained unmoved.

"Okay," she said. "I'll get tested. But I have a condition. If we go together, I want the Master and the Nest destroyed. I'll need some time alone with him, but after I'm done, it should all be razed to the ground. We need weapons, and I mean very destructive type. We only get one shot at this, and if we don't destroy him on the first attempt, we'll never get a second chance. Our only advantage is the element of surprise."

"All right, we can guarantee you some time with the Master. We can also destroy the Nest, but only after studying the technology. If you get tested, and we have proof that you are trustworthy," Olonda said firmly.

Vietra nodded. It didn't mean she'd have to abide by the rules when the time came. She didn't care about the Orchids' interest in the technology, but she was satisfied that she'd get the weapons. It would be difficult to do on her own and would take more time. However, she was dreading the upcoming tests. There was something she really disliked about the idea, even though she didn't understand what exactly it was. They all shook hands, and Vietra retreated to the dull grey room she'd been assigned temporarily.

The tests were scheduled for 5pm that day, and she was sitting at the edge of an old desk, tense and ready to run away any moment, her arms crossed and her brow furrowed. She was battling with herself, on the verge of making a different decision every second. *Stay. Leave. Do it on my own. Use the help I can get. Be free. Fuck it!*

However, when the time came, Vietra was still there. A short, plump woman with attentive dark eyes and sunburned skin came to escort her, explaining that she would have to be blindfolded. Vietra almost kicked her. There was a barely perceptible twitch of her muscles that could have ended in her knocking the woman down and running, but Vietra stopped herself with a deep breath.

Even blindfolded, she could orient herself pretty well and would have no trouble finding her way there again, but the Orchids didn't need to know that. She was led into a spacious white room with shelves and cupboards full of medical equipment, most of which was unidentifiable to her. Everything looked new and shiny, the room was immaculately clean, and the light was too bright for her taste. A pleasant fat man wearing a white coat was waiting for her there. He was quite tall, had kind blue eyes, curly white hair and a belly that for some reason made Vietra want to put her head on it and fall asleep. He smiled broadly.

"Vietra, good to see you. Welcome to my kingdom!" he laughed spreading his arms, clearly pleased with his joke, and was a bit discouraged by her lack of response.

"I am doctor Jommaly, but you can call me Jom. Do you need anything to be more comfortable?"

"To get this over with," Vietra replied.

Jom laughed and shook his head.

"Yeah, okay. Tell me if you change your mind. You've got water here, and some snacks over there, if you need a toilet break or something, just let me know. We'll start with a brain scan. It is mainly to make sure you haven't got an implant, but we'll also see if everything is physically all right with your brain. Later we'll proceed to psychological evaluation."

Vietra sighed as she allowed Jom to put a helmet on her head instead of kicking him in the nuts. A slight smile touched her lips at the thought. The helmet performed a scan within a couple of minutes. It was a straightforward and easy part, unlike the rest of the procedures, which took all of Vietra's willpower to follow without breaking anything. Jom had her sit in front of a machine that shone light in her eyes, showed her strange pictures while measuring her physical reactions, asked her to track movement of a holographic dot and had her listen to different sounds while measuring her brainwaves. All that seemed meaningless to Vietra and made her really tired.

When she thought she couldn't take any more of this nonsense, Jom smiled encouragingly.

"Okay, good job, Vietra. Now, there is only one last part left. I'll just ask you some questions," he said.

Vietra braced herself.

"Do you ever hear voices?" Jom began.

"What?"

"For example, when you are alone in a room and aren't using any devices to talk remotely, does anyone speak to you?"

"Are you kidding me?" Vietra was staring at him angrily, and Jom shuffled uncomfortably.

"It's standard procedure, Vietra, it has nothing to do with my opinion about you, I just have to ask you this," he smiled a bit nervously. "Answer sincerely please, there is no shame in it either way."

"No, I don't hear voices," Vietra rolled her eyes and crossed her arms.

"Do you ever feel that other people can hear your thoughts?"

"No."

"Do you ever feel like they are talking about you in the news holos or Internet programs?"

"No."

"Good," Jom brightened, intensifying Vietra's distaste for him. "Now we'll talk about your memories a bit. What do you remember about your parents?"

"Nothing, I've already told that lady. What I remember is living in the Nest since I was a little girl with other kids and the Master."

"So... the Master was the only parental figure in your life?"

"I guess so."

"What was he like?"

"An asshole."

"Can you tell me more?"

"We were like his soldiers. We had to obey him unquestioningly, and we were punished if we didn't. It was usually the sensory deprivation room, but it could be going without food or sleep for a couple of days, running for an entire day or doing some exercises until we fell and couldn't move. All he cared about was preparing us to fulfill our purpose, but he never told us what it was."

Jom made some notes with a concerned expression. It made Vietra want to punch him in the face.

"Did you have any friends in the Nest?"

"No, we were not allowed to be weak, and that included expressing emotions and caring about anything or anyone. We weren't really close, we didn't talk much, apart from sharing relevant information, and we didn't have time for all that. We were basically training from dusk till dawn... I guess I had one friend though, despite everything. He was kind to me, and he was the one who got me out of there. His name is Tyss, and I hope I can get him out, too."

"What about the rest of them?"

"I don't give a shit what happens to them."

Jom made some notes again, but Vietra was focusing on the warm feeling in her chest that she got thinking about reuniting with Tyss. She hadn't realized that she cared about him, and now she was anticipating their meeting.

"Were you involved in any romantic relationships?"

"Dude, I just told you. No friends and nothing romantic either. There were some who tried, but they were put in their place fast. The Master was really against us bonding with each other. He said it was no good for the mission."

"O-kay, and what about sex?"

"We had it sometimes, when we weren't too tired and when we thought we could get away with it."

"What was your first sexual experience like?"

"I was about seventeen, and there was this girl whom I'd been working on some martial arts stuff with. We were throwing each other around and sitting on top of each other, and I guess that got us excited, so after the practice we went to the shower and did it right there."

"Did you have sex with her again after?"

"Yeah, from time to time."

"How did you feel about her?"

"I don't know, like the rest of them," Vietra shrugged.

"You didn't care about her?"

"Not really. It was purely physical, I didn't even like her as a person, in fact, as I'm thinking about her now, she was quite annoying. We just used sex to get rid of tension or feel better for a little while."

"Did you have any other partners?"

"Yes, three more women and five men."

"Did you feel anything more for any of them?"

"No," Vietra shrugged again. "We all knew we couldn't get attached to each other, we did it with this thought. I don't know, maybe we were looking for some sort of connection, but because we couldn't really have it, we were all aware it was just a temporary substitute."

Saying it aloud made Vietra sad for some reason. She thought about her conversation with Limea, and how she spoke about Cay. She used to have a deep connection with him, but that was in another life that was inaccessible to her.

"Anyway, why does any of this matter?" she said to distract herself from these thoughts. "It all happened in a sim anyway, so none of it was real."

"Have you ever loved anyone?" Jam asked, looking her in the eye as if he hadn't heard her.

That caught Vietra off guard. She didn't understand what had happened, it was like an avalanche of frighteningly strong feelings that swept through her entire body and made her burst into tears. She never cried, it was the biggest disgrace for the Nestlings, the most shameful show of emotions. She didn't allow herself that weakness even when she was alone, and suddenly she did it in front of another human. Vietra was embarrassed, and the fact that Jom was looking at her sympathetically as if it was okay only made it worse. The questioning stopped there, and Vietra was escorted back to the grey room to wait for the results.

CHAPTER 22

Cay still couldn't believe what was happening. Everything was changing and buzzing around him, events kept developing unpredictable curves, and he was struggling to keep up. After Vietra's tests, Olonda invited him to talk in her office. He was taken there without a blindfold for the first time. Even though there were a lot of doors on the way that his implant wouldn't open, he realized it was a sign of trust.

Olonda's office was spacious and stylish, with walls in soft blue and violet hues, large windows, comfortable cream armchairs, a striped rug matching the colors of the walls, a large bookcase and cozy lamps in the corners. She was standing in the middle if it with a helmet on her head and raised her hand for Cay to wait. She was talking to someone, but Cay couldn't hear a word. He wanted to inspect the books, as he believed that what someone read always provided a glimpse into their personality. Besides, not so many people kept bulky printed books these days, and he was wondering whether there were any old editions that didn't exist in the digital world. He only managed to take a couple of steps to the bookcase when Olonda took her helmet off and gestured for him to seat down. He did it, casting a slightly regretful look at the bookcase. Maybe he'd have a chance to go through it in the future. The armchair was comfortable. Olonda took a seat as well.

"It's time for us to talk," she said.

"What's up?"

"You've proven to be trustworthy. We want you to keep working with us. And I want to reveal something to you. We use brain implants of our own design. They are more advanced than the ones people used to have in the past, so they are way safer and faster, but their properties are similar. They allow mind to mind and mind to computer communication as well as managing your memories and knowledge. I'd like to offer one to you. The installation is simple and safe. If you accept it, you'll get access to our entire facility and data. You can still leave us after getting it, but we'll delete the memories about us and take the implant out. I don't expect the answer immediately, you can think about it."

Cay was stunned. He realized that he was clutching the armrests and let go with an exhalation, leaning back.

"That's... unexpected. Do you have an implant too?"

"We all have them. They allow us to be much more effective and solve problems others can't."

"Right. Okay. I'll think about it. Can I ask you something unrelated? How is Vietra? What did her test show?"

"Well, she's not insane, though she clearly has some issues, but it seems unlikely that she can be hallucinating or experiencing intense delusions, so we don't really know what to think. We just have to investigate the Nest and see for ourselves. Her brain is in a good shape, so we are going to offer her an implant as well. We think it will allow her better control of herself to tackle the mental issues that might intensify before and during our raid on the Nest. We'll also be able to manage her memories in case we want her to forget about us."

"Oh. That's good to know."

Cay was curious about the implant and a bit tempted, but he remembered his friend Martil and all the other horrible stories. He would probably say no, but the fact that Vietra might get one complicated the issue. If he declined and she accepted, there would be a huge gap between them that he would never be able to bridge.

He was lying in his bed that night, staring at the ceiling, unable to stop the constant onslaught of thoughts. He couldn't find Vietra to talk to her about the implant, and he was thinking about her when suddenly someone slipped into his room. He raised on his elbow and clicked his fingers to switch on the soft, dim light that would be tolerable for the eyes used to darkness. He was surprised to see Vietra.

"What are you doing here?" he asked, squinting a bit.

Vietra was standing there motionless, looking at him. She was still wearing her plain black clothes that contrasted with the whiteness of her skin. She looked good, as if the simplicity of her outfit underscored her beauty. Without a word she got undressed and took a step closer. Her skin was shining softly, embracing some of the redness of the walls, and her curls seemed darker on her shoulders. Cay's heart accelerated. It seemed to have been ages since he'd seen her like that. She put her hand on his shoulder, and as he touched her hand, she suddenly broke into tears.

"What's wrong?" Cay whispered, sitting up, but Vietra kept sobbing without saying anything.

He got up and wrapped his blanket around her, holding her tight.

"It's okay," he said.

He kept embracing her until she stopped sobbing and lay down on his bed, hugging her knees and pressing them to her chest. She was shivering, and Cay felt lost. He tucked her in and sat on the floor near the bed, caressing her head until she fell asleep. He dozed off but woke when Vietra got up a couple of hours later, put her clothes on and left without saying a word. He watched the door close behind her and got into his bed, still holding her warmth. He had no idea what any of that meant, but he was too tired to think and too comfortable after sitting on the hard floor. He fell asleep and dreamt about his previous life with Limea.

***

It was a tough time for Vietra. She didn't understand what was going on with her, and why she was so overwhelmed, but she couldn't shake off the feeling of helplessness after the tests. It seemed to her that she was losing control, that all her composure was slipping through her fingers, and she could break down any time. In a moment of extreme weakness when she needed someone's support, she came to Cay. She didn't know what she was going to do. She found him in bed and thought that he might be asleep, but he turned the light on immediately. He looked handsome with his unkempt hair and an inquisitive look in his slightly narrowed grey eyes. He wasn't wearing a T-shirt and she wondered briefly if he was completely naked under the blanket. His body looked good, and Vietra felt excited at the thought. For a minute she thought she wanted to have sex with him and took her clothes off on an impulse, but she realized it was rather a desperate search for connection, an attempt to get distracted from herself. It wasn't how Vietra wanted to build her relationship with Cay, and she felt so pathetic that she burst into tears. Again! The shame of it intensified the feeling of helplessness and misery. Cay got out of bed and wrapped her in his blanket, revealing that he was wearing blue boxers after all. Even in the midst of her mental breakdown, Vietra managed to feel slightly disappointed with the lack of nudity. She also noted his athletic build. Cay looked fit, and she thought he probably worked out casually, maybe jogged or rode a bike as well. All of that remained in the background, as Vietra never stopped being perceptive, even when she was falling apart. She let Cay console her, and for a little while she felt so safe that she even fell asleep. She didn't remember ever feeling this way with another human being, and it scared her. It was a mistake, and when she woke up, she was so ashamed of her behavior that she left still without saying anything.

She realized she needed an implant if she wanted to keep it together. Nothing seemed more frightening than losing control to Vietra, so she went to look for a solution immediately after leaving Cay's apartment. There were always engineers working at night, and Vietra found them in the kitchen, sipping that disgusting coffee substitute of theirs. They didn't mind helping her out and took her to their lab that was a colorful, cluttered space, covered with graffiti and filled with unmatching furniture, gadgets she couldn't identify, lamps of all colors, sizes and shapes and empty mugs that had probably been there for days. They didn't blindfold her, explaining that before leaving she would have all the memories related to the Orchids deleted with the help of the implant. They were all pumped and overly excited because of the drink.

"All right, all right, all right!" one of them said, rubbing his hands and swiping some cables off a chair, waving for Vietra to take a seat. He was a short white man in his mid-twenties, of an average build, with brown eyes and long dark hair gathered in a bun. "The procedure is super easy, but a bit unpleasant. We won't have to drill your skull though," he added with a laugh.

Vietra didn't smile. She sat down, trying to compose herself, trying not to think about what had happened with Cay earlier, trying to appear calm.

"You'll handle it?" another engineer asked. She was an extremely beautiful woman in her late thirties, with dark skin, short curly hair and red lips, wearing a tight top and jeans that underscored her slim yet voluptuous figure. Vietra would be attracted to her if she didn't feel so empty.

"Sure!" the guy answered enthusiastically. "Are we hanging later?"

"I have to finish this, but I should be done in a couple of hours," the woman smiled and jerked a helmet on, diving into work.

"I'll be working until morning," the third engineer, a tired looking woman in her fifties, with greasy hair collected in a messy ponytail, dark circles under her glistering eyes and olive skin sighed.

"Next time then!"

"Next time," she nodded enthusiastically several times and picked up an instrument Vietra didn't know.

The guy turned to her.

"I'm Sib,", he introduced himself with a slight bow and a wide smile.

230

"Vietra."

"Where was it?" he mumbled, going through various things on a cluttered desk. "Ah, there it is!"

He was holding a small black box of about 2 centimeters on each side.

"Let me just configure it for you real quick," Sib said and kept standing there with the box between his fingers, his eyes glazed over. Vietra realized he was probably using his own brain implant to do the job.

"Okay, now," Sib said, squatting near Vietra and holding the box up. "I'll open it and put it close to your ear. The implant is something like an ant in size and shape. It will jump into your ear and find a way to your brain. The sensation is... you can imagine," he chuckled. "But it's completely safe, and it will be over in ten minutes. You just have to endure it. Ready?"

Vietra didn't like it. She wanted to say no, but she saw in his eyes and body language that he was sincere, that she could trust him. She needed this.

"Yes," she said.

"Here we go then," Sib grinned and put the box near her left ear.

Vietra heard a click and a felt a tickling sensation in her ear. Something was crawling in, and her impulse was to jump up and shake her head to get it out, but she remained motionless. It was as if an insect got trapped in there and was burrowing in. She took a deep breath, calming herself and relaxing her neck muscles. It was rustling, tingling, moving, but just as Sib said, it was over in ten minutes.

"Good, it's in. I'm seeing its position through my implant, it's in the right place, attached correctly. Now give it about an hour to adjust and establish connections, and you will start feeling the first changes. It's very intuitive, and you'll know how to use it, but if you have any questions, look me up," Sib smiled.

Sure enough, within an hour the world started opening up in front of Vietra, laying the connections out, becoming more logical and structured. She soon discovered that she could interface with all the computers in the facility by just imagining what she wanted done. In the next couple of hours, she could also see her own mental processes and analyze them in a way she'd never been able before. The powers of the implant were amplified by her training and skills. Everything started falling into place. She could see how her psyche was significantly damaged by the life imposed on her by the Master, how the subconscious currents of her previous personality were still flowing through her, even though she didn't remember their origins. She saw that she could take steps to heal the mental wounds and work on her trauma. She was tempted to erase at least some of the sickest things from her memory, but she understood it wouldn't undo the damage. It was better to know where it came from to be able to deal with it.

***

When Cay woke up next morning, he found out from a grumpy, middle-aged engineer, who looked like she could use some sleep, that Vietra had an implant installed at night. He felt even more confused than before. What did last night mean? He knew that he had to get an implant if he wanted to keep up with Vietra, but he was scared. He asked the engineer to describe the safety protocols they had in place in detail.

"Dude," the engineer said in a hoarse voice. "I've been up all night, and I can't wait to go to bed. I can send you the specs if you have the training to understand them. Or you can just believe me: our protocols are top-notch. They are created by people with implants against people without implants, who have no idea that we have them anyway. You'll be fine."

That didn't reassure Cay at all, but after struggling for an entire afternoon with the specs and talking to a couple more engineers, he had an implant installed with a heavy heart.

CHAPTER 23

Vietra looked calm on the outside while fighting her own shadows on the inside. She felt she was getting stronger, but she knew she needed more time to improve. She also realized with sudden clarity that she had feelings for Cay. She wondered how she could have ignored all the signs and signals her mind had been sending her all along. The dreams, the visions, the sparkles of attraction, the unreasonable trust. She'd been angry with herself for feeling that before because she didn't understand what was going on, and deep inside she believed she had no right to love him. She thought this right belonged to Limea alone. Now Vietra could finally accept it as it was, but she still felt the need to become a better, a more "normal" person before she could burden Cay with her feelings. She wanted to give him someone he could admire and respect, someone more like the woman he used to know. She was worried that if she just opened up to him, he'd get disappointed and stop loving her.

Working on her past was painful and exasperating at times, while the positive change came way too slowly. Sometimes Vietra felt frustrated and exhausted. She needed support, but connecting with people and trusting them didn't come naturally to her. The only person she was ready to really bond with was Limea, but she was gone. Vietra realized how bizarre that was, but it didn't alleviate the pain of loss in the slightest.

As the Orchids were supposed to help her deal with the Master, and preparations were taking time, she couldn't take the risk of them being busted. Vietra knew who the undercover agent was. The police managed to work their way through admission procedures and send a talented person who gained trust of the Orchids, offering them her engineering skills.

The agent's name was Tranilla. She was a petite woman with black hair in a neat bob cut, deep, dark eyes with an epicanthic fold and healthy-looking fair skin. She always wore oversized, brightly colored clothes that made her look like a child from a distance. It was hard to tell her age, she could be in her mid-twenties as well as in her thirties or even forties. Vietra felt a sort of respect for her: she managed to get to the Orchids and maintain her cover for several months, something no one had ever achieved before.

The good news was that the police didn't know where the facility was yet, as Tranilla couldn't contact them directly after receiving a confirmation from the Orchids. She had to get rid of her implant, and after that they only sent her one encoded, handwritten message through a carefully envisioned, complicated channel that was supposed to keep them anonymous. The message that said to find a way in for Vietra. It was delivered to a secret location outside of the Orchids' facility. Tranilla hadn't yet shared any sensitive details with the police. It was too soon and too dangerous. She had to gather enough information and evidence to put them into prison before she could risk exposure. She had to gain more trust and access to more data.

Vietra couldn't afford waiting, as the police were going to discover she'd manipulated them pretty soon and try to contact their agent. She considered telling the Orchids about the impostor, but that would involve revealing too much information that Vietra didn't want to share with them, giving them an insight into her abilities. She realized she had to deal with the situation herself.

She found a moment when Tranilla was alone and offered her to take a walk together. The woman didn't suspect anything, as she was expecting to receive orders from her chief. Vietra took her to the place where she'd last talked to Limea, making sure no one saw them on the way. She was planning to push the woman into the predatory forest below quietly. She'd never killed anyone before, and as she was standing there, listening to Tranilla's report of the work she'd done so far, Vietra felt nauseous and repelled by herself. Part of her was excited by the power that slaughtering another human would give her. At the same time, it was hard to accept she was about to become a murderer, and the inner conflict was tearing her apart. She knew she had to get rid of the agent to be safe. The Orchids changed the channels of admission pretty often, and it was the first time the police managed to get someone through. By the time they'd realize their undercover agent wasn't going to contact them ever again, their information on getting in touch with the Orchids would be obsolete, the people able to get them in long gone, the routes changed.

Viera took a deep breath, preparing herself for the push. Her body was tingling with tension in anticipation of violence. Tranilla turned to her, looking her in the eye somewhat sheepishly.

"Can I be frank with you, chief?" she asked, and her voice faltered.

"What is it, agent?" Vietra focused her attention on the woman, sensing hesitation and fear.

236

"I... my period didn't come on time after I started here. I thought it was the stress, because of this job. But... it didn't come next month either and... I got a test and..." Tranilla exhaled sharply and closed her fists. "I'm pregnant."

"Fuck!" terror pierced Vietra as she realized what she'd almost done.

"I know, I wasn't supposed to, it's in the contract, I'm so sorry!" the agent burst into tears, still clenching her fists. "I swear, I didn't mean to, my doctor told me I was infertile, that's why I took the job! My partner and I broke up because of it... because we wanted a family... and I... He said we could adopt, but I felt... inadequate for him... I knew how he wanted to be... a father... so I said... it was over, and he was so devastated, and now I'm pregnant, and I... this job is too dangerous, I don't want to risk my baby's life, and I want to tell Lomi he's a father, and I can't even contact him!"

Tranilla pressed her palms to her eyes, sobbing and shaking. Vietra felt paralyzed for a moment, still terrified of how close she came to taking two innocent lives. She took control of herself with the help of her implant, forcing herself to think logically.

"It's okay," she said softly, hugging the agent, feeling uncomfortable doing it. "You are out. You can go home."

"Are you serious?" Tranilla looked up at her in disbelief.

"Yes, you can go. Tell them it's my orders. I'll do the rest of the job myself."

"Really?"

"How many times do I have to say it?"

"Oh, thank you, thank you so much, chief!" Tranilla pressed Vietra closer to herself. "I'll never forget your kindness!"

Vietra was thinking quickly. If Tranilla returned home, the police would figure out what had happened and try to get another agent in. There was a high probability they'd already discovered her deception and would try to make a move against her and the Orchids. They'd learn where the Orchids resided from the agent, which would mean getting busted.

Vietra suddenly realized that she was sensing something from Tranilla, a sort of field, like an imprint of her personality and emotions. She probed it carefully with her implant, seeing the options of sharing information, thoughts and files unfold in front of her mind's eye. The woman had an implant too! Vietra smiled as everything fell into place.

"You have a brain implant, is that correct, agent?"

"Yes, they gave me one."

"Good. We'll have to do something before you leave. Go to your quarters and pack. I'll find you there."

"Yes, chief."

Vietra took a moment to compose herself. She wasn't sure she could do it if it wasn't for her implant, but luckily, she didn't have to find out. She found Sib and told him a story of a pregnant woman who wanted to leave the criminal life to give her baby a safe future.

"We need to erase her memories, and she's good to go, right?" Vietra asked casually, masking her anxiety under a layer of opaqueness that her implant allowed.

"Yes," Sib shrugged. "It's easy to do with an implant, that's why anyone who gets it is free to leave whenever they want

238

She won't remember a thing about us. We don't keep anyone by force here."

"Great, can you do it now?" Vietra said.

"I'm a bit busy, but I guess I could. It doesn't take long."

"One more thing, I need her to forget me too. We had a couple of conversations I don't want to leave the premises of this building."

"Oh, no worries. She'll forget everything about being here and everyone she met here."

"Good. I'll bring her in then."

Vietra found Tranilla in her small apartment, with her travel bag on her lap, sitting on the edge of her bed in complete readiness and anticipation.

"They'll have to erase your memories so that you can leave quietly without raising suspicions," Vietra said.

"But..."

"Do you want your baby to be safe? If you leave without doing it, they'll find you and kill you for everything you know about them. You know they are capable of it," she saw fear in Tranilla's eyes. "Besides, if they suspect anything, they might uncover our entire operation. I'll take over from here. Your work won't be for nothing. It's an order, agent," she added, sensing hesitation.

"Yes, chief."

And just like that, it was done. After erasing Tranilla's memory, the Orchids' security gave her a safe sedative and delivered her to the central part of the city, leaving her on a bench on a public roof. She would come to her senses within 20 minutes and would be confused about how she'd got there. Her last memory would be before she contacted the person who got her to the Orchids. She would remember nothing about getting there, being there and getting out. Several months of her life would be missing as if they'd never happened. Vietra experienced a sense of relief that was almost physical in its nature. She didn't become a killer. She still felt the darkness within her, knowing now that all the abuse she'd experienced being the Master's puppet was looking for a way out, but there was another day when it didn't turn into violence, and that was victory. Yes, the poor agent would lose her job, but she and her baby would live. She was a smart woman and would figure something out.

CHAPTER 24

Several weeks passed since Vietra found herself in Cay's bed, and they still hadn't talked about it. Preparations to the raid on the Nest were intense, and both of them were busy. Whenever they met, there were other people around and important issues to discuss. Besides, Cay was working on finishing his solar system for the Orchids, so he didn't participate in all of the meetings. Vietra was rather happy about it because she felt really uncomfortable around him and wouldn't know how to start the conversation anyway.

Presently, they were in a meeting in the tactics room. They were sitting at a round table, a hologram of the Nest in front of them. Vietra was clenching her fists under the table. Cay was looking at her, and she tried not to meet his gaze.

The Orchids were in the habit of discussing their decisions and plans even though they could just exchange their thoughts directly through the implants. It served two purposes. Firstly, it gave them time to really think everything through because this type of communication was much slower but also more deliberate. The spoken opinion could be changed, while a thought sent right into another's brain had some finality about it. It was a good way to exchange precise data but not opinions and ideas. Secondly, they had to stay in practice, as they still dealt with lots of people from the outside, and Olonda always emphasized how important effective communication was for business and human relationship in general.

There were six of them at the table. The people who comprised the tactical group that was going to participate in the raid of the Nest.

Sais was a middle-aged man with olive skin, dark hair and deep eyes, his features rough and angular. He was the Orchids' soldier, who always looked confident and reserved. Being around him made others feel more secure. If something went wrong, Sais would know what to do, at least such was everyone's assumption. But there was dark void behind his black eyes, and even though he never talked about himself, it was clear that he'd suffered a great loss that he couldn't put behind him. It made Vietra uneasy.

There were Maltara and Syong, twin sisters who lost their whole family to the plague and were rescued by Olonda when they were teenagers. They were in their twenties now, beautiful, tall, with bright blue eyes, shining from their small, feminine faces. Their loyalty was limitless, they'd give their lives for Olonda and the Orchids without blinking an eye.

Maltara was a technological genius who participated in designing and making most of the devices used by Olonda's people. She built robots for fun and staged comedy shows with them. She usually kept her long, blue and violet hair in a ponytail, and a frown of concentration often crossed her forehead. But when she went out of her head into the outside world, she was a cheerful person who laughed a lot and shared smiles generously.

Syong worked security. She was fast and strong, watchful and graceful like one of those pre-plague wild cats. She could do scary tricks with knives, knew martial arts and shot a target faultlessly from several hundred meters. Her sandy blond hair was cut short, and her lips were always tight. She looked out for Maltara, feeling responsible for her both as a sister and a valuable asset of the organization.

There was also Gono, a quiet guy of an indefinite age, who always had a confused look on his face and gave an apologetic smile to anyone who tried to talk to him, as he usually wasn't listening. When it came to software, there was no one better than him, and Olonda relied on him and Maltara to investigate the Master's technology, find out what could be useful and figure out a way to replicate it for their needs. Gono didn't look like it, but he'd studied ancient martial arts and was very good at fighting when it came to it. He preferred not to, as he was a peaceful creature, but he wouldn't let anyone hurt him or those he felt loyal to. Vietra didn't know him long enough to see him in action, but she heard rumors of him turning into a completely different person in times of need. His face became a mask of concentration, his movements precise and swift, even though he was usually quite clumsy. He managed to stop three armed men once and got shot but saved a couple of the Orchids' members and some of their secrets. He had a scar running across his neck and shoulder down to his lower back from another fight when he was attacked by members of a rival organization. It didn't exist anymore, and no one talked about it, but everyone knew Olonda's people eliminated all of them after that unfortunate attack.

And then there was Cay, a person Vietra deliberately ignored. She'd prefer that he didn't take part in the mission at all. They could do without him, as the only reason he did it was for her, and Vietra was worried about his safety.

243

"All right, let's go over it one more time," Syong said. "After we get onto the bridge leading to the Nest, it's the Master's territory and it's booby trapped."

"Yes," Vietra confirmed, feeling the burn of Cay's gaze on her. She magnified the area on the hologram. "The bridge is fenced, but we'll get over it no problem. There are some warning signs to keep the general public away, but there are only abandoned buildings around anyway, so no one really goes there."

"What kinds of booby traps he got?" Sais asked.

"Different kinds, and they move around occasionally. You should only step onto safe zones, but it took years of training to be able to identify those. Subjective time, of course, but still, I won't be able to teach you. If you make a wrong step, you'll either get shot or electrocuted or poisoned with gas. You never know which one it will be."

"Right," Syong said. "So, we have to follow your steps precisely."

"Yes, you should place your feet exactly where I place mine, it can be a matter of centimeters."

"My team could make tracker shoes for you," Maltara said a bit slowly, looking up, her gaze darting from left to right. She pursed her lips, nodded to herself, smiled and looked at Vietra, continuing faster and more confidently, "They will measure the exact placement of your feet and share the information with our implants that will highlight your steps with virtual markers we'll see on the ground as if they were imprints in the sand."

"That should work," Vietra nodded. "There is also a problem with cameras. There are drones patrolling the territory 24/7,

244

and if they see you, you'll get killed anyway because you are unauthorized."

"Does anyone watch the footage?" Gono asked thoughtfully.

"No, it's all autonomous."

"We could make suits that would prevent the algorithms from identifying us as people. The cameras will see us, but we'll be classified as inanimate objects," Gono said.

"Okay, if that works, we'll be able to get into the Nest," Vietra said. "What weapons have you got for the inside?"

"Based on what you told us before, besides the usual guns and knives, we prepared a real treat," Sais smiled wolfishly, and the hologram changed to a flat grey disc with holes and dents in it. "This is our latest innovation in bombs, tweaked to the peculiarities of the Nest. It will help us destroy it when it's time. You throw it sort of like a frisbee."

The hologram depicted a silhouette of a person throwing the disc inside a large domed building that looked like the Nest. The person was on the ground floor, where the main room, the gym, the study and practice rooms, the kitchen, the bedrooms and the sensory deprivation room were. The upper floor, Vietra knew, contained the sim-caskets with all the Nestlings, some labs and manufacturing equipment. The holographic building was divided into rooms accurately, as it was reconstructed from her descriptions. The disc flew several meters, hovered in the middle of the main room, scanned it and released smaller copies of itself from the dents. Most of the smaller parts as well as the disc attached themselves to the walls and ceiling and detonated. The building collapsed, and some of the smaller discs that were still hovering in the air attached themselves to the remaining constructions detonating again.

"The bomb and its children find the most vulnerable places in the building to ensure its destruction," Sais explained. "Some of the children stand by in case initial damage is insufficient and finish the job. The holo is slow, in reality, it all takes about three seconds. We'll have to get out before we activate it, and the person activating it should stand in the doorway and run like hell after throwing it."

"This is good", Vietra was impressed. She was worried about the destruction of the Nest, and this technology made it look like it could work.

They spent some more time talking about the details of the operation, arguing and sharing responsibilities. The plan was becoming more and more solid, which gave Vietra some hope.

She wasn't feeling very confident, even though she didn't show it to anyone. She wasn't so sure she wanted to meet the Master anymore. She was afraid it would undo the brittle progress she'd made. She was also terrified that he could capture her again. What if she had to stay in the Nest forever? What if this time there wouldn't be a way out? But she knew she had to do it. Tyss was waiting for her there, and she had to go back if only to set him free. She would have to kick his ass later for having created the horrible sensory deprivation room experiences, but she felt they could be friends afterwards.

***

There came a moment when suddenly the preparations were over. They'd manufactured all the tools and weapons they could think of, they went through every possible scenario and made arrangements for those, they had a plan and a dozen of backup ones. They were as ready as they were ever going to be. It was time to move. It was scheduled for later that night. They had several hours to rest before leaving.

Vietra couldn't sleep. She was too nervous, too agitated for too many reasons. She was wandering around the building, that she'd gotten to know well, until she found herself in the familiar room with a collapsed wall where she last saw Limea. The room where she almost became a murderer later. She was looking at the plants, breaking their way into the fragile human world. She could sense their hostility. They made her feel uneasy, and even on a warm night as it was Vietra felt the chill creeping on her skin. She knew it was either humans or the plants, and so far, her kind had been losing the battle. The greenery was going to kick them out of their home, and nothing would ever be the way it had been even if people managed to escape. Colonies on other planets and moons as well as the orbital station would be able to sustain only a fraction of the population. The majority would die. So many people had died already. How many lost their children, parents, loved ones and friends? How many had she lost, even if she didn't remember them? It was hard not to hate the plants for that. She knew that if she could destroy them, she wouldn't hesitate a moment.

"Can't sleep?" Cay's calm and quiet voice almost made Vietra jump. She was so lost in thought that didn't hear him coming, nor did he indicate his presence through the implant.

"Why are you creeping up on me like that?" she snapped but quickly took control of her emotions. "Sorry, I'm a little edgy before meeting the Master. And you? Why aren't you sleeping?"

"I can't," Cay shrugged. "Sorry I startled you. I turned the implant off to feel human again. Maybe it's for the last time."

"You think you are going to die?"

"It's possible."

"How do you like it without the implant?"

"Not much. It's like everything is blurred and chaotic, and there is little I can do. The world has shrunk around me and presses against my chest. Anyway, I wanted to talk to you before we left. Because, you know, we might never get another chance."

Vietra sighed. It sounded a little too dramatic for her taste, but she knew he was right.

"Can you turn your implant back on? It'll be easier if we are on the same level, and I don't want to turn mine off. It gives me the little control that I have over myself, and I'm afraid I'm going to fall apart if I lose it."

"Sure."

No visible change happened, but Vietra felt Cay's presence in her mental field as his implant resumed its functions. She looked at him for a moment and suddenly let go. Maybe it was because she realized it could actually be their last meeting. Maybe because she was tired and stressed. Whatever the reason, she just opened up to him without a warning and without thinking it through. She simply gave all her feelings and fears, all the mess her inner world was to him through the implant.

It was like a sudden waterfall that rushed right into his brain. In that moment he knew exactly who she was and what it was like to be her. It was what he wanted, she realized. As startled as he was, Cay took it in looking at her with his eyes wide open. Then he did the same for her. And Vietra suddenly knew how agonizing it had been for him, how he longed for connection with her, and how he still loved her even though she was a different person.

It was so easy. It didn't matter how they got where they were. What mattered was how irresistibly they were drawn to each other, how pure and deep their feeling was and had always been. The exchange was so intense that even though it lasted for no longer than a couple of seconds, it left them exhausted. They sat down with their backs to the wall, shoulder to shoulder. Was it even real? Vietra touched Cay's hand gently. He was sitting without movement for a while before touching hers. Then they were caressing each other, gently moving their fingers along each other's bodies. She touched his neck and shoulders. He touched her face. They were slowly getting closer until their lips met, and they fell into each other's arms. They had sex right there, in the dark room with the plants gradually making their way to kill them, and the stars sending their light from unreachable depths of space. Their implants intensified the experience, making their sensations mix, causing a chaotic expansion of pleasure into dimensions previously unknown to them. When they were finished, their implants told them it was time to move out. They got up and went to their rooms to grab the things they might need. Connected. Tickled and pushed by streams of wild energy from the inside.

"It would be so unfortunate to die now," a thought appeared in their common mind space, and they didn't know which one of them it belonged to.

CHAPTER 25

They came as close as they could to the Master's Nest and stopped in front of a bridge protected by a tall fence with a sign saying entry was forbidden, as the bridge could collapse any moment. They knew it wasn't true. Real danger began on the other side: open ground filled with cameras, tracking devices and traps. Even though they were ready for it, it was quite discouraging to see.

Vietra was shivering. It seemed to her that she'd never been so scared in her life. Terror enveloped her and penetrated every nerve and every cell of her body. There was not a single part of her that wasn't taken over by fear. A thin analytical voice was fighting its way through the chaos, trying to reason her feelings, courtesy of the implant.

Before her escape from the Nest, Vietra didn't know what life actually was, she was only familiar with a distorted version of it. Since then, she'd had a chance to taste what it was like. Human relationship and laughter, being in control of her actions and, of course, love. She had just gained Cay. They hadn't had enough time to enjoy each other, and Vietra knew there was still so much for them to do together and so much for her to learn about life. All of it could end any moment. She could be captured by the Master and never be able to escape again. Cay could die. She'd had nothing to lose before, but it was different now. Life in the Nest seemed absolutely unbearable since she'd had a glimpse of the outside world.

"Are you okay?" Cay asked, putting his arm around her shoulders.

"Yes," Vietra said. She wanted to tell him the truth, but there were other people around. People who depended on her to make their plan a reality. Cay knew anyway.

"You are shivering."

"I'm just a little cold. It's the wind."

"You don't have to do it, you know," he said quietly.

"Yes, I do," she said firmly and stopped shivering with an effort of will that was, in fact, force of the implant applied to the right region of her brain. "See? I'm already better."

Cay said nothing, but she saw in his eyes that he shared her fear. He didn't want her to go either. He was afraid he could lose her again. He would try to go instead of her, Vietra knew, if only it made any sense. But they'd agreed on a plan before, the one that gave them the best chance of success according to their simulations. Cay couldn't act on his own even if he wanted to, no one would let him because their lives and the whole operation depended on everyone doing exactly the right thing.

"Are you ready?" Sais asked.

"Yes," Vietra said even though she felt otherwise.

"Good," Sais nodded. "You know what to do. Good luck."

"Thanks."

Vietra looked at her group. Sais, Maltara and Syong, Gono–the people she'd been spending most of her time with lately, feeling like she was getting to know them, beginning to understand them and even caring about them despite herself.

And, of course, Cay, the man she loved more that she thought was possible, the man who could die just because he

252

refused to stay behind. The man who accepted her for who she was, in spite of everything she'd been through. Tall, graceful, reserved. His brown hair fluttered by the wind, his grey eyes focused, lips tight, arms crossed. He looked so handsome standing there, peering at the Nest. Would life even matter if he was gone? Vietra smiled at him, and he smiled back. He believed in her, and that gave her strength.

She took a deep breath, climbed over the fence and stepped onto the bridge. Some of the traps had been moved around since she'd left, but she had enough skills to recognize them. Her brain reinforced with the implant was a machine for picking out every detail of the environment that other people would never notice. She'd been trained to do that for decades of subjective time, and even though it happened in a simulation, those skills were hard-wired in her neural pathways.

Vietra was walking slowly, avoiding the traps that could kill her in an instant. Drones were buzzing high above, capturing her on video. She was walking openly, without concealing herself with a suit the rest of the group were wearing. She wanted the Master to know that she was coming. And there she was, in front of a smooth, solid, white wall. She pressed her hands to the wall, wondering whether her fingertips and the lines on her palms could open the door hidden in it. It was so in the sim, but she wasn't sure that it worked in reality or, if it did, that she hadn't been erased from the database. After a couple seconds of scanning, the wall slid sideways silently, making an entrance for her. She hesitated before walking in and fought the urge to look back. It could be the last time she saw the outside world. She took a step, and the wall closed behind her.

"Vietra," the voice she kept hearing in her nightmares said. "It's good to have you back."

The Master was standing there, in the middle of an empty room with his arms crossed, staring at her. She tried to say something, but there was a lump in her throat.

"How was the outside world?" the Master continued.

"Dis..." Vietra had to make an effort of will to push the word through. "Disappointing."

"I knew that," the Master faked a smile.

The polite conversation was getting on Vietra's nerves more than anything else. She would rather he got down to punishing her.

"So, would you like to rejoin us?"

"Yes."

"What a fortunate surprise. We are in the final stage of our preparations, and we need you to fulfill your duty."

"Will you finally tell me what it is?"

"You will know when the time is right."

Vietra felt rage spreading in her like poison. She had to reduce the functions of her implant before entering the Nest so that the Master's machines couldn't detect it. She didn't know if they were capable of that, but the group agreed to do that as a precaution. The implant recognized the chemicals her fury consisted of but couldn't contain them. The voice of reason drowned in the outburst, and for the first time since she got the implant, Vietra lost control of herself completely.

"I'm so sick of this!" she shouted. "You keep saying the same thing, over and over, over and over, like a fucking robot on a loop! You make me sick! What the fuck have you done to us!?

254

Do you think there is anything that can justify the way you treat us? How can you expect us to do anything for you? I hate you, and I will never do what you want! Do whatever you wish to me, I want you to die, and to fail, and to drown in your own shit, and to suffer for eternity, and this won't be enough!"

Vietra realized she screwed up, but she couldn't stop her fervent speech even though she knew she had to stick to the plan. She didn't care about the plan at that moment. Emotions were in control.

"I understand," the Master said very calmly. "You weren't the perfect choice, and I recognize my mistake now. But I can't afford to start over just because of you. The other Nestlings are good, and we are ready to go. There is actually something that justifies what I did to you. If I show that to you, will you do your part?"

Vietra was speechless for a moment. This was her chance to actually draw the Master's attention to herself and distract him from what was going to happen outside of the Nest. But that only flashed in her mind as a background thought. More importantly, she was given an opportunity to finally get a closure, to find some meaning in what had happened to her. Would she want to help him afterwards? She didn't want to think about it, such a possibility terrified her, so she stuck it into her mental closet and focused on the present moment.

"Maybe," Vietra said feeling unreal like in a dream.

The Master sighed and nodded, looking like he had to indulge a nasty child.

"All right. But you'll have to get into the sim-casket."

"No!"

"It's just…"

"You think I'm stupid? I see what you are doing!"

"I'm trying to keep my part of our agreement," the Master pointed out.

"No, you are trying to trick me! As soon as I get there, you'll never let me leave again. You'll turn a second of actual time into a million of subjective years, and you'll keep torturing me until I agree to help you."

"That's not true."

"Of course it is. I know you well enough to never trust you. But you know what? Even if you got me into your fucking sim again, I'd never give up! Give me an eternity of suffering, you are not going to get what you want, you can be damn sure of it!" Vietra said glaring fiercely into his eyes. And she was convinced it was true, but after she finished talking, she realized she could actually break down. The thought was unbearable. She'd rather die.

The Master stared at her for a moment with his eyes blank and devoid of emotion. It was impossible to guess what he was thinking.

"Dealing with you is such an ordeal. I promise I'll do what I said."

"No way I'm getting in there. Why would I believe your word? After everything you've done!"

"But there is no other way to show you."

"You don't have to show me anything. Just tell the story."

"You won't understand. You have to see."

"Start speaking. If at some point I am unable to grasp something, I'll think about your offer."

"It's not an offer. Either I plug you to the sim-casket and tell you the whole truth, or you never find out."

"You won't get me to do what you need then. Whatever you do to me. I'll. Never. Do it."

"I believe you call such people a pain in the ass," the Master said. "But you know, Vietra, I actually like it. There is something about you... I think I'm beginning to understand what it's like to be..."

"To be what?"

He didn't answer. He stared at some point in space, zoned out.

"It's your choice, Vietra. Find out the truth or don't. There won't be a second chance," the Master finally said.

"No, it's your choice. You can tell me the truth, and maybe I'll help you, or you won't, and your whole plan will fail without me."

"I can do without you. It would be good to have you to increase the chances of success, but we are also likely to succeed without your participation."

"You are bluffing. You need me," Vietra was desperately hoping this was actually the case. In fact, it was her who was bluffing. She was on the verge of abandoning everything just for a slight chance of learning the truth. If it wasn't for Cay who depended on her, she would have done it already.

"All right," the Master finally said. "I'll tell you. I've never tried this before, and maybe that's the secret ingredient of success. Maybe I should treat you more... humanely so that you can sympathize with my goals and do your part. Maybe a different approach is the key. Come, take a sit. It's quite a long story."

Vietra tried hard not to give away her astonishment and triumph. The Master had never indulged anyone. Something had changed about him, and she didn't know what the reason was. It frightened her. She headed to a large black couch in the middle of the oval room that she remembered so well. The couch felt exactly the way it felt in a simulation. It made her uneasy. What if she never actually left the Nest? What if it was still a sim?

"Where do I start?" the Master began. "You are not who you think you are. You had a different personality before, but I wiped it out along with your memories. Tyssdin has already told you that, hasn't he?"

Vietra was hoping the Master didn't know about that. But there was no point pretending, so she just nodded briefly, urging him to continue with a stare.

"That's so curious," the Master shook his head slowly in a dreamy way. "But it doesn't matter now. And that wasn't a good start either. Let's try again. Imagine you live in a relatively prosperous world, technologically advanced, filled with intelligent beings that dominate the planet and multiple other species."

"Done," Vietra said with a sarcastic smile.

"Yes, that should be easy," the Master nodded. "Imagine you belong to the dominant species, and nothing has really threatened you for hundreds of thousands of years. You have it all under control. You are practically immortal and can only die from an unlucky accident. You've eliminated diseases as you are able to edit your DNA and every cell in your body. You can basically program your body to be healthy, to fight and repair whatever damage comes its way. Suddenly, several of your kind die young. It starts happening all over the planet. No one knows why. There is a great investigation with more and more dying along the way. It quickly becomes an epidemic.

"Eventually, you discover that what's killing you is actually an integral part of your own cell, so small that it's extremely hard to detect. For an unknown reason it stops cooperating with the cell and starts remaking its building blocks in such a way that it stops functioning properly. It happens in multiple cells simultaneously, all over the organism, in different parts of your body. Since it's a natural compound of your body, the regular protective mechanisms fail to work.

"You don't know what triggers the process, studying it is onerous, more and more of your kind die on the way. It spreads fast, and you never know who is affected until it's too late. It always takes different time to kill, sometimes it happens within days, sometimes it takes years. It's a struggle to even figure out what the problem is, since the change happens deep within your cells. But eventually you find ways. And what you find is striking.

"When you look close enough, the integral part of your own cell that causes the damage turns out to be sentient. It uses technology and builds inside of you, lives in organized groups, even studies you. It changes the cell in such a way that more of it can live there, which disrupts the balance of the cell and, eventually, causes it to fail. The more you find out about it, the scarier it gets. You don't know what causes it to turn on you, scientists speculate that there must be some trigger that activates it. You don't know what it is yet. Maybe some changes in your environment. Something you are exposed to. Maybe it's a

259

genetic mutation. What you know is that once it is activated, it begins to spread, and it's not going to stop. Your species is in danger of extinction.

"You try everything your medicine can come up with, but it doesn't work because essentially you're fighting against your own body. You can only slow the change down in the best-case scenario, and in the worst case, what you do helps it evolve even faster. Spreading inside your cells is like space travel for it, it colonizes one planet after another and establishes control. It's very arrogant, bringing new rules and changing the environment for its needs wherever it goes. Destroying, polluting, disrupting the ecosystem of your cells," the Master fell silent.

"Okay," Vietra said when the silence started getting uncomfortable. "I can imagine that. It's a strange concept, but strange things happen all the time. Is there a point to that?"

The Master glared at her.

"There is," he said. "You are the part of the cell I'm talking about, Vietra."

"Me?"

"Your entire species. Humans. You are not in the Universe as you imagine it. You live inside my species' bodies. The stars and planets, the galaxies and those clusters or whatever you call them are just an inner structure of one cell."

"You are crazy," Vietra shook her head in disbelief and indignation. "You should see a fixer."

"I told you it was going to be hard to understand, that's why I wanted to show it to you from the very beginning."

"How is it going to convince me?" Vietra let out a short hysterical laugh. She was beginning to lose patience. "How will it be different from any other simulation?"

"It will be very different," the Master said with great conviction. He wasn't moved by her reaction. "Let me show you, and you'll decide for yourself."

Vietra didn't know what was guiding her at that moment. It might have been curiosity or the urge to make sure the Master was a nutcase, even though it was clear. Maybe it was because of her disturbed nerves. But she said "okay" and let him plug her to the sim-casket. When she was in there, she realized it had probably been his plan all along. She saw his image in front of her and heard his voice a moment later.

"I don't need you in the machine, Vietra. You all have to come out for the final stage of the plan, so there is no point in keeping you there. I want you to understand. You humans like to understand the reasons for everything, isn't that right? I've been learning about you all this time, and you are still a mystery. But if that increases the odds of your cooperation, I'm ready to take this chance. Let me show you."

What she saw could be just a simulation, but there was something utterly inhumane about it, something alien that made Vietra feel like even the most insane person couldn't have created it. She wasn't able to explain it, and she knew no words for what she saw. If it wasn't for the Master's commentary that sounded in her head all along, she wouldn't understand any of it. It made her nauseous. It was so uncomfortable that she wanted it to stop, and at the same time she couldn't help looking.

She saw death of millions of creatures that resembled stains of mud to her. She called them Brandstocks for herself, as they were making sounds resembling the word when they communicated. The Master explained they were the victims of the change happening in their bodies.

She watched them do inexplicable things, and the Master described how they were looking for the cause of death and studying the inner structure of their cells. She couldn't distinguish the tools they used from the environment, but at a certain point she started seeing through their eyes, getting deeper into their bodies, until they found something she vaguely recognized as human constructions and networks. It looked utterly bizarre from the perspective of those creatures, they couldn't understand what it was or how it functioned, and the way they saw it influenced Vietra.

The Brandstocks realized it was something hostile, they knew it was the reason their species was endangered, and Vietra couldn't help but feel part of their rage. There was something perverse in the act of destruction of living cells caused by their integral part.

Humans repeatedly polluted and abandoned what they saw as "their planet" for a new one when it was drained of resources and incapable of sustaining them. Just moving on to devastate the next one. Traveling to new places, finding new homes. First in their own solar systems, later, as technology evolved, to farther destinations. More spaceships, more planets at a time. Colonizing the Universe at exponential speed. If they met other humans who were on a lower stage of development, they often turned them into slaves or exterminated them. They destroyed whole species of animals and plants if they turned out to be inconvenient or just by accident, and if that happened to disrupt the ecosystem, well, there were lots of other planets out there.

If they met other humans who were technologically advanced, they started a war, destroying the structure of the cell even faster.

Some of the humans even found ways to get out of their own cell into a neighboring one. Visit a parallel Universe. They were always on the move. The changes they made inside the cells impeded their functioning. When enough cells stopped working properly, the organism died. Vietra felt disgusted and impressed at the same time.

No means the hosts normally used to fight diseases worked. Anything that could kill humans also killed the cells they were part of, which eventually resulted in the death of the organism anyway.

They started testing everyone, even those who looked healthy, and were terrified to find changes in almost two thirds of the population. It didn't mean that the rest were safe, just that humans haven't done enough damage yet or were still living in harmony with their cells. There was no guarantee it would stay that way though.

The most horrible news for the Brandstocks was that the Old Ones were affected. It hadn't been too destructive yet, but taking into account how fast it could spread, the Brandstocks knew they were on the verge of calamity.

The Old Ones were their source of wisdom and information. They stored all the memories of their species since the early days. It was too much for regular Brandstocks, who weren't capable of keeping memories for longer than a couple of months. Even that was a great effort, and they only did it in case of necessity. An average memory was kept for no longer than a day or two. The structure of their brain didn't allow for longer storage. That impeded the Brandstocks' development, and they had remained primitive creatures for billions of years before the First One emerged.

Maybe it was a mutation, but the First One was capable of remembering. It (the Brandstocks didn't have a sex) quickly united the rest of the species around itself and helped them make some steps to development using and managing their memories. Thanks to the First One their population increased, as they didn't have to repeat the same mistakes over and over again and learned how to avoid dangers. They started using primitive tools, perfecting them day by day, as the First One reminded them of the process of creation and the possibilities a certain tool represented. The First One multiplied itself before it died, and two of its children had the same capabilities, so the tradition continued. Descendants of the First One became sacred in Brandstock culture, guiding and helping the rest of the population. They were worshiped and protected, as the fragile development of the whole species depended on their abilities. Thanks to the emerging medicine and special care they received they were able to have much longer lives than others of their kind and were called the Old Ones. The name stuck around even after everyone's life expectancy increased.

The Old Ones made every important decision. Whatever they said became a law. They were revered like gods by the

Brandstocks. There came a moment when technology that allowed direct brain to brain communication was created. Now regular Brandstocks could share the memories of the Old Ones. It turned out to be a nightmare. The Old Ones could handle it as their brain functioned differently, but it was a torture resulting in mental disorders and even death for the rest of the population. Needless to say, this brought even more reverence to the Old Ones. The whole culture was built around making them comfortable, happy and safe. Anything they wished for was done, even if it meant death of hundreds of Brandstocks. There wasn't a single life that meant as much.

Thanks to the Old Ones the species became dominant on the planet. All the Brandstock technology and way of living was owed to them. The Old Ones controlled it all. Now that there was so much to remember and so many Brandstocks to manage, they merged themselves with machines. They handled common memories: who should remember what every single day to do their job, function properly in the society and bring prosperity to their global community. They only made small bits of memories that could be dealt with by the general population available and quickly changed them to the next ones when it was necessary. Sometimes a memory had to be stored longer for some reason, but the Old Ones tried to minimize the ordeal of it by all possible means. Everyone depended on them and was happy to obey. Now they were in danger.

"Couldn't they just transfer all their memories into the machines?" Vietra asked.

"The machines?" the Master seemed repulsed. "Who would know which memories were useful at a given moment? Someone should manage the data using their judgment. How can that be trusted to a machine? A mind enhanced by a machine is good, but a machine that makes decisions... How can you be sure its decisions are right for your species, not the machine itself? How can you know it understands what you really need?"

"All right, all right, relax," Vietra said. "It's just some human thinking."

She brought her attention back to the simulation. She got used to it by now and distinguished some of the things in the Brandstock world, but she still had to rely on the Master's explanations.

The fact that the Old Ones were infected was the greatest tragedy for the Brandstocks. Without them, even if some managed to survive, they'd just quickly fall back to the primitive state. Everything they'd achieved would be for nothing. It would be the end of their civilization, and there would be no one to remember their great deeds.

Naturally, they pulled all their resources to cure the Old Ones. They were trying different approaches until a young and ambitious scientist came up with an outrageous and brilliant idea to fight the problem on its level. After many trials and errors, they managed to create a viable specimen of the rebellious part of the cell. An artificial human. They replicated it into several copies meant to be controlled by the Old Ones. Basically, they tried to put the consciousness of the Old Ones into human brain. It didn't function as intended, as the brain structure of the two species was too different, but after multiple procedures that Vietra didn't understand they somehow made it work.

Artificially created humans were placed inside the bodies of the Old Ones. Every Old One had control of all human agents inside it, sharing its consciousness with them. It was a sort of a hive mind analyzing the methods of the individuals it consisted of and deciding on the best strategy to save the Brandstock in whose body they operated.

The Old Ones embedded themselves in human culture through the agents and started studying it in order to understand the problem and create a solution. The more they learned, the more complicated it seemed. In the end they set out to change the biochemistry of the cell in such a way that would strengthen the cell and allow it to function, while eliminating the rebellious part. It wasn't trivial. In fact, it was next to impossible. What was home planets for humans, for Brandstock was a component so deep inside a cell that they hadn't even been aware it existed before. Modifying it from the outside was impossible just because of its scale. Altering it from the inside was an extremely tough problem without an obvious solution.

The Master was one of many soldiers living in many different cells, in different organisms, serving the sole purpose of saving the Old Ones by destroying humans. He was from the seventy-second generation of artificial agents. The previous ones couldn't survive or assimilate, couldn't adapt and take control of the necessary resources, but his was the first successful batch relying on the experience of their predecessors. The good news was that time flowed differently inside the organism, and what took the Master and his fellow soldiers decades to achieve, was merely a couple of minutes in the Brandstock world.

Others like him were working in other parts of the planet to set the plan in motion at the same time. Even more of them were on other "planets" inside the same cell as well as in other cells of the organism. The Master had already tried different approaches, and most of them failed.

First, he attempted to create artificial humans of his own and share the Old Ones' consciousness with them too. It was easier to do it on their scale, since creating such elaborate and precise biological machines out in the Brandstock world was extremely strenuous and required too many resources. But creating them as such wasn't very helpful, since they didn't have any knowledge about their environment or any insights about possible solutions. Their brain was blank, and they were essentially useless. The Master had to change that.

He tried to record some skills and knowledge right into their minds, but it turned out to be hopeless. His creations weren't viable. They died in packs. Their brain had to be more human-like to be able to take care of the vital functions of their organisms. Then they needed basic skills to stay alive and perform outside of his lab. They needed training. When he got that covered, his creations were still incapable of any elaborate activities. Later he learned it was important for humans to know a language, as it developed some functions of their brain and made more intricate thinking processes possible. He managed to record language and some basic knowledge into their brain with the help of Brandstock technology used for managing memories. He did the same for himself to be able to communicate with them. He had to change his brain in the process, and it was painful and strange. The world looked differently after that and being part of the hive mind became more complicated.

Even with all this done, most of the things still had to be taught. It was taking too long, so he adopted another machine from the Brandstock culture they could be plugged to, which slowed their subjective time, kept them alive and allowed them to learn in a simulation.

It wasn't enough. They wondered who they were and what their purpose was, they needed a personal history to find their place in the world. Making memories and skills for them turned out to be grueling. Even the humans themselves didn't know much about their own brain, and it was a total mystery to the Master. Most of his creations malfunctioned, lost their mind or turned against him.

Then, following the experience of other agents operating elsewhere in the organism, he adopted a new technique. It was better to take a fully formed human with developed brain possessing all the basic functions along with the skills necessary for the attack. Rewire their brain partially to erase memories of who they used to be, replace them with new memories created in a simulator while simultaneously enhancing their existing skills and teaching additional ones, including martial arts and obedience. It turned out to be the most effective method, but there were some scandals involving missing people. The Brandstocks didn't need unnecessary obstacles, that's why, eventually, they came up with the idea of replacing the people they took with clones.

"Why didn't you take the clones for your purposes and let the real people go back to their lives?" Vietra asked.

The Master pondered it for a moment.

"What difference does it make?" he asked. "I suppose we could do that too. But clones are less stable, who knows what can go wrong with them. Cloning isn't a big deal in my world, but it's not easy to make proper equipment here. Our analysis showed that real humans with real memories were more trouble-proof. Anyway, I chose you because you have knowledge of botany and plant genetics," he continued.

"Your predecessors from different parts of the world created what you call the plague. The plants were supposed to kill specifically humans and take over the planet but make life possible for other species, though we had to modify them too. The idea was to preserve the ecosystem in a slightly different state that didn't affect the work of the cell and eliminated humans. But you were too fast again. It even spurred your space program in search of a new home, which is exactly the opposite of what we want.

"That's why we need a massive attack on several fronts this time. I've gathered specialists in different fields who will ensure the complete and immediate destruction of your species. And I need you on board to make sure humans stand no chance of survival. We have to accelerate the growth of the plants to such an extent, that they'll get to every single human who somehow manages to survive our attack within a couple of days. If you remember the work that you did in training, you know that it's possible, and you only need to complete the final stage of creating the plague modification. The others will do their jobs. I want to remind you, in case you want to sabotage the whole thing, that my plan is very likely to work without you. You are improving the odds, but I don't believe you are crucial. Now, what do you say?"

Vietra was silent for about a minute. She needed to gather her thoughts and adjust to her new place in the Universe. She wanted to dismiss what the Master had told her as a delusion, but what she'd seen convinced her that it was real. It explained the plague, the Master's weirdness and disregard for the Nestlings. It explained the cruelty of what he'd done to her. It didn't make her feel better though.

"So, you are basically the Old One in the body of an artificially created human?" she finally said.

"That's almost correct. My consciousness is shared by all the artificially created humans working to destroy your kind inside my body."

"The civilizations you showed me... do they all live in your cells?"

"Yes, and there are many more. There are several other civilizations in this cell alone, or this Universe, as you call it. Some are more advanced than you, and some are more primitive. A couple of them have already been destroyed."

"Why didn't you use the same method on us then?"

"Some methods that worked elsewhere are absolutely impossible here. You like to change and enhance yourselves and the environment, especially where you are more advanced, so individual approach is required. But we're using a similar idea."

"And we also exist in other Universes?"

"Yes, I told you, you are everywhere."

"What do we look like out there? I only had a glimpse of a couple of civilizations through your microscopes, if I can call them that. But what is it like on the ground level?"

"Unfortunately, as you are highly adaptive, how you look depends greatly on the environment, which is different in different types of cells and different organisms. It's a problem for us because we had to create many different kinds of artificial humans. They had to be plausible, just like I am to you. Some of them look like you, but others are so distinct that you might not recognize them as your species. That's one more reason why you are so hard to fight."

Vietra pondered it for a while and felt a faint signal in her implant. Her group was approaching. She needed more time with the Master though.

"Why are you telling me this?"

"I want you to understand."

"Why?"

"I don't know. The longer I am among you, the more difficult it is to understand myself. I just want to survive, I want my species to survive! And I'm trying as hard as I can. I have failed so many times already! I just hope that if you understand, you'll agree it has to be done."

Vietra stayed silent for a little while, then asked, "And there are others like you on this planet?"

"Yes, we are going to carry out a massive assault in different parts of it to ensure success."

"Where exactly?"

"Why would I tell you?"

"Because I might have insights as to where your assaults would be more effective. Maybe I know something about my planet and my kind that you don't. You think you understand it, but I'm afraid it's not so easy for you to think on this scale. For you it's still a tiny building block of your cell that you hadn't even been aware of before we happened. For me it's a vast network of connections, and I might understand which ones can be severed to harm humans the most."

"So, you agree to help me?"

"If you let me."

"You should understand that I'm a little skeptical after you left."

"I've been there, and I've seen what people are like. You are right, we destroy everything on our way. This planet deserves another chance without us. I want it to survive even if it means extinction for my species. This planet is something... like the Old Ones for your culture, it's a treasure and the biggest value for some of us. Not all humans, unfortunately most of us are assholes who don't deserve to live."

"But you understand you'll have to die too."

"Of course, I'm ready to pay the price. By the way, I think we could use Tyssdin's help on this."

The Master made a sound that somewhat resembled a laugh of a broken toy. It made Vietra's skin creep.

"Tyssdin," he repeated in a strange voice, "was deleted."

"What do you mean?"

"He was just a computer program, Vietra. He took care of your simulation, but he malfunctioned. He rebuilt himself and started making his own decisions. He helped you escape."

273

"A... program? But he..." Vietra couldn't breathe for moment, overwhelmed. He'd been her only human connection in all the subjective years in the Nest. He treated her like a friend and seemed to like her. None of the other Nestlings had ever been so good to her. How could he have been a program?

She remembered that he said he was unable to leave the Nest with her, and how he could track the Master's movements, finding moments to talk to her and console her. How the scary simulation about her mother suddenly ended with blackness, even though she felt there was more to come. He cared for her. He wasn't human. And he didn't exist anymore because he helped her. Because of her.

"Was pretty human-like, wasn't he? He was a smart program that learned and improved himself to understand you humans better. One of your predecessors created him, and Tyss surpassed his creator pretty quickly. Initially, it was necessary to maintain the simulation. Later he was also tasked with finding a way to influence you in the most effective ways in the sensory deprivation room. But I think it got too far at a certain point. He became too good at understanding you, too similar to you. He started to care about you."

Vietra was still speechless. There was so much new information in such a short time. Her brain wasn't coping. She'd lost a friend. Her feelings for Tyss didn't change when she found out he was a program meant to torture her and other Nestlings, manipulate them into submitting to the Master's will. He was good to her. He saved her from this place despite the cost. Of course, he knew the Master would find out, but he still did it.

274

Had she ever had better friends in her previous life? But she had to shake the pain off, there was no time for it.

"Okay," Vietra said. "Then, I guess, we'll have to do without him. Show me your plans."

She studied the holographic maps carefully, allowing her implant to save them in short snaps of activity.

"What do you say?" the Master asked.

"The points are adjusted well on the globe," Vietra said. "But I have a couple of ideas on how to make the attack more effective. I'd like to know the details though. What tools and methods are you going to use?"

"Can't do that, sorry. You already know too much. I'd like to share more information with you, but I've got some experience that tells me not to."

"What kind of experience?"

"Of my kind being deceived or even killed by your kind. That's not what's going to happen, is it, Vietra?" he turned to her and looked her straight in the eye. Vietra finally knew why in spite of being acquainted with the Master for her entire subjective life she'd always found him unnatural and eerie. She couldn't quite grasp it or put it into words, it was subtle and elusive, yet ever present. Now she could see clearly in his eyes that he wasn't human deep inside. He didn't belong. And he never understood what really drove them or was important to them. He was doing guess work, experimental work, but he could never fully grasp what it was like to be a human. He came among them, but he remained a stranger, and it probably couldn't have been any other way.

"No," she said. "You can trust me."

"I don't really want to destroy you," the Master said. "But you should understand I don't have a choice."

"Of course," Vietra nodded. "What if we changed though? What if we could live in harmony with our environment? What if we could make our impact invisible or even strengthen you from the inside?"

"That happens quite often. But we still have to eliminate you, it's too much of a risk to keep you around."

"How often?"

"About 50% of the cells where you are present."

"So... you have eliminated friendly human civilizations, too?"

"Some of them. It's not that easy, I've told you."

"How do they do it?"

"Do what?"

"Live in harmony with the nature."

"It's a complicated subject, but in short, they either don't evolve technologically, staying part of the ecosystem or use what you call clean technology and build their economy on respect to the environment."

"Can you show one of those to me?"

"Why would you want that?" the Master seemed to be getting annoyed.

"I want to see what it's like. I think it's something I've always wanted. There must be an agent like you among them, right? I'd like to see it through his eyes, from the ground level."

"No matter how hard we try to erase your personalities when we take you, there is always something that sneaks in. I recognize the woman you used to be in these words."

276

"Well, she's gone now," Vietra said. "But I still want to indulge in this one last pleasure before we go on and destroy humanity. Let it be my death row wish."

"Okay, if that ensures your cooperation, I'll do it for you," the Master sighed, and Vietra was immersed in a world of color without a warning. The creatures she saw weren't very similar to people as she knew them, but the shape of their bodies, the number of limbs and the way they moved looked familiar.

"They looked quite like you initially, but they've come a long way since then. Their technology allows them to acquire any form and color, and many of them use it actively," the Master explained.

Vietra could see it now. Many of those people looked like fantasy characters and mythical creatures. Their bodies displayed a variety of colors and patterns, some possessed wings, horns, tails, fluffy ears and other attributes uncharacteristic of human physique. It was hard to tell whether those were body modifications or costumes. Others looked quite normal, only slightly different from what she was used to, their skin tones a bit off and their bodies slightly elongated.

Vietra watched them interacting with each other, smiling and touching one another, offering little help or just stopping in the middle of something to have a chat with a passerby. She was struck by how curious they were about each other, how spontaneous, just like children when meeting something unknown. A sequence of scenes flashed before her.

A man took a woman's tail in his hand to inspect, commenting on it, and the woman laughed. She wiggled the tail to tickle his nose. He burst into laughing, too.

Children and adults were running around, chasing each other, shooting each other from water pistols, hiding in tree branches and behind bushes, screaming and giggling.

A young man was sitting under a tree, crying. A pair passing him by stopped and sat by him, put their hands on his shoulders, inquiring. He started talking, still crying, and they listened. When he finished, they hugged him, caressing his head and neck, whispering something in his ear, and he clutched at them as if his life depended on it, still shaking in his pain but not alone anymore.

There was no rush or hurry. People were lying or sitting here and there, right on the lawns or tree branches, on the roofs of their many-shaped houses. Others were playing games or music, painting, tending to plants, chatting, dancing, building things Vietra didn't understand, cooking and sharing food, teaching and learning, giving each other massages or what looked like medical treatment. Others still were busy doing incomprehensible things that might have been work or play. They interacted with the environment, changing it in real time, having things pop up right from the ground or some parts roll out from the buildings. They seemed to be taking measurements, analyzing data they received, discussing them with each other waving their hands.

A group of kids were wandering around a field full of various objects of different colors and shapes. They were wearing what might have been AR goggles. They examined the objects, tried them out, showed them to each other, forming teams, clearly trying to make sense of them. They were rearranging the objects, to which the environment reacted by changing colors, having new objects appear from the ground or displaying colorful patterns. The children cheered when it happened. An adult was strolling among them, stopping here and there, making suggestions and jokes.

There was greenery everywhere, and human habitat was integrated with it in a sort of organic way. Their buildings were covered with plants all around and sometimes almost indistinguishable from the environment. Others stood out because of their peculiar shape and color.

Vietra didn't understand much of what these people were doing, but one thing was clear to her: whatever it was, it looked like they were enjoying themselves. Their world seemed like a big playground full of elaborate toys, scientific equipment and fascinating characters. Even though Vietra had no idea what their problems, challenges and struggles were, she could see how much love those creatures had for each other and their planet, how much passion for what they were doing. How at ease they were, how unselfconscious and sincere, how genuinely and easily happy. How come, she thought, that in her world it took an effort of will to be happy and enjoy life? That they were often so disintegrated and lonely in their own bubbles, even when there were lots of people around? That so many had to suffer?

The picture broke down, and the Master appeared in front of her, alone in the dark.

"How did they achieve this?" Vietra asked him.

"It's irrelevant, Vietra."

"Please? Do me this last favor before I die," Vietra looked him in the eye searching for humanity that couldn't be there.

The Master sighed, "They used to have a system resembling yours in a way, that's why I chose them for you. They live in the same cell and on a similar planet inside my body, so their environment and resources are akin to yours. What's quite fascinating though is that their culture and history are also like yours in many different ways. That doesn't happen so often. You wouldn't have understood much if I showed you some of those other civilizations. The ones you've seen almost ruined their world, but they realized it wasn't the way to go and changed their ways in time."

"But how? Can I see it?"

"Vietra...".

"Please! I will be dead soon. We all will. Can you do this last thing for me?"

There was a long pause, and Vietra thought the Master had lost his patience. She could tell he was quite displeased, when he finally said, "Just a quick look. If that's a strategy to make you cooperate, I'll relate it to other agents elsewhere. I have their history overview obtained by one of the agents who used to operate there. It was made by the locals. It's the story they tell about themselves, so it might not be entirely objective, but much of it has been confirmed by my kind."

The story began unfolding in front of Vietra like a fast-forwarded experiential 5d movie. She saw humans as an insignificant species of foragers roaming wild plains. She saw them discover and tame fire, develop language and art, form distinct cultures built on beliefs in the imaginary, develop elaborate tools and means of hunting that drove other species extinct wherever they went. She saw them spread all over the globe.

She saw them wipe out other species of humans. She saw them settle down and discover agriculture, build larger settlements, towns, kingdoms, empires. She saw them fighting and conquering each other, spreading their beliefs by force, unifying and reshaping the world. She saw rivers of blood and immense suffering. She saw cultures blooming and disappearing. She saw the emergence of science and technology, of economy and politics that represented the few while depriving the many. They kept changing the environment, bringing it closer to collapse each year, kept driving animals and plants extinct, kept committing atrocities in the name of greater good the understanding of which was constantly shifting.

They created industry and economy dependent on fossil fuels. They were depleting those finite resources, destroying ecosystems, unable to see their planet as a complex biosphere where every action led to a change that in turn triggered more changes.

They seemed to view other species as commodities, not living beings, and treated them accordingly. Farm animals were mass-produced as if they were items on an assembly line. Their bodies were shaped according to the needs of industry. There were tens of billions of them, living their short lives in pain and horror before they died a dreadful death. They required huge amounts of water. 80% of all land used in agriculture was dedicated to raising animals and producing feed. Humans were cutting down their forests to make more room for those fields, destroying habitats, upsetting fragile ecological balance, driving more species to extinction, releasing more carbon dioxide into the atmosphere. Farm animals created potent amounts of methane that was a powerful greenhouse gas as well.

All in all, it was a pretty inefficient method of food production, and it looked unbelievably cruel to Vietra. Fifty billion of those animals were slaughtered each year. The length and quality of their lives was dictated by profits of the corporations owning them. There were no efficient laws to protect them, so atrocities were considered industry standard.

Male piglets were castrated without anesthesia. Male chicks were asphyxiated in gas chambers. Cows were impregnated artificially and separated almost immediately from their calves so that humans could take their milk. Male calves were put into small cages where they couldn't move for several months before they were killed for meat. Females were standing knee-deep in their own excrement, given food and antibiotics before they grew enough to be impregnated, their udders sore and infected from machinery constantly pumping milk. They were denied their basic needs and lived an average of four years before they collapsed and couldn't get up anymore. Then heavy machinery took them to slaughterhouses where their throats got slit.

Vietra couldn't get their screams out of her head. She wanted it to stop, but it wouldn't. She felt physically sick, weak in the knees. Drinking other animals milk seemed like a barbaric perversion, as in her world only some tribes living outside of civilization used to do it before the plague. But her people had meat industry, and there were still a couple of farms left making the exotic delicacy for the super-rich. She had never thought about what the industry was like and was now wishing with all

282

her heart it was different from what she'd seen. As bad as they were, her people weren't like that, they couldn't be.

Vietra was shaking. The scenes looked bizarre to her because chickens and pigs weren't eaten by her people, and she was only used to seeing them in the wild. All the animals also looked slightly different: size, color, patterns of their skins made the experience even more surreal. She couldn't watch it anymore, she had to turn away, take a deep breath to alleviate the sickness. Luckily, the story took another direction, and she focused on the narrative.

All of the above created a better life for about a half of their population, while the other half was living in extreme poverty, without electricity or running water, seemingly worse off than their ancestors had been before the industrial revolution.

Vietra saw great inequality everywhere. Sixty-two of the wealthiest humans had as much money as 3,5 billion poor people. A small group of individuals were hoarding the resources they'd never be able to use. Waging wars, killing millions, escalating conflicts, manipulating governments, destroying their environment, abusing workers—all for the sake of profits and power. The assets they possessed could solve most of the world's problems if they were put into infrastructure, education, healthcare, solutions. Instead, they were used to produce more money by depleting resources. Vietra sneered. If she was hoping for the story to get better, she was bitterly mistaken. She had to brace herself for more. Maybe the Master had a point with what he was doing after all. If her civilization was like that too, maybe they deserved to go.

They created a culture of disposable products that littered their streets, choked their oceans, poisoned their air. Millions of them were dying each year because their air and water were full of toxins. Their industrial way of life and consumerism produced more and more carbon dioxide, methane, nitrous oxide, and Vietra watched the gases cloak the planet, preventing the Sun's heat from leaving the atmosphere. She saw their planet slowly heating up, the climate changing, leading to changes in the water cycles all over the globe. That meant snowfalls and rainfalls more violent than ever before, but also less frequent, prolonged droughts followed by downpours destroying their crops. Ice was melting in their polar regions changing ocean currents, which lead to severe storms that would only become worse every year. It also meant that their coastal cities would go underwater within several decades.

Vietra saw fierce winter storms paralyzing their traffic, trapping people in the middle of nowhere, freezing. She saw spring floods sweeping thought their cities, killing people, ravaging their homes. She saw summer droughts getting longer, leading to loss of crops and hunger, giving rise to civil wars and mass migration. She saw more and more powerful hurricanes destroying their infrastructure, taking lives. She saw more fierce wildfires consuming millions of acres of forests all over the globe, burning people and animals alive, choking them, wiping whole species from the face of the planet.

There was so much pain in the eyes of the mother whose home was swiped away with both her children and her partner. She didn't understand.

There was hurt resignation in the eyes of the boy dying of starvation in the desert. He hadn't known what it was like not to be hungry in his short lifetime.

There was so much terror in the eyes of the man drowning in a flooded metro station. He hadn't told his father that he'd forgiven him.

There was so much anguish in the scream of the firefighter who had just seen an animal burned alive before the fire enclosed him. He'd thought he was ready to give his life for his country, but he wanted to live.

There was grim determination in the eyes of the rescuers excavating survivors and the dead from the rubble of what used to be a beautiful city. They didn't allow themselves the luxury of tears, not until the work was done.

So much suffering. Only more to come. Tears were running down Vietra's cheeks.

Suddenly she found herself alone in the dark, with the feeling of utmost wrongness in her entire body. It wasn't even pain, it was something else, some profound sickness. She could barely breathe, it seemed that the whole world was pressing on her chest. And she needed to breathe so badly, just one deep breath would suffice, but she couldn't, just couldn't, she only barely managed to take short, shallow gasps that didn't even seem to reach her lungs, that only suffocated her more. It was dark, so dark. Was she buried alive? She tried to move and couldn't, but the effort caused acute pain to run like a razor blade through her spine. The feeling of sickness intensified. Fear was swelling inside, and there was no way for her to release it, so it was pressing on her from the inside, and she felt that she could burst like a bubble.

Trying to remember what had happened to her, she recalled a hurricane warning and waiting for her partner, Tamara, to get back from work so that they could go to a shelter together. But it was getting late, and Tamara wasn't coming, and the hurricane was already there, and she was watching TV, holding little Oksana in her arms, gripped by fear. She couldn't go out now. The reporter was saying something about fallen trees blocking the road, maybe that's where Tamara was stuck.

Suddenly the TV screen turned black, and the lights went out. She was sitting there for a while, pressing Oksana to her chest, and Oksana started crying, and she couldn't calm her down because she was so scared herself, because she realized she couldn't protect her little girl. She heard glass break in the other room. She couldn't stay there anymore, it wasn't safe. She had to go down, to hide in the basement. She needed some water and diapers for Oksana, but it was hard to find them in the dark, there should have been a candle somewhere, she was rushing around... And then her memory went blank.

Did it mean that the house collapsed on her? And where was Oksana? She did seem to feel something warm and wet on her chest, something that could have been a small body crushed by the rubble. She wanted to scream, but she couldn't, she needed a break from it, but there was none, she couldn't take it, couldn't take it, couldn't take it!

"Vietra," someone said from far away, and then closer, "Vietra."

286

It was the Master. Vietra didn't think she'd ever be so happy to hear his voice. Was she in the sensory deprivation room again?

"You're experiencing immersion. It happens with those things if you get too emotionally invested."

"Immersion?" Vietra whispered. She wasn't under the rubble anymore, and she didn't have a dead daughter crushed on her chest. That was a major improvement. She recalled that she was watching one human civilization's history.

"Yes, you got sucked into it. Let's finish this, we've got work to do."

"No. Wait. You promised. I want to see it."

The Master stayed silent, but he could as well have sighed loudly.

"Then focus on the story," he finally said. "You're in control of what you see and how intensely you experience it. The more invested you get in something, the more detail you see, and the more personal it gets."

"Got it," ignoring the violent shudders of her body and the sore lump in her throat, Vietra focused on the broader picture. The planet was heating up. That caused natural calamities.

As an impartial observer again, Vietra heard the concerned voices of thousands of scientists all over the globe warning others about climate change and mass extinction of species. Saying it was the result of their way of life, calling for a change. And she saw fossil fuel corporations fighting hard for their place in business, even as green technology emerged. She couldn't believe it, but it seemed that the fate of humanity didn't concern them as long as they could keep earning money. Even if it was leading to mass extinction that threatened to destroy as much as 50% of life on their planet. Even if humans, the young species, could be among those animals and plants gone forever. Even if it could lead to famine, diseases, mass migration, deaths, collapse of civilization and destruction of the world as they knew it.

They brought corrupt politicians into power taking advantage of the technologies that connected the world, and all the personal data that the tech giants possessed. These politicians promoted more pollution and deforestation, igniting more hate and intolerance, causing more violence, creating more enemies.

They spent huge amounts of money to found institutes and hire scientists who claimed climate change wasn't real, think tanks whose goal was to shape public opinions, make people believe there was nothing to worry about, disseminate doubt and confusion. They were using successful techniques that some industry producing a toxic, addictive product had implemented decades before even as science presented more and more evidence that it was killing people.

Vietra found it hard to comprehend how much effort, resources and funding went into sabotaging actions and regulations that could still save humanity, discrediting all scientific data and human suffering. They still had a little time to avert the disaster. And the people who had money and resources to contribute in a major way were instead spending those on deceiving others. Not just doing nothing but delaying important action. Not just contributing to climate change but doing their best to make sure nothing was done about it as long as possible, even though they were among the first ones to learn about it.

288

Vietra had trouble understanding this level of evil. She would have thought in such circumstances people would pull together regardless of their beliefs, but they were more polarized than ever, their arguments fueled by information wars.

Unexpectedly to herself, Vietra felt a touch of pride for her world. It wasn't perfect, there were lots of problems and injustices, and they weren't fair to the nature either, but as far as she knew, they'd never reached such a level of insanity. Thinking about the people who knowingly and methodically took part in destroying their home made her freeze on the inside. Her grief was turning into rage.

The propaganda did its job. Instead of working together to solve the greatest crisis of their time, people were arguing whether it was happening at all, even as they felt the rising heat on their skins, even as millions were dying and losing their homes, forced to flee their countries.

Their oil supply was dwindling while the demand was growing. Their economy relied on fossil fuels that were finite, dangerous and dirty. Their fertilizers and pesticides, construction materials, pharmaceutical products, synthetic fibers, power, heating and lights were made of fossil fuels. The surge of oil prices caused the collapse of the economy as it led to all other prices skyrocketing. That meant people losing homes, losing their life savings, unable to buy basic goods, hungry, paralyzed with fear.

The civilization they'd build looked dangerous and shortsighted. Their power stations worked around the clock, heating up their planet to produce food and clothes they threw away uneaten and unworn, to light empty rooms, to run water no one was using. They created a greedy, selfish lifestyle of excess and were made to believe that was what happiness looked like, that they were entitled to it. Meanwhile their economy was going through its final convulsions. Its constant growth was leading to inevitable collapse.

At the same time, while many people were losing their sleep and hope to survive, Vietra noticed something new emerging in different corners of the world.

Biosphere consciousness was taking root. New generations saw their world as a complex ecosystem where everything was interconnected and interdependent. They didn't see their planet as a commodity anymore, it was their precious home that they dearly loved. They realized it was like a space station with finite resources, alone in the cold, unforgiving void. They didn't see themselves as lords of the nature but as an organic part of it, as the nature itself.

They cared about forests and oceans and treated their resources with care, saving water and power, recycling, reusing and sharing. They cared about people from all over the world seeing them as part of the human family instead of weird strangers. They cared about their working conditions and education, about their rights and powers. They refused to buy products that were made exploiting other human beings.

They cared about other creatures, recognizing their right to be there, seeing them as similar to themselves instead of different and more primitive. They refused to hurt them, refused to eat and exploit them, refused to support the corporations that did. They protected endangered species and treated life with respect. They had love for their planet, love for each other, love for other beings. They wanted to be fair and just.

They donated, volunteered, supported causes that mattered to them, helped out those in need. They were kind to strangers. They didn't see themselves as separate individuals whose comfort mattered above all, rather as equal contributors in the global network.

They were sharing their cars, toys, clothes, food and knowledge with others for free. Power was different to them: they didn't want it to be distributed from the top down, they saw how damaging and unfair it could be. Instead, they wanted it to be lateral and manifest itself through networks where they could benefit each other.

They didn't want to compete with other individuals and countries for finite resources. They saw clearly that their well-being depended on the well-being of the whole system and everyone in it. They didn't want anyone to suffer for them to have a nice life. Instead, they wanted a world where everyone could have access to resources, education, medicine, power and technology, and they wanted this world to live in harmony with their planet and other beings. They were ready to rearrange their lives and give up their habits to achieve that. They were ready to do the necessary work. Of course, just changing their lifestyle wasn't enough. Solving global problems required system changes.

Scientists, economists, politicians, entrepreneurs, engineers and average people started working on the new ideas in different ways. Vietra could see how in this complex, interconnected system different powers, movements and processes were pushing against each other. She saw that the outcome was not determined at all, saw how events could move in various directions, how the slightest change of power could result in a huge difference of outcome.

While some of them kept trashing the planet, and most of them were walking around clueless, others got down to business. They studied scientific data and identified major causes of climate change. Buildings and their excessive energy consumption; meat and dairy industry; transport; energy sources. They looked at historic and economic data, analyzed the existing and emerging technologies and trends to come up with solutions.

The problem was that even though solutions were created, governments were often reluctant to use them. Even when they were ready to do something, it was never enough, and in many cases, it was nothing at all or the opposite of what needed to be done.

But there were enough people who refused to helplessly watch their home destroyed. Grassroots movements were emerging all over the world. Regular people from all walks of life came together to demand change. Among themselves they created communities where power was distributed laterally, where mutual respect and equality were the basis of all further action and cooperation.

It was a new kind of revolution, and people were gaining power, standing strong together. They tried to make their fellow humans understand that it wasn't about political views, religion or any personal preferences. It was about survival. It was about preserving the world that could still sustain human population and other species that were already disappearing in a mass extinction. It was about love, compassion and collaboration. It was about giving the power back to the people and ensuring safety and survival for themselves as well as future generations.

It was snowballing. The governments couldn't ignore them. In some places they used brutal force against the activists. Some got killed or were thrown into prison. It didn't work. They couldn't be intimidated because they knew they were fighting for life. They stayed strong, having created a culture of support and acceptance, a culture where no one was left to deal with troubles on their own. Their community and common goal were their strength.

And, to Vietra's awe and surprise, they made it happen. Once people were shown how their home and their future were being destroyed on their watch and that there was an alternative, a way to channel their frustration and turn it into positive action, a global revolution was ignited. The old ways that were standing in the way of survival were burned in this fire of rage, and new flowers grew out of ashes.

Some countries took up the task of rebuilding their whole infrastructure and switching to renewable energies. More and more organizations and businesses popped up here and there with new goals in mind. Old companies were restructuring and reenvisioning their strategies.

Together they started tackling the problems they'd identified. Vietra watched them remaking buildings and turning them into mini power plants collecting solar and wind, recycling waste and water, storing energy surplus. They installed sensors that monitored the equipment. They put plants and gardens everywhere. Every building became a node connected into a new, smart, digital grid, sharing data and power with other buildings. That was so much work and brought so many people together that Vietra felt her throat tightening as she watched them slowly pave their way to a better future. It was healing after everything she'd experienced so far. She took a deep breath. There was no time to get sucked into the story again, even though it could be something nice for a change.

They were rebuilding their cities, making them into self-sustainable little economies where most of the fruit, vegetables, grains and mushrooms were grown locally, using local renewable energy. They created more parks and gardens in every district of those first, experimental cities. There were also agricultural areas with open-air country markets and restaurants, featuring local, plant-based cuisine. They held cooking workshops, food festivals and educational campaigns, teaching people about the footprint their eating habits had. They were rethinking agriculture and food production, making those more sustainable, interweaving them into strong, resilient ecosystems.

There were national parks, nature reserves and animal sanctuaries where people could reconnect with the environment. Vietra saw kids throwing a large ball to a cow that galloped after it only to push it back, waiting eagerly for the game to continue. The kids were laughing. She saw a middle-aged man touching a pig's ear, looking into her intelligent eyes as she seemed to be smiling at him. He wiped a tear discretely. She saw people playing with domestic animals, grooming and feeding them, sitting with them on vast lawns, walking with them, hugging and interacting with them with newly found tenderness and fondness. There was a real connection forming between

294

those beings belonging to different species that was pure and beautiful.

Vietra felt something loosen in her chest. She was getting warmer on the inside.

People were visiting wild animal sanctuaries and reserves where they could watch the animals in their natural habitat, unrestrained, or help take care of those who needed it. No more cages, no more breaking animals mentally to make them perform tricks for people's entertainment. Instead, people were taking care of those animals, treating their wounds, easing their pain, preparing them to reenter the wilderness when it was possible. And those people looked so genuinely happy, so serene, as if they rediscovered some deep truth that set them free. In those places and slowly all over the world, meat and dairy consumption dropped to its record low.

There were also large-scale renewable energy projects that made use of solar, wind and biomass energies, making the cities self-sustainable. They attracted scientists and entrepreneurs from all over the world, as well as farmers looking to implement the new technology in their home countries.

Cities were rebuilt to make them more convenient for walking and riding bikes. Their historical centers were made completely walkable, and industrial parts, containing universities, biosphere science and technology parks, companies and start-ups whose aim was new, green commerce turned into attractive working environments. They were full of plants and art and produced their own energy. People from all over the world were striving to come and work there, breath the fresh air and just see it all with their own eyes.

Those first green, high-tech cities became huge tourist attractions and a major inspiration for others to follow. No city was exactly the same, and depending on its climate, geographical region, specific needs and economic conditions, each one had its own challenges and solutions, but after the first few, they started popping up like mushrooms all around the globe.

Transport was changing, too. New companies were emerging while the old ones remade themselves to produce electric and hydrogen vehicles. Charging stations were put everywhere, in every building and in the middle of every remote road. Public transport, boats and aircraft were turning electric or hydrogen. Vehicles were also being made autonomous, reducing the number of accidents.

Poor countries were developing extremely fast, as they didn't have an infrastructure to rebuild and could skip right to the cutting-edge technology. They gained power, access to running water and education. For the first time they were rising above their poverty and looking around with curious eyes. They brought new perspectives and original ideas into the world of business and technology. The population stopped growing so fast, as more and more people got education, more and more women got jobs, investing their time and energy into the exciting, emerging new world, relying on science, technology, big data and human connection. They were inventing new materials, little by little abandoning disposable plastics and rethinking their culture.

Many companies that failed to adjust disappeared, but the intelligent ones repurposed themselves. Because the new energy system required lots of small players to unite and collect energy everywhere where it was available, smart energy companies that now produced only a small percentage of power turned into consultants, helping other companies and individuals manage their big data, offering solutions, apps and technology.

This was a revolution. There was a shift of power, as the nations that used to be world leaders found themselves behind those who turned more progressive on the issue and started way earlier. But power was also becoming more and more decentralized, as economic data became available to everyone worldwide through the internet of things. It was like a nervous system connecting everyone in the world into one complex organism. Sensors gathering data were now everywhere: monitoring real-time activities of devices and machines, monitoring crop growth and soil salinity in agricultural fields, monitoring economic data in factories, monitoring the use of energy in buildings. There were sensors in their vehicles, warehouses and roads. All these data were used to manage, power and move their economy and were available to everyone, empowering social entrepreneurship and making it more effective and widespread than ever.

This system was designed to be collaborative, open and transparent, but, of course, there were companies and governments that wanted to exploit it for their purposes, wanted to conceal or change their data. Data security, privacy, cybercrimes and cyberterrorism became huge issues. They gave rise to new political movements fighting hard to ensure equal access, security and transparency for everyone. It required a change in the international legislative system, a mass of new laws, practices and tools, and an ongoing fight against people who always managed to find new ways of exploitation. So many times, they almost failed, almost gave up, almost outlawed the international internet of things. There were public scandals, personal tragedies, manipulation and mass, global protests.

Political changes in some parts of the world were slow and painful, as their governments wanted to keep authoritarian control over the people, which was made easier than ever through constant monitoring and the internet of things. There was a lot of suffering, and even though the world altogether was getting better, cleaner, safer, and life was improving for the majority of population, some people's lives became even harder because of it. Those political systems took hundreds of years and millions of lives to adopt the new values.

It was surprising to Vietra, but somehow, they managed to make it work mostly in their favor and to create huge difficulties for those who wanted to do harm through the new system. Attacks, breaches and exploitation never completely stopped, they only evolved and changed, but most of the people, businesses and organizations benefited from the internet of things most of the time. The new platform gave rise to an enormity of tools, apps, technologies and services that helped everyone interested dramatically increase their productivity and aggregate efficiency while effectively decreasing their ecological footprint and marginal costs.

There came another turning point in the story. Vietra watched as the marginal cost of renewable energy, transport and logistics plummeted to zero or near zero all over the world. It meant everyone could afford a computer, everyone could produce their own green energy, even in the poorest corners of the world that were rapidly developing. Companies were now

298

plugged to the smart grid where energy cost them almost nothing. The rise of new materials and 3D printing allowed everyone to produce almost everything themselves or with the help of local communities for free and with zero imprint on the environment, using mostly recycled materials. The new culture of sharing was now at its prime: no good things were thrown away and piling up in the landfills anymore. What could still be used by other people was given to them through efficient networks. What couldn't, was recycled or remade into something new. Most people didn't need to own cars anymore, instead, they relied on high-quality public transport and car-sharing networks. Within two generations 80% of cars were eliminated, recycled, and the materials they were made of repurposed, while all the remaining vehicles turned electric or hydrogen and were operated at near zero marginal cost.

And just like that they tackled the problems they'd identified and created the infrastructure for the new economy. It was hard to believe they were capable of that, and yet in a common, titanic effort, people who cared tipped the scale in favor of their world.

Vietra couldn't but feel proud of them, even though they were just aliens. She saw what it had cost them, saw the struggle and pain, saw new problems emerging while they were grappling with the old ones. They started too late, and climate change had wreaked havoc in many places in the world. Too many people had to die, suffer of thirst and hunger, see the horrors of war for the precious resources. Too many lost their homes and had to migrate to strange places. Too many species were gone forever.

And yet, they fought for their right to live with passion and determination that she could only admire. They fought for the whole humanity, including those who tried to destroy them. They fought for other creatures. They fought for their home. They fell and rose to their feet again and again, together, learning to connect and work with one another, to figure out solutions, to compromise, to resolve arguments, to accept and listen to each other. Being creative and doing lots of guess work, making tons of mistakes. Doubting themselves and the reality of their cause. On the verge of giving up. They were getting up again because they knew it was their only chance to survive. Searching for their new place in the world together. Step by step until success.

Their history books called all the people who worked for this transition heroes. Everyone, from scientists who studied the problem to inventors who were creating new technologies, from builders who retrofitted their buildings to engineers who worked on solutions, from entrepreneurs who established new businesses to those who adjusted their existing companies to the new needs, from government officials who didn't bend to bribes and power games to activists who devoted their time and energy to solving the problem, often risking their freedom and even life. Everyone who took a stand, who spoke out and chose their part in history–all of them were heroes because humanity could have failed even if a couple of them had made a different choice, because they could have only got there together, only when everyone used their skills, knowledge, platforms and means available to do the best they could. They established an international holiday to celebrate life on their planet. They spent that day with their families and friends in national parks, engaging in conservation projects and learning, enjoying the company of their loved ones, surrounded by nature.

After two generations of mass employment in construction, transport, logistics, telecommunication, cable, ICT, electronics, real estate and other spheres they got the new infrastructure laid out and working. Their energy complex was converted to 100% renewable technology connected into a smart, digital grid. They lived in smart cities. They ate 98% plant-based, locally grown, organic diet. They cleaned up their water and air, got rid of disposable plastics and got really good at recycling what they couldn't reuse.

New technologies that had grown on the internet of things platform had changed their lives in unprecedented ways, and the standard of living of the previously poor countries and individuals had improved dramatically. The immensity of the transformation left Vietra deeply impressed.

Most of production was now performed automatically, with the help of analytics, big data, apps and algorithms, run by small supervisory crews. That meant that millions of people lost their jobs and the skills they had lost their relevance. The new economy took care of their physical needs in most cases, but there was a surge in crime, suicide and addiction rates, as there seemed to be whole generations of people who'd lost their purpose. The transition was, as always, a painful process with multiple forces and worldviews colliding, and while they were trying to figure it out, there was immense suffering and turmoil.

After several decades of uncertainty, the majority of humans found themselves in the fields where they could directly benefit each other and share their knowledge or skills with others. Huge numbers of them were working in non-profit, sharing and social economy.

Now most of the people could do what they actually cared about, directly engaging with others. It was finding out what was important to them and learning to enjoy their new roles that took time, effort and profound changes in the education system.

After a while, they unleashed the full power of their creative potential in education, healthcare, culture and science. Their space program got a huge boost, and they soon established their first viable colonies on one of their solar system planets and the Moon. Before Vietra knew, the colonies turned self-sufficient, and the first babies were born there. The colonists demanded independence and established their own political systems. They expanded further to the moons of their gas giants. Space travel within the solar system became a popular holiday activity. They reached such a level of understanding of their genetics and biology that they could change the properties of their bodies to adapt better to living on other planets. They were editing their genes to increase their lifespan, enjoy good health and just for fun. Knowing that those changes could be reversed over time made it easy.

They also reached a much greater understanding of their own psychology and made social intelligence, dealing with difficult emotions and managing conflict part of their education system. Kids were taught how to take care of themselves, other people, animals, plants and the planet on multiple levels, how to help others in times of difficulty, how to process negative emotions and recognize stress in themselves and others, how to maintain a healthy body and a healthy mind. From an early age they were learning to see each other as human beings, vulnerable and real, to form deep connections and bonds, and that had a huge impact on their mentality and society. All of that, combined with improvement of their living conditions and overall access to goods had caused crime to drop to unprecedentedly low levels.

It wasn't a paradise, of course. There were still lots of problems, injustices and inequalities. They now discriminated against each other not on the basis of their race, sexual orientation or gender, but the planet or moon of origin. Religious conflicts never completely subsided, even though the population was becoming more and more secular. New religions and belief systems were taking root, claiming, as always, that it was their god that was the only real one, their values and way of life that were the only right ones. People were still dying and suffering in many ways. There were new diseases, new problems, new challenges, new threats, new unanswered questions. Life was still life, but all in all, it was a much more tolerant and happy society than it had ever been. There was more understanding between them than ever. Many countries even refused prisons and took a new approach to reforming criminals, offering them therapy, community and meaningful work. It proved much more effective, further reducing the number of crimes. Borders were melting. The meaning of countries and nationalities was dissolving. They were now citizens of different planets or moons, rather than nations, united in tight-knit local communities.

Generation after generation their world was becoming less and less familiar to Vietra, with more bizarre things in it, with inexplicable art, technologies and entertainment, until it reached the point when she first glimpsed it: something that looked like a colorful fairy tale. She could now see that it was, in fact, no fairy tale, with general artificial intelligence lurking as a real and tangible threat, manipulation and deceit brought to a new level with the help of technology and many other perils Vietra didn't really understand. And yet, there was something about it...

Vietra found herself sitting on a tree, enjoying the setting sun caressing her skin, inhaling the freshness of the upcoming evening.

"Can I join you up there?"

She looked down and saw a curvy young woman wearing large boots, one of which was orange and the other striped green, blue and yellow. She had butterfly wings on her back, her torso was tied with blue bands only partially covering her breasts. She was also wearing a loose, knee-length, yellow skirt. Her hair, eyes and skin were dark.

"Sure," Vietra said with a smile. She was feeling relaxed and curious.

The woman jumped unnaturally high, boosted by something in her boots and used her wings to steer herself on a branch next to Vietra that was about two meters above the ground.

"Cool, huh?" she said, clearly pleased with her trick.

"Impressive," Vietra confirmed.

"Booster boots," the woman explained. "Work way better on the Moon where I could literally fly with these wings. Here I can only jump higher and slow down my fall."

"You are from the Moon?"

"No, I'm from here, but I lived on the Moon for the last five years."

"Why did you come back?"

"Because of love," she laughed somewhat bitterly. "Moon girl," she rolled her eyes and waved her hand. "You know what they are like. It was good while it lasted, but then she dumped me. She was somewhat famous out there, and you know, Moon is a small piece of rock. I kept bumping into holos of her everywhere I went, it was difficult to forget her, so I thought it was better to go."

"I'm sorry. Are you okay?"

"I don't know. I mean..."

"Vietra," the familiar hoarse voice cut through the image. "Vietra, that's enough."

"You are right. Thank you for showing it to me," she said tearing herself from the dream, turning her attention to the Master.

The simulation ended abruptly, leaving her in the dark.

It would be nice to learn more details, but it was sufficient for now. Vietra noted that much of the technology, some of the problems and many of the structures were similar to her world. At the same time, a lot of their political and social life was completely alien and weird to her, but she could learn from them, could adapt some of their strategies. It was more than she was hoping to get. It was a road map.

"It's weird how many things my world has in common with theirs," Vietra said into the void.

"Yes," the Master responded. "It might appear to you that yours is a natural way of living because you don't know anything else, but it's not. You can't imagine how different it can get. But their historical choices were similar to yours, they came to some of the same conclusions and ways of organizing themselves."

"Thank you," Vietra said. Gratitude to the Master made her feel uncomfortable. Part of her wanted to like him for showing her the world she could understand. She couldn't afford it.

"What's odd for me," the Master snorted, unaware of Vietra's struggle, "is that every single one of my kind who was sent to this place just disappeared from the hive mind after a while, so we couldn't set anything in motion there. And we didn't feel them die as is usually the case when it happens. It's more like they sever the connection. They are probably being killed by the locals, but in a way we can't identify. They must have detected us and used their technology against us."

"Or your friends just like it there," Vietra shrugged and immediately realized it was the wrong thing to say.

"Even if they do, it's not justifiable. We come to these worlds to save our species, and nothing can be more important than that!" the Master said more vehemently than Vietra had ever heard from him.

"You are right, of course," she uttered hastily to calm him down.

"It's so strange, but the longer I'm staying here, the more I feel like an individual. I'm still part of a hive mind, still an Old

One, and at the same time... I'm just me, separate from all that. Is this what you call cognitive dissonance?"

This was bewildering. The Master had never been so open and vulnerable with Vietra, never seemed so human, even though she now knew that he wasn't. She thought she couldn't feel compassion for him, and yet, she did, despite everything he did to her, despite Tyssdin's death, despite his plan to destroy humanity. Empathy was waking up in her, urging her to help him, to soothe him. She shook her head to clear her mind.

"Are you doubting your cause?" she asked cautiously.

"No!" he barked. "How could I? Have your forgotten who I am? I want to live. My life depends on destroying you. Even if I don't want to," he added quietly.

"Okay then. Let's get down to business."

"I'm listening to your ideas."

"I can't make it very precise unless I know your exact plan, but I can give you some feedback on relocating the points of attack to make more damage. I'd like to get out of the simulation."

"Why? It will be faster here."

"I know, I just want you to show me some good will. I want to know I'm not your prisoner, and you are not going to use my insights and keep me here forever until I'm completely nuts."

"All right," the Master said. "You know, you humans are complicated. It took me a long time to even begin to understand you, and I believe there is still a lot beyond my grasp."

"I think you are doing quite a good job taking into account who you are."

"Thanks," the Master said. "I shouldn't be indulging you, but that's almost the end. I can do it once."

Vietra wanted to respond, but she felt the darkness break apart around her as she woke up from her machine induced sleep and sat down with a violent inhalation. It was like emerging from under water, light rushing into her face in a hazy blur, slowly reassembling itself into the world she knew. It reminded her of the last time she woke up like that. Of Tyss. Her implant informed her once again that her team was already at the Master's doorstep attempting to enter. She felt relief descending upon her as she realized they managed to follow her steps without getting into any of the Master's traps, and the technology of their suits didn't fail to conceal them. Cay was alive, and Vietra felt a tender touch of his consciousness along with his own relief when contact with her was reestablished and he knew she was all right. The group was at the entrance now, and a scan of Vietra's palms that Syong was carrying on her gloves was to ensure their access to the building.

Vietra knew she had very little time and no right for a mistake. She had to act as quickly and precisely as possible. Her timing had to be perfect. Even a second of a slip could ruin it all. It was the Master's training combined with the analytical and tracking abilities of her implant that made it achievable. She half smirked thinking about the irony of that. The next moment was time to act.

She knocked the Master down with a series of precise, hard hits into the most vulnerable parts of his body and skillfully evaded mechanical arms that immediately reached out to her, trying to capture her. She ran down the stairs and got to the front door the moment it was open. She knocked down Sais and Syong before they had a chance of reacting to her and grabbed the disc bomb that Sais was carrying on his back. While they were getting up, not yet aware of what had happened, she threw the bomb into a flying trajectory, activating it with her implant. The group began rushing into the building, the Master rose to his knees on the upper floor, and a couple of mechanical arms missed their grip on her as Vietra set the bomb to its maximum destructive force, confirming the command before it could be overridden. She jumped out of the door, trying to catch Cay and Maltara, who also happened to be on her way, pulling them back out of the building with her, screaming "Out!" to the rest of the group, hoping they would manage to react. There was devastating noise and heat, she was kicked harshly in her back, and then there was blackness.

CHAPTER 26

Aisami was talking to the spirits of the forest, floating in clouds of green smoke. It felt like she was several centimeters above the ground, weightless and serene. The shamans of the tribe taught her this practice. It was important because the spirits could help her solve some of the tribal problems and answer some of her questions, but it was also extremely pleasant and relaxing, and she indulged in the activity just to feel the weightlessness and the calm wrapping her like a warm blanket. Nothing could hurt her when she talked to the spirits. Even wild animals would leave her alone at least until she was done.

It would be nice to stay there forever, but it was a trap of mind. She had responsibilities as a shaman now, and she still had a lot to learn. The tribe depended on her. Yet, this moment belonged to her alone. No one would bother her. And that was one more reason why she liked doing it so much. People of the tribe always needed her attention when she was available. There were always ailments of body and mind to heal, ceremonies to hold, questions to answer, plants to gather... The responsibilities came with her newly acquired role of a shaman, and she embraced them fully. But it was tiring, and even though she loved every single member of her tribe, she needed some mental space to let her mind expand and comprehend the vastness of the world once in a while. She needed the quiet. The spirits understood and were silent until she started talking to them. They were touching her gently, which felt pleasant and soothing. They didn't accept her at once, they tested and tormented her before they decided she was worthy, and it cost Aisami a lot of ordeal, but it was all in the past now.

Suddenly, the air around her started trembling. Pain pierced her body with multiple needles, and she gasped for breath. Aisami knew the instant it happened that something was wrong. She shook the impressions away and jumped to her feet, seeing the world clearly again. She didn't have time to think anything through, she just started running, only realizing what was happening on her way.

"This shouldn't hurt," she thought. "It doesn't matter."

But the pain didn't stop as the destruction happening dozens of kilometers away shook her. Something was falling apart, and she sensed the connection that held her to this world break. Through the spirits that were still following her, she felt those of the tribe who came from the same lab as her, sharing the sensation, others growing uneasy around them.

At the same time, the spirits focused on a place inside her womb where life was beginning after the recent tribe orgy. Pain mixed with excitement. There was a new life that would have a place in this world and that would tie her back to it as well. Unable to contain her emotions, Aisami kept running.

CHAPTER 27

When Vietra opened her eyes, she couldn't understand where she was. Her ears were ringing, her eyesight was blurry, and her mind felt hazy. She figured out she was lying with her nose in the sand and tried to raise her head. That reminded her body how much it hurt, but she bit her lip and pushed herself up onto her knees. She turned around and saw Cay lying unconscious a little behind her. She crawled to him and put her head on his chest to listen to his heart. That was when she managed to reestablish communication with her implant which told her Cay's life parameters. He wasn't hurt too badly and was definitely going to survive. The rest of the group was in a similar condition, except for Sais, who managed to get farther into the building. Vietra rose to her feet and came up to him. His right arm and leg were ripped off by the explosion, and his face didn't have any recognizable human features anymore. His implant managed to stop the bleeding and was working on sterilizing the wounds, but it didn't guarantee survival. There was nothing she could do.

The Nest was destroyed. It lay in ruins in front of Vietra, and she couldn't believe her eyes. How long she was preparing for it, and how quickly it happened! She half expected to be pulled out of the simulation and reprimanded by the Master for betraying him. A small part of her was hoping for it. But nothing happened. Her implant told her there were no survivors in the rubble. The Master was gone along with his crazy lab, and so were all the Nestlings still plugged to their sim-caskets, unsuspecting. Vietra was acutely aware of the fact that she was responsible for their deaths. She became a murderer, after all. She hadn't realized that fully yet, but it was going to catch up with her soon enough. Still, it was a price she was willing to pay.

Olonda and the members of the team were sure to think of her as a traitor: not only did she stop them from studying the Master's equipment, but she also risked their lives and maimed one of them. She had no choice. It was their survival as a species at stake. They'd have to get to the rest of the Master's accomplices around the planet as soon as possible and destroy them before they had a chance to start their massive assault. Then they had to change the world quickly to remove it from the Brandstocks' priority list and to protect themselves well against the next invasion. Use the example of the people the Master had shown to her. Develop their space program even faster, find others like them, connect, share expertise, form a common front of resistance... Vietra sighed. She was thinking too far ahead. Maybe the Brandstocks had already started the assault, seeing the Master's death. Maybe they only had a minute left to live.

"We could change," she whispered into the curling smoke enshrouding the ruins of the Nest and turned back. She came up to Cay and put her head on his chest again, listening to his heartbeat, waiting for him to awaken.

GRATITUDE

I'm grateful to you for having bought and/or read the book, and I sincerely hope that you enjoyed it. Sorry if you didn't! But if you are here, something kept you reading, so I'm sending you a virtual high five.

I'm grateful to my husband for being an inspiration to write this book, for always being there for me and supporting me, for setting an example of persistence and creativity and for being an awesome human. I love you!

I'm grateful to Maria Levene for creating a beautiful cover that captures the mood of the book so well. If you are looking for a graphic or interior designer who is also a wonderful person, check out her website: https://www.marialevene.com/. High five, Maria! Good luck with everything you do!

I'm grateful to Julie Chipko, Kat, Magda, Lukas and Sveta for reading the book and sharing their critical feedback that allowed me to see it from different perspectives unattainable to me before and make it better. They made suggestions that influenced the way the story was told, enriched the book and, hopefully, made it more enjoyable for you. Great job, you guys!

I'm grateful to Jeremy Rifkin and Yuval Noah Harari, whose books and ideas created a foundation for most of the problems and solutions of the civilization whose story Vietra was watching. They are great at what they do.

I'm grateful to my parents, friends, the Extinction Rebellion movement and all of the authors whose books I've read for influencing me in various ways and shaping my views, beliefs and values.

The book wouldn't be what it is without all the people mentioned above, they kick ass, so I'm going to take a moment to appreciate their impact, while you can appreciate someone important in your life.

I'm also grateful that I was able to write this book, that I had enough time and resources to make it happen, that the world as it is now allowed me to self-publish and reach some readers.

Thanks for reading. If you enjoyed the book, please consider leaving me a review on Amazon and/or Goodreads. As an indie author without a budget that big publishers have, I need all the help I can get, and reviews are a great way to interest other readers in the book.

I wish you all the best! Be happy, spend time with the people you love, do things you care about, make your dreams come true and be the change you are waiting for. Peace and love <3

STAY IN TOUCH WITH THE AUTHOR

You can find me on Twitter (@AlinaLeonovaSF) and Goodreads: goodreads.com/author/show/20846255.Alina_Leonova

Check out my website where I review sci-fi by female and non-binary authors, create lists and recommendations and do interviews: alinaleonova.net. I explore books by famous as well as indie and self-published authors, so, if you'd like to expand your horizons, join me on my quest!

Subscribe to my newsletter to discover new sci-fi authors and enter an occasional giveaway to win awesome books. You'll get an email about once or twice a month:

alinaleonova.net/newsletter

You can also write to my email: contact@alinaleonova.net

And if you liked this book, don't forget to write an honest review! It will help me a great deal, and I'll be really grateful. I read all the reviews, so I won't miss yours.

Hope to hear from you soon!

Made in the USA
Monee, IL
04 February 2021

59618039R00187